Thirteen

Sebastian Beaumont

MYRMIDON

Myrmidon Books Ltd
Rotterdam House
116 Quayside
Newcastle upon Tyne
NE1 3DY
www.myrmidonbooks.com

Published by Myrmidon 2008

A catalogue record for this book is available from the British Library.

ISBN 9781905802128

Set in 11/14.5 Goudy by
Falcon Oast Graphic Art Limited, East Hoathly, East Sussex

Printed and bound in Great Britain
by Mackays of Chatham Ltd, Chatham, Kent

1 3 5 7 9 10 8 6 4 2

To my sisters, Kate and Nicola

Acknowledgements:

First and foremost to everyone who rode in my cab and, however unwittingly, allowed me to witness the spontaneous living of their lives. Also, to Clare Armstrong, Keith Elliot (yet again!), Cordelia Feldman, Janet Glass, Alex Merrett, Neil Parker, Lulu Russell, Lisa Touzel and to Anne Westgarth my editor. To John McLean (posthumously) for the snowdrop information. To Peter Burton for well over a decade of unstinting support and encouragement. And to Simon Lovat, of course, who has accompanied me on this journey.

CONTENTS

'This is the zone. Enter at your own risk.'

The taxi incidents in this novel (with one exception) are all real, experienced by myself while working as a licensed Brighton & Hove taxi driver.

SB

8 year old girl: When I grow up I'm going to be an artist in the morning, a farmer in the afternoon and a taxi driver in the evening.
SB: That's a lot to fit in.
Girl: And I'll travel the world, of course. Holmes Avenue, West Blatchington, December 23rd.

1. The Three Ds

Once, after driving my taxi for eight hours non-stop, in heavy city traffic, I saw a cat having death throes in the road ahead of me. When I slowed down to avoid it, I realised that it was just a grey bin liner whose ripped edge had caught the wind to look like a paw, spasming rhythmically. This intense mis-recognition – and others like it – made me feel weird. Other drivers had told me about this unnerving night-time blurring of reality. Some refused to drive at night, full stop. Come two o'clock in the morning, after a difficult shift, I would notice a rich, tarry yellow smudge at the edges of buildings. Then, I would know that soon my eyes would stop tracking in unison, and I'd begin to see things that weren't there. It wasn't unpleasant. In fact, I think I liked it. One of my customers – a painfully beautiful, distraught girl who'd sat, sobbing, as I drove her across the city on the night of the cat episode – replied, in utter disbelief, 'Goodnight?' when I said goodbye to her. But night, to me, then, was a rich, dark place that left me exhausted and strangely thrilled, especially when I worked until the world began to shimmer. Because then I left behind the three Ds.

The three Ds.

Dread, despair and debris. Dread of the future, despair in the present and debris from the past. The three Ds, of course, make up the *big* D. Depression. But I found that I couldn't be depressed when I was mentally exhausted – a discovery that was a revelation. If I wanted to stop being unhappy, I just had to work an hour or two longer on my already long shift, and my bike ride home after dropping off the cab – a three-year-old Ford Galaxy – whether star-gilded or rain-soaked, would be characterised by an extraordinary inner peace. I would pedal past the Budgens at the end of Portland Road and see those lost souls buying cigarettes, or chocolate or magazines, or whatever it took to make them feel less alone, and I would smile to myself with relief and release.

Of course, I knew that I was using these unhealthily long shifts as a way of hiding from my unhappiness. But I told myself I was working so hard because I needed the money. Well, actually, I *did* need money, to service my spectacular debts, and taxiing, let me tell you, is far less lucrative than most people imagine. If you own your cab, plus your hackney plate (if you've got the small fortune required to purchase these things), drive your cab twelve hours a day and get a night driver to take it for the rest, you can make genuinely good money – so long as you can keep the cab clean and deal

14

with the endless maintenance on a vehicle that's doing over 1000 miles a week. But otherwise it's just another trap of a job that gives only modest returns unless you put in long, long hours. Still, at that time, long hours suited me. I could sleep the days away and drive at night when the rest of the world – the world in which I was so relentlessly unhappy – slumbered.

One thing I hadn't realised when I started doing late shifts is that you never get used to them. I've asked all kinds of night workers, not just other taxi drivers, and even if you've been doing it for thirty years, it never comes to feel normal, ordinary. Human beings are diurnal animals. Stay awake at night – particularly between midnight and 4.00am – and weird things will begin to happen to your consciousness. It's true of everyone. Those who tell you they're innately nocturnal are just people who prefer to function away from the starkness and rigidity of 'ordinary' states of mind. Drive a cab during the day and your passengers, so often passive victims of our culture of complaint, will grumble about the weather, the news, the traffic. Drive at night and they'll talk about their recent nervous breakdowns, their broken dreams, their painfully unrealised hopes, their latest all-encompassing love affairs. Either that or you'll be listening to drunken mumblings, or perhaps disjointed drug conversations, which can actually be strangely moving, or entertaining, or surreal.

After my first month of nights I noticed how pale I'd become. This was not because of my nocturnal lifestyle but because I was washed out with exhaustion, the constant bedfellow of work of this kind. Unexpectedly, though perhaps unsurprisingly, alcohol became an almost indispensable inter-face between taxiing and sleeping, so that I found myself opening a welcome can of beer as soon as I arrived home and before I sat on the carpet to count my money. My *filthy lucre*,

as I called it. No, seriously. Just look at a taxi driver's hands at
the end of a long shift of handling money. It's disgusting.
Hand-washing became a significant ritual for me – it was the
second thing I did, after pouring myself a beer – and watching
those grey suds being rinsed away by clean water was like
removing a stain from my soul. Sometimes, I would be caught
by a sense of astonishment at what I was doing, as I snapped a
rubber band over my pile of notes, or collected my fuel
receipts into sequence.

I never thought I'd be a taxi driver. Four or five years ago,
when I was solvent, when my life seemed utterly secure and
stable, when I basked in the comforting glow of my future, if
you'd told me then that I'd end up broke and a taxi driver, I'd
have laughed. At some point I'll tell you something of that –
my demise. But not yet. I need to build up to it, to steel myself.
It's amazing what you can push away just by ignoring it, or by
opening another can of beer – or by working extra hours on
the night shift.

People have sometimes asked me, 'Isn't it dangerous, being
a taxi driver at night?' and I say, 'Sometimes.' People also say,
'You must meet some wacky people out there,' and I say, 'Yes.'
Sometimes it's difficult not to experience events, even as they
happen, as anecdotes to be told later. But I lost touch with all
my friends in those early weeks and months of my depression,
and so I never had a chance to regale anyone with what was
happening to me.

Here's an incident off the top of my head:

I pick up four blokes from a private party in Westbourne
Gardens. They are all huge – rugby players, I imagine, as
they are clearly extremely fit and have sports bags with
them. They are also extremely drunk. And high on

cocaine. They are laughing amongst themselves as they get in, and, once the doors are closed, the one in the passenger seat turns to me and says, 'You're going to take us to West Street, Shoreham, and don't bother to put the meter on, because we're only going to give you five quid.' I don't know whether he's joking or not, and as a kind of un-considered reflex, as I put the car into gear, I lean forward and flick the meter on. Instantly, I am punched in the face so that my glasses are knocked askew and I have to catch them as they fall off. It's not a hard punch, but it has a precision that is shocking, considering how drunk I'd assumed them all to be. 'What the fuck did you do that for?' the man asks, quietly. I stammer something, and they all laugh, but not in a friendly way, and I set off for Shoreham extremely aware that if I displease them something nasty might happen. They ignore me and banter amongst them-selves as I drive down the Old Shoreham Road, past Southlands Hospital, which looks particularly other-worldly tonight, being so lit up and yet so deserted. As I continue, I feel a trickle of blood on my upper lip and wipe it away with the back of my hand. I also feel the dull pres-sure of some swelling burgeoning at the bridge of my nose. The punch was obviously harder than I'd first thought. My passenger asks me to 'Speed up a bit, mate', but I tell him there's a speed-camera on the next bend, and he grunts, 'Oh yeah.' Once I'm onto Eastern Avenue I speed up to fifty miles an hour and they seem happier. When we get to our destination, the fare is £8.60. I stop the meter and look at my passengers. I wonder how much they've spent between them on drink and drugs tonight. 'That'll be . . .' I look briefly at the meter. '. . . um . . . five pounds please.' The man beside me beams as though I'm his best friend.

'Thanks mate,' he says as he hands me a fiver. He laughs in a friendly way and leans over to pat my shoulder. They get out of the cab and one of them leans in and says, 'Take care.' I sit and take a long breath and, although I note which house they go into, I also know not to report the assault – it'll take ninety minutes out of my shift, if I'm lucky, three hours if I'm not, and I can't afford to lose the time. Besides, although I have some swelling at the bridge of my nose, it's hardly something that the police would consider serious.

Now, I want to tell you what began to happen to me towards the end of some of my shifts, when exhaustion started to set in.

I began to see things that weren't there. Not as in actual hallucinations. It was a question of misinterpretation, like with the bin liner that I saw as a dying cat. I'd see a vehicle hurtling towards me, and, just before swerving out of its way, I'd realise it was the reflection of my own cab in the windows of the showroom across the road. Or I'd misrecognise a street and suddenly have the conviction – accompanied by an unpleasant feeling, similar to vertigo – that I was in another part of town altogether; that I'd taken my passenger to the wrong place. Sometimes I'd notice in my rear view mirror that my passenger was staring at me, fixedly – fearfully, or perhaps murderously. I'd flinch and look round, only to realise that they weren't looking at me at all.

Of course, even after you've realised that what has just happened is not *actually* weird, but a trick of the senses, you're still left feeling strange, with a skin-prickling sensation that something even stranger may happen to you at any moment. And once you've felt this way, the atmosphere doesn't diminish as your shift progresses. You're stuck with it for the rest of the night. Only sleep will make that kind of feeling go away.

I was once given a warning about this by another driver. But at the time it was given, I didn't have enough experience to know it was a warning.

Sometimes, mid-week, when trade was quiet, I'd end up dropping by at the office to have a piss and grab a coffee from the vending machine in the back lobby, and I'd meet other drivers doing the same, and maybe I'd stay and chat for a while. I mentioned these odd visual disturbances a couple of times and was given the advice to stop plying trade before it got to that point, that I should knock off before my driving became dangerous and I started to be a liability, to myself as well as others. Good advice. But then I mentioned the same thing to Phil, a driver who'd been on the rank for over fifteen years, and he looked at me with wary intensity and said, 'Don't go there.'

It was eerie, the way the hairs stood up on my forearms. Not particularly at what he said, but at the way he said it.

'What do you mean?' I asked.

'Just don't go there,' he said. 'It's not only tiredness, it's something else as well. If you don't know what I mean, then I'm not going to say any more. You'll know if it happens to you, and all I can say is *don't*, that's all.'

Don't.

I'm not superstitious, but being told this at 3.00am, in the quiet of the night, by someone so serious it was scary, made me feel creepy. Don't? Don't *what*? But Phil just picked up his cigarettes and nodded slightly to emphasise his point, and left me in the vague fug of the over-bright back lobby at the office, the dregs of my coffee bitter and tepid in my mouth, the flushing of the toilet upstairs a seemingly random sound in the night.

Later that evening, I found business had been too quiet to propel me into my calm fugue, and I cycled home pensive and curiously dissatisfied. I wondered what Phil had meant, but soon realised that pondering his words was pointless. He'd been deliberately evasive.

I picked up something hot and greasy and satisfying at the Golden Grill, at the Palmeira end of Church Road, just before it closed at 4.00am, and took it to my small, shabby, but breathtakingly expensive rented basement flat on Lansdowne Street, where the impossibly bright, naked bulb in the sitting room rendered everything stark and unwelcoming. I grabbed a beer from the fridge, then went through to empty my money onto the sitting room floor, and lit a couple of candles, turning the light off, and making a mental note – yet again – to buy a dimmer bulb and a suitable shade as soon as possible.

It took a while to start recognising the regulars. There was Deirdre – ageing, asthmatically breathless – always booked in from either The Regency or The Farm Tavern, with her walking stick, thick lipstick and aching, widowed loneliness. She was always grateful, but unpopular with the drivers because she lived so close that it was always minimum fare, despite the lengthy process of getting her in and out of the cab. She never tipped.

There was Mark – unstable on his feet whether sober or drunk, because of a medical condition that made him unable to fully control his movements – who would sometimes cry with gratitude at the help that taxi drivers were prepared to give him.

There were the girls from the lap-dancing club on Church Road who always travelled home in pairs and who talked in whispers, shocked at themselves for what they were doing; hating it, but stuck with it because they needed to make good money fast, usually because of debt, a situation that inspired a kind of sad, quiet empathy in me.

But perhaps the most memorable of all my early regular fares was an obviously ill, though serenely beautiful woman, perhaps in her late twenties, who travelled from 13 Wish Road to the Cornerstone Community Centre on Palmeira Square every Thursday evening for her 'positive thinking' classes. What was it about her that touched my imagination? What made me want to be the one to collect her and take her to her class? It wasn't just because I was attracted to her quiet beauty, but also because she seemed to be lit internally by something so subtle that I would find myself feeling that it was something in me that I was seeing. She would smile as she came haltingly down the garden path, leaning on her stick, and giving me a casual wave, her frail fingers fluttering as though communicating an esoteric message.

She never seemed concerned or surprised that it was so often me who picked her up, and we would always say hello, and I'd say something trivial about the weather, and she would answer with a comment that was light and optimistic. And after I'd dropped her off, coming round and opening the door for her, or, as the months passed, taking her arm and assisting her up the wheelchair ramp and into the building, I would sit for a while and breathe the scent that she left behind – lavender, but with a hint of citrus – and, for those minutes, I couldn't help but see my own problems as trivial. It was the only time, other than when exhausted, that I felt genuinely alive. Here was a woman who was clearly dying, but dying so *gracefully*, and without any apparent hint of regret; who, instead of giving in to self-pity, as I had when faced with problems, could bring herself to give the gift of her smile, and of her courage. If she hadn't been declining in the way she was, I would certainly have told her that I found her attractive. But there was something so frail about her that I wanted to spare her as many burdens as possible.

I would find myself waiting by Wish Park at around 7.15pm on Thursdays, soon after the start of my shift, just so that I would be the one to be allocated the fare. This would some-times mean logging out of the system for a while. But I became fascinated by the way in which, as she grew weaker, her radiance grew stronger. I wondered, once or twice, whether I was in falling in love with her, and was disturbed by the thought. There is something involuntary about love, I know, and there were so many things about her that were easy to admire – her beauty, the simple way in which she spoke of the world around her, and her attentiveness towards me . . . but a part of me was frightened by the fact that I was becoming obsessed by someone who was *dying*. Was I falling for her precisely because of this, because commitment – or con-summation – would never be an issue?

She never told me her name, and I never asked, so I referred to her in my thoughts as Valerie because she reminded me of someone of that name from my school days. And it was through her that the first, fleeting hints of my own recovery from depression began to become apparent.

In fact, there were other people whose terrible circum-stances helped me decide to get my act together, but I never saw them on a regular basis, so their effect on me wasn't some-thing ongoing and organic. It was a surprise to me how many elderly, sick and disabled people I carried in my cab. I'd expected to be back and forth to the station all the time, and to pubs and clubs and hotels – all of which I did, of course, but sick and elderly people take taxis too; they are dependent on them if they are unable, for whatever reason, to drive their own cars or walk to and from a bus stop.

Mother with two sons.
Younger son: Is Gary our dad?
Mother: No.
Older son: Gary used to be our dad, but he isn't any more.
Eastern Road, December 29th.

2. My mother ran out on us and my father drank himself to death

Okay, I'd better get the 'How I ended up in this predicament' bit over with. I thought I might say something dramatic and tragic like: 'My mother ran out on us when I was ten and my father drank himself to death', but that would just be a case of me trying to make capital out of something that affected me a lot less than other people I was at school with, who were genuinely fucked-up by their families' dysfunction. And I know I was a nightmare child – always in trouble, always going off when I shouldn't, getting up to pranks of one kind or another with my arch conspirator and best friend, Graham. But I was like that from the word go, and would never blame this aspect of my character on the fact that my mother walked out on us. So I might as well just cut to the actual life-changing incident, which didn't happen because of anything that was, or was not, dysfunctional in my family.

I thought, when I found myself reticent to go into details about this before, that it might be because I was embarrassed by it. But, actually, I'm not. I'm just *bored* of it. When misfortune happens, it keeps coming back into your mind over and over again, endlessly in fact, like the waves that break on Brighton beach. I kept thinking, 'Why?' And, like waves, questions like these can crash into your consciousness, blasting everything else away, but they can just as easily lap, quietly but insistently, until you go half mad with the need to think of something else.

In my case, I was running a small company, Downs Electrical, that had a manufacturing unit in Lower Bevendean. I'd inherited it from my father, who'd pioneered a simple electrical switching device which he manufactured and supplied to the automotive industry. He died unexpectedly, aged fifty-five, of various things, none of which he did particularly to excess but which, combined with his extreme sedentariness, managed to kill him.

I'd been working in 'the family firm' (which sounds grand but we only had seven employees) for three or four years by then, and I took it over just after my twenty-first birthday. There was a romantically tragic aspect to this because I had no current girlfriend, and I suddenly looked very good on paper – a twenty-one-year-old, single, solvent, company director. And, in some ways, it felt good too. I was virtually an orphan; I'd never loved my mother, so her absence in my life was a relief rather than a tension (she had temper trouble – I really can't be bothered to say any more than that). And I could turn on the tragic-young-man thing any time I wanted to if it looked like being effective.

What made this easier was that I'd genuinely liked my dad. I know I'm sounding a bit glib about how I landed up owning a successful little company when I was only twenty-one, but losing Dad was a major blow. I wouldn't have gone into the company if I hadn't liked him. I'm not one of those people who can do the hypocrisy thing – you know, dragging yourself into work every day, hating it, and wishing the old codger dead. No, I liked him. The job? Well, I wasn't so bothered about that, but you can't have everything in life, can you? Dad looked after me when Mum left, and he did it well, and it never occurred to me for as much as a nanosecond that I wouldn't follow him into the firm. And when he died . . . I took over.

I was never into the club or drug scene in a major way, but I did do that a bit, then, and I did sleep with a few women – not very successfully, I have to add. I guess the simplest thing to say on that subject is that I've always been self-conscious about my body. That's a fairly major understatement, by the way, but it's not something I'm particularly keen to discuss here. Even taking my shirt off, either in a club or on the beach, has been a big deal for me, and something that I have never had the confidence to do. I've always had trouble with being naked around others, especially strangers. I might tell you a bit more about that later on. Maybe.

As far as being a young executive went, my friends would say things like, 'You were handed all this on a plate, you were,' and they were right. And I *did* appreciate it, up to a point. Up to a point. Maybe I could only do anything *up to a point*. Even caning it. And I didn't manage to do that in the

27

systematic sort of way that young brash men in my position were expected to do. Within a couple of years I settled down to work hard, run my company and make good money, though I had very little time to spend any of it. And that's how things remained for a number of years.

And then it was taken away from me.

Why didn't I foresee it? Because I was young? No, because I was human. The cause was *progress*, in its most narrow definition. The switches that I was manufacturing were made redundant by new, sophisticated computerised switching devices. I mean, our switches were partly computerised, but it was more to do with compatibility and what might be described as 'loyalty technology'. They were made redundant, and so was I, along with my seven employees.

What finished me off was that I allowed myself to be persuaded into a decision by a friend of my father's – a man who had, like me, made a good living from automotive products, and who had, like me, suddenly lost his business for exactly the same reasons. He persuaded me to fight back, to invest everything – and I mean *everything* – I had in fully computerised technology, to produce world-class switches again. And so I did, and we did. But – and this was the point – they were no *better*. Who's going to buy switches from two blokes in Brighton when they've got them, shall we say, *heavily promoted*, by an international corporation?

Bitter? Me? Yes, it does make me go off on one when I think about it. So, I try not to think about it too much. What a waste of time. It won't bring back my house, will it? Or my car, or my – as I now realise it – more or less effortless income. I'm sometimes haunted by those 'friends' who told me I'd had it all handed to me on a plate, because when the plate was taken away, they fucked off pretty sharpish.

My business partner at this time – Derek – refused to give up his quest for recognition of our switches, and had taken out several lawsuits against the company that had 'stolen' a number of our contracts, as well as against the companies that had dumped us. But, unlike Derek, who had only invested part of his capital in the initial venture, I had no money left. And, anyway, I felt that large corporations could afford large lawyers, and that our chances of success in the courtroom were zero. Still, Derek would come round to the flat occasionally and tell me how things were going, which was always 'We're getting there, Stephen, getting there.' I tried to be as polite as possible, but Derek just made me feel worse. We wouldn't get our money back, and hoping for that to happen would ruin him, and drag the misery out for both of us. Because I felt sorry for him, I didn't feel able to tell him to leave me alone, but that was how I felt.

And here I am, at exactly that point in my story that I didn't want to find myself. At the, 'I lost my job, my house, my car . . .' point. The *Oh, the pain! The pain!* point. I did sometimes refer to this as my 'ecstasy of despair', and I hate it, because the only thing that I want to convey is that I became unhappy. Just that clinical fact. I don't want pity, or a gleeful 'serves him right' response; I just want you to know that I came to a moment when I woke up one morning and realised that I was unhappy. I also realised, by the way, that my previous state of mind hadn't been *actively* the opposite – it wasn't a neat binary opposition, or anything as simple as that. These distinctions can become fantastically important when you're sifting through your own personal debris.

I realised that I had done nothing to deserve my job and my salary; they were simply an accident of birth. And now they were gone. I was only twenty-seven, and I kept telling myself that there was plenty of time in which to do something else. There was no reason to be overly concerned. But depression had always been a part of my make up, and depression is not a happy bedfellow of rational thought. It now came to the fore, this time in a different way from the occasional cycles of despondency and weird exhilaration that had always come and gone in the past for no apparent reason.

Some people used to tell me it was biorhythms, or the phases of the moon, but my symptoms weren't as regular as that. I could go for months at a time, perhaps even as much as a year, with no sign. I'd always assumed the condition was genetic. But then I would, wouldn't I, so that I could elect not to examine the causes any more closely?

On the day I handed over the keys of my house to the new owners and took up residence in my rented basement in Lansdowne Street, I could feel myself slipping into the haunted shadow of depression. And, for the first time in my life, I felt that I should resist it with every psychological resource at my disposal. In the past I'd known that, like a cold, my depression would pass. But I could feel that this new echoing cavern of self-pity had no bounds. But even as I tried to stop myself from slipping into it, another part of me was giving myself permission to be relentlessly miserable. After all, and for the first time ever, I could say to myself, *I've got good reason to be pissed off.*

It was a couple of appalling months later that I bumped into Graham. He was the childhood best-friend and mischief-maker that I mentioned earlier, but he'd moved to the US after we'd taken our 'A' levels, and that was the last I'd heard of him. Interestingly, this meant that he predated the whole Downs Electronics thing – both my rise *and* my fall. It was refreshing to meet someone who knew me, but who knew nothing of all that. I'd always remembered him as a forthright person, and that clearly hadn't changed. Almost as soon as he saw me, he described me, accurately, as 'a total fucking mess'.

We met on a sparkling afternoon in August when I was returning from signing on. I'd been through the usual harassment about looking for work and was walking along the seafront feeling dejected. The sun was warm, the light breeze blowing up from the crowded beach was scented with brine and factor twenty-five. And I resented it all. By this stage, I couldn't even bring myself to have a genuine sense of tragedy about the way I felt, just a rather numbing boredom.

It was Graham who stopped and caught my arm. 'Stephen?' he said. 'Stephen Bardot?'

'Yes,' I said, surprised.

'You must remember me – Graham Kingsley?'

It took me a moment, but he'd hardly changed so it was only a question of getting my brain into gear. Although it was ten years since I'd last seen him, he still retained his surety, his candid openness. 'Hey,' I said, 'Graham. I thought you were in America.'

'I'm here on holiday,' he told me.

And so we ended up having a happy-hour pint in the dark, womb-like basement bar, Ali Cats, with him telling me I was a total fucking mess, and me agreeing and explaining a little bit about why. He was staying in a bed-and-breakfast, so I invited him over for a meal at my flat – and we ended up spending the next couple of days together.

It was such a relief having someone around to talk to who could interrupt my despondent cycle of thought. We talked a bit about our schooldays, though very little about my life now, or much about his, come to think of it. He was doing quite well at the American headquarters of the company in which his father was now a top UK executive. A company that made high quality luggage. 'I'm in the baggage business,' Graham laughed. 'There's not much to say about it, except that it's a job. I was kind of resentful at being shipped out to the States just because my parents found me hard to deal with. But at least over there I can be both a "strategic engineer" and have an alternative lifestyle. Still, I guess you get a lot of dope-smoking executives in the UK these days.'

I don't remember much else about our conversations, apart from laughing about how dreadful we'd been as kids. I hadn't thought about it for years and found myself caught up in an absurd nostalgia. We'd been such merry pranksters, always getting into trouble, always being punished, both at home and at school. There was one time we threw bricks through someone's window just because we thought he looked shifty. What a nightmare we must have been.

But the all-important conversation we had was on the evening before Graham returned to the States, which eclipsed everything else that had happened over the previous forty-eight hours. I'd cooked us a junky kind of meal and we'd shared a bottle of wine, and we started talking about what I should do with myself. I'd applied for a few jobs, but my qualifications and experience didn't really add up to anything coherent, and the jobs that they advertised on the terminals at the Job Centre were an insult.

I was currently thinking of going to university and getting myself a degree.

'For someone of your age, there are only two good reasons for getting a degree,' Graham told me. 'Of course, for eighteen-year-olds, there's the whole thing of getting away from home and fucking around for the first time, or getting pissed up and taking drugs without your parents finding out. But for you, it should either be for the simple pleasure of studying, or to gain a qualification that will help you get the sort of job you want.'

He looked down at his curiously long brown toes as he stretched his legs, then slouched deeper into the, rented, IKEA sofa.

'"Because I can't think of anything else to do" is a bad reason,' he added with a laugh.

'It's as good a reason as I'm likely to come up with,' I said.

He sat up at this, as though reminded of something shocking, and looked at me carefully.

'If you really can't think of anything,' he said quietly, 'would you be prepared to try something that I suggest?'

I wasn't sure what he meant.

'Such as?'

'No,' he said, 'it's okay, I shouldn't have said anything. Forget it.'

'What were you going to say?' I asked.

'It's nothing.'

'No, tell me.'

He thought for a moment, then ran his fingers through his hair, knotting his eyebrows in concentration. He suddenly looked just as he had a decade earlier: absurdly young, but oddly mature and knowing.

'You were thinking of giving up three years of your life to get a degree for no other reason than that you couldn't think of anything else to do?'

'Pretty well,' I agreed.

'Okay,' he said, 'give a portion of that time to me. Say, half the time you would give to getting a degree. Eighteen months. Or maybe only a year—'

'What do you mean, "give" you that time?'

'I mean, give up all responsibility for your life. You're sitting there anguishing about what to do with yourself. So stop it. Stop wondering. Let me suggest something.'

I laughed.

'You mean, "do whatever I say"?'

'Don't you trust me?' he asked.

'Yes, but . . .'

'I know you. I respect you. I want the best for you. As you can't think of what to do, give me one reason why I shouldn't decide for you.'

I shrugged.

'Okay,' he said. 'Think about it. If you agree, I'll tell you to do something, and you *must* do it – unless you can think of a good reason not to. And "because I don't want to" isn't a good enough reason. You've got to be able to say, in all honesty, that what I suggest would be damaging to you, psychologically. Only then will I let you off, and try to think of something else.'

I stared at him, breathless, because I knew he was serious, and breathless, too, because I was so tempted to take him up on his suggestion.

'Give me a year. A *year*,' he said. 'I'll give you my email address in California and you can send me regular bulletins. And any time you feel that you need to stop, then you must stop. But only if you *need* to. You'd have to define what you mean by "need", not me.'

I got up and went to have a piss, then went through to the kitchen to make us both coffee. In that short time, in just four or five minutes, I made my decision. Looking back on it, the way I jumped at his suggestion was not because I thought he would solve my life for me: make me happy. It was just that things right then were so shit, that even if they remained shit after I'd started doing whatever it was that I'd agreed to do, at least they'd be no worse. And what bliss it would be to stop wondering, however briefly, what to do with myself.

My amateur psychologist side said, 'You're just refusing to take responsibility for your life.'

Well, alright, but this was at least finite.

One year.

One year.

'Okay,' I said when I came back into the room, 'I'll do it. I'll give you one year. When are you going to tell me what to do?'

'Now, if you like.'

'Okay.'

He shifted slightly, as though uncomfortable, and took a sip of coffee before looking at me, watching for my reaction.

'Become a taxi driver,' he said. 'Working on a night shift.'

Mother to arguing children: This'll end in tears. (Wistful pause.) Probably mine. Hangleton Way, January 3rd.

3. The aroma of medication

I get a call at 2.45am, on a frosty December Saturday night, to go and get someone a take-away meal. This is not a regular Citicabs customer, and so it's a question of collecting the money first before going on the food run. I pull up outside a large, converted house on The Drive and, as there isn't an intercom, let myself into the lobby, looking for flat 14. As I go upstairs, I see a woman of about 25 standing on the landing, wearing only a nightdress. She is doing a sort of dance, partly out of agitation and partly because she has bare feet and the concrete floor is freezing. She is obviously stoned. And distraught. 'Oh my God, oh my God,' she says, 'I've locked myself out.' She has ginger hair piled up on her head, a nose ring, and I can see a barbell in her tongue as she moans, 'I came out and the door swung closed behind me.' She is trying hard not to cry. 'That's terrible,' I tell her, 'how are you going to get back in?' 'I woke my neighbour up and used her phone,' she says, 'a friend of mine is driving over from Shoreham, even as we speak, with my spare keys.' 'Oh,' I say, wondering why she's so upset, 'that's alright then.' 'No, it isn't!' she exclaims, a tear squeezing itself out as she blinks, 'my money's still in the flat, and *Burger King closes in NINE minutes!*' I understand her predicament. 'It's okay,' I tell her, 'I'll trust you. I'll go and get what you want, and you can give me the money when I get back.' 'Will you?' 'Yes,' I say. She gives a little scream of euphoria and, literally, leaps into my arms, kissing me desperately on the lips. I drive recklessly to Burger King, arriving with only a minute to spare, and buy a Double Bacon Cheesburger, fries and Coca-Cola, thus earning myself fanatical gratitude, as well as a handsome tip. Later, when I have to radio the office, Sal laughs. 'I don't know what you did earlier this evening, Stephen,' she says, 'but a woman phoned to say you'd saved her life.'

One of the disappointing things about becoming a taxi driver was that Brighton lost all its topographical secrets. When I was doing my knowledge, I was charmed to find the old Jewish burial ground half way up Ditchling Road, at the top of Hollingdean Lane, and Foredown Tower, and the twittens and passages in the city centre. But after that there was nothing left for me to discover. The physical side of doing the knowledge had been fun, as well as hard work – riding the streets on my bicycle, memorising the 2,300 street names, along with pubs, clubs, hotels, hospitals, churches and so on. It kept me occupied for nearly three months, and it made my brain tingle as though the stimulation was waking it up in some new way. Plus, it was physically tiring too, so that I slept well during that time, a welcome release from my previous insomnia and inertia. And then, I passed my test and was out driving within twenty-four hours.

Of course, it was going to take months for all that knowledge to settle in my mind, even working ten, eleven, twelve hours a night – I rented my cab from 6.00pm to 6.00am and could work as much or as little of that time as I pleased.

Those mid-week hours, when it's quiet and you're waiting for your next fare, can be a nightmare. You don't know whether you're going to be waiting for a minute or an hour. I tried reading novels, but found the on-off-on-off nature of my reading more frustrating than satisfying, and so I would sit in my cab and think. It can be a seriously reflective kind of job at times. I would sometimes wonder if it was going to be a kill-or-cure scenario, given my only partially dormant depressive state.

The radio was no solace, either. Music would always, eventually, make me want to scream, and talk radio wasn't sufficiently consistent in interest value. So, I sat and tried to face my unhappiness in silence; tried to pull together some idea as to what I might do once my year was up. One possibility, of course, was to remain a taxi driver. Not a bad profession, if it suits you . . . I just needed to find out if it suited me – a sane me, that is. If that was possible.

There was a psychiatric hospital in the city that gave our rank a lot of business. It seemed curious to me, especially in the first weeks of driving – before I discovered the shimmering refuge of exhaustion – that I would be giving lifts to people who appeared to have become institutionalised because of conditions so similar to my own. My heart would sometimes ache with pity for these helpless people. I'd heard other drivers moan about them, saying, 'They should get out and do an honest day's work. Most of them are just mad with boredom.' But I could see the trapped look in their faces, a bewilderment, a tenderness perpetually inflamed by the blows of life.

It was always in the first couple of hours of my shift that I picked up the psychiatric cases – people who would never be out later than 7.00 or 8.00pm because they were in sheltered accommodation – and it was odd because after a while it was possible to recognise some of them because of their smell. I've always had a particularly acute sense of smell, and in a taxi you have plenty of opportunity to experience what people smell like, from the ageing, designer-label-wearing, perfectly made-up women who are so liberally drenched with perfume that it makes you gag, through lighter scents, to soap, cosmetics and that fresh laundry smell. Then there's food, beer, garlic (*garlic!*), common or garden dirt, BO, piss, dried vomit, and more subtle, and even disturbing smells. It was in this olfactory landscape that I began to realise that some psychiatric cases have a smell that is identical from individual to individual. Not an unclean smell, but – and it took me a while to pinpoint it – a sort of sour, fatty smell. I guess it's the result of certain specific kinds of medication, and it was a little sad to think that they were unaware of this invisible haze that surrounded them.

Once I took a woman of about thirty-five home after a stint in hospital. She was on this odd, fatty medication, and was monosyllabic in reply to my attempts at gentle conversation – cheery conversation, I quickly discovered, can be embarrassingly inappropriate at times – and when I got her home, her husband/partner came out, and they looked at each other as she pulled herself, with medicated slowness, from the cab. Their expressions were something I shall never forget. There was shock, and fear, and 'What the fuck is happening to us?' and 'I love you but I don't know what to say; this thing is outside anything that life has prepared me for'. They both tried to pay me. The woman more insistently, being so desperate to be in control of *something* in her life. I drove away, slowly because of the punitive speed bumps on Southover Street, and realised that I would never, ever again be able to generalise about what 'people' are like.

It was at around that time that I began to be intrigued by 'Valerie'. Her scent of lavender and citrus was one of those lingering smells that would surprise me long after I'd dropped her off at her positive thinking classes. I would get a haunting echo of it, reverberating somehow as it diminished throughout the evening.

One of the things about Valerie that I found shocking was that, although I knew she was deteriorating, I was still totally unprepared for the first time I saw her genuinely, desperately sick. She was helped out of the house by a nurse, who smiled at me appreciatively when I opened the cab door, and said: 'Could you get them to help at the other end? They're expecting you, and they've got a wheelchair ready.'

'Of course,' I told the nurse, whose dark blue uniform made Valerie's illness seem suddenly, intensely real.

Valerie herself was as serene as ever, though she spoke in a near-whisper. I couldn't think of anything to say, so she was the first to break the silence.

'Snowdrops are going to be out soon,' she said. 'The shoots are coming up in the garden. I hope I'll get to see them bloom. They're so delicate, aren't they?'

I glanced across at her, at her frailty, and wondered at how gracefully she could refer to her impending death.

'Yes,' I said, and added after a pause, 'though I think I prefer bluebells. Have you seen some of the bluebell woods out towards Haywards Heath?'

'Yes,' she said with pleasure. 'I really think that, in profusion, they are the most . . . wonderful colour.'

When I stopped the cab I said, 'Do you know when your class finishes this evening? I'd be happy to come back and collect you.'

She smiled, and leaned over slightly to pat my arm. 'It's okay,' she told me, 'Malcolm, the man who runs the course, will be giving me a lift home this evening. But thank you.'

The next time I saw her, she had to be helped down the path by the nurse, who accompanied her in the taxi and who went off to get a wheelchair at the other end. I got out as usual and opened the passenger door and Valerie took my hand. And, as I helped her up, her body buckled slightly so that I had to catch her round the waist. She was emaciated, and clutched at me slightly as she righted herself, and she smiled with gratitude and said 'Thank you'. I looked at her, just looked at her, as the nurse came down the ramp with a wheelchair and whisked her away.

I was never asked to collect her again.

A couple of weeks later, the subject of Valerie came up when I radioed Sal at the office, to order a return lift for the fare I'd just dropped off. Sal was one of the night staff in the radio room, and had often allocated me the Wish Road job. As it was a soporifically quiet evening, I knew she wasn't busy, so I chatted for a while and then asked, 'Oh, by the way, Sal, do you remember that sick girl who used to go to the Cornerstone Community Centre? Did she die? I haven't picked her up for a while, and I just wondered.'

'Doesn't ring a bell, Stephen,' she said. 'Where did she live?'

'13 Wish Road,' I said.

And then Sal said the words that would change everything.

'But Stephen,' she told me, 'there is no such address. Wish Road doesn't have a number 13.'

I stared at the hand set. 'Are you *sure*?'

'Yup,' she told me. 'Sorry I can't be more helpful, Stephen. This one hasn't come through us. Are you sure she wasn't one of your private clients?'

I drove to Wish Road, mystified by Sal's assertion that there was no number 13. But she was right. Someone had been sufficiently superstitious to make sure there wasn't a number 13. The odd numbers went: 7,9,11,11a,15,17 . . . There was no 13, and number 11a was a totally different house from the one that I'd been visiting all this time to collect Valerie. It was a plain building, from the fifties probably, with a built-in garage that had a brand new metal door painted white, and a small garden full of roses. Number 13 had been a standard but shabby 1930s semi, with diamond-leaded windows.

If the house I'd been collecting Valerie from wasn't on Wish Road, where was it? I felt a curious feeling of horror at this thought, because it seemed so bizarre and impossible. Okay, I would agree that I've led a sheltered life, and that, because of this, I can accept that there are some things I haven't experienced. But houses that disappear?

My first reaction was to assume that I must have been waiting in an adjacent road, mistakenly thinking of it as Wish Road. But no, Wish Road was beside Wish Park, and there – as I looked round – was the tree, whose shade I'd so often parked beneath as I waited for Valerie's bookings to come through. And, though Sal had said so casually that it must have been one of my private clients, at this stage in my taxiing career I had no private clients.

I sat at the wheel of my cab and logged the computer onto 'manual', so that I was off-system, and sat looking at 11a Wish Road, and thought, *What does this mean?*

And then I remembered. The driver. Phil. He'd said those enigmatic words to me when I'd talked to him about my oddly altered perception when I was exhausted. What had he said? 'Don't go there.' He'd known something.

I radioed Sal once more.

'Is Phil on this evening?' I asked her, and when she told me that he was, I drove back to Boundary Road and staked out the office. I parked up by the Audi franchise near the tennis courts, where I could be inconspicuous, then logged out and waited. If anything was guaranteed to make me feel strange, it was sitting in my cab in silence as the calm of the dead of night settled precariously around me. The only sound was that of the engine, which I would run every now and then to keep the cab warm. It seemed that I had to wait an incredibly long time, but it can't have been more than an hour or so before I saw Phil park up and go into the office. I got out of the cab, crossed over, and followed him in.

He was by the coffee machine as I came down the corridor.

'Hi, Stephen,' he said, 'coffee?'

I nodded and he pressed a button on the machine and I watched the desultory trickle of coffee dribble down into the brown ribbed plastic cup.

'Quiet night,' he said.

'Phil,' I said, 'I'm glad I bumped into you, because I wanted to ask you something . . .'

He glanced at me questioningly as he passed me my coffee.

'Something's happened,' I said.

He saw my expression, raised his hand to silence me, and said, 'Don't tell me. I don't want to know.'

He was, I don't know, kind of *glaring* at me. I was so surprised by his reaction that I was speechless for a moment.

'I can see,' he said, 'that you've crossed the threshold. I did it once or twice in my early days as a driver. A lot of drivers who've done the night shift have come pretty close to it, though most of them will deny it. One or two that I've known over the years have dabbled in it. But I've only known one person who really tried to find out about it. A good friend of mine.'

'What happened to him?'

'He died.'

He gulped down his coffee and winced as it scalded him, and he said, 'Don't say I didn't warn you.'

'But warn me of *what?*'

'I don't know,' he said. 'All I can tell you is that you know when you're crossing the threshold. You know because something happens that can't happen. And when you notice, when you realise, you can make sure you don't go any further. By stopping, dropping off your cab and going home. And,' he added, 'I have no more advice to offer you. I don't know any more than that because . . .' He looked at me carefully. '. . . I didn't go there.'

I looked down at my coffee, scummy with beige froth.

'And please,' he said as he picked up his keys, 'don't mention this to me again. It freaks me out.'

It freaked *him* out? What about me? I drove over to Mile Oak, dropped the cab off and cycled home feeling weird to say the least. I was tempted to go and have another look at 11a

Wish Road. I was only a block away from it as I returned along Portland Road, past the bingo hall and the Venetian-looking church on the corner of Tamworth Road. But I didn't want to face, yet again, the fact that the house I was sure I'd been visiting seemed no longer to be there.

Over the next couple of weeks, I knocked off the long hours. But, although I felt rested and my sense of physical health drastically improved, my earnings fell so much that I realised it would be more and more difficult to service my debts. Plus, I had more time on my hands. I know I should have used this time to start seeing my friends again: people like Lou, my closest remaining friend from school, or Katherine, another friend from my youth, a lesbian who always talked sense. Or one of those friends I didn't know particularly well, but whom I could always join for an evening if I came across them in places like the Great Eastern or the Prince Albert. But I didn't. Although I wasn't suffering from exhaustion any more, I found that I didn't feel sociable.

As time passed – inevitably, I suppose – I began to become more and more curious about what I'd been warned against. This is partly a human trait, to want to do whatever it is that you've been told not to. But for me it was also a depression thing. When you're well, stable and happy, you wouldn't consider jeopardising your happiness by doing something that you know, in your heart, is psychologically dangerous. But when you're unhappy, you can say to yourself, 'My life's crap as it is, so I might as well do X, Y or Z. I mean, how much worse can things get?' The answer, as we all know, is usually a *hell of a lot*, but unhappy people are amazingly adept at self-deception, and so we avoid telling ourselves these truths.

On the third Friday after I'd reduced my hours, I just knew

that there was a question I needed to answer, and the only state in which I had any hope of trying to answer it was one of utter exhaustion.

It was now early February, and at the start of my shift that night I felt some change in myself, felt a vibrant energy, a creeping excitement, and I knew, I *knew* that I was going to work twelve hours straight through without a break, and that on Saturday, when business was going to be hectic, I would push myself even further into exhaustion, because the day driver never picked the cab up before 8.00am on a Sunday, and so I could have it for fourteen hours straight if I wanted to.

In the end, I collapsed into bed at 8.30am on Sunday, having worked twenty-six hours in two days. Nothing even remotely strange had happened to me, and I fell into a deep sleep, waking up feeling empty and enervated at six o'clock. Instead of taking the evening off, as I usually did on Sundays, I forced myself to work again, stopping to pick up a burger on Church Road on my way to Mile Oak and eating it as I pedalled down Portland Road into a stinging, westerly rain.

I kept this workload up all through the week, then forced myself to do twenty-six hours over the following Friday and Saturday, and when I got home on Sunday morning I couldn't sleep. My whole being yearned to rest, but I was so frazzled from driving that all I could do was sit, bug-eyed, on my bed and stare at the wall. *But nothing had happened.* Not a shimmer. Not so much as a moment of confusion.

On Sunday evening I drove into the back of another cab. I should have expected this, the way I was behaving. The Galaxy's front bumper was cracked, but I'd managed to bash the other driver's rear bumper half off. Still, I was lucky – *I* wasn't kept off the road while waiting for a new bumper to be delivered. But I had to pay the other driver handsomely – in cash – thus neatly eclipsing any financial advantage that might have been mine from working all these extra hours.

But I kept on driving. And still nothing happened.

The more tired I became, the more irritating I found the perennial taxi hassles to be – the classic several-times-a-night-during-busy-periods business of turning up to collect someone only to find that they've already left, usually by having ordered taxis from more than one rank. Those minutes of waiting, when you know no-one is going to come out, when you've radioed through a no-show and have been told to wait 'just another couple of minutes' started to make me feel like punching someone. Then there were people who would say, 'Look, I've only got £5.60. Can you take me as far as the money lasts.' In the early days, I would always take the person to their doorstep. It usually only meant a few extra minutes for me, but for them it could be a real life-saver, and it always gave me a warm feeling to so easily earn such genuine gratitude. But now, I started to resent it. One evening, I made a sad, drunken youth get out, coatless, in the late-February rain, at the foot of Hangleton Way, when he had that long hill to walk up. And I thought, then, that by working so hard while so tired, I was losing something in me that I couldn't name, but which was precious above all else.

At last, after seventeen days on the go, things finally began to change. This time it was different in that I didn't see things that weren't there, I just found that, from time to time, I was incapable of keeping my eyes open. I would sometimes have to pull into a lay-by and close my eyes for a while, and then I would have the bizarre sensation of being propelled, forcibly, into a dream-state. I called these happenings 'dream-punctures'. I think they were a result of not getting enough dream-time when I slept – fitfully – during the day. I would find myself with an utter imperative to close my eyes, especially during that time of night between midnight and 4.00am when the human body's circadian rhythm is set for sleep. It was a sufficiently short fuse that, sometimes, it was agony to wait until I'd dropped off my fare, and then, once I'd pulled up somewhere, and even before I'd closed my eyes, I would start to dream. Intense, mundane flickers would pass through my consciousness with incredible speed – *bang, bang, bang* – so that I could hardly recognise the images that they contained. It was an unpleasant experience, because it was so clearly born of desperation.

These incidents of imperative dream-punctures were useful, though, because even if I only slept for ten minutes, I would wake up, if not actually refreshed, then at least properly functional again. Once I'd had one of these stops, the rest of my shift would be fine.

The only problem was that I would sometimes wake up in a different place to where I'd gone to sleep.

The first time this happened to me, I'd pulled up at the foot of Victoria Park, in the quiet turning circle there, and had fallen asleep within seconds. When I woke up only ten minutes later – I'd set the alarm on my phone – I was parked up on the seafront by Shoreham Harbour.

Freaky.

But the weird part was that, each time I experienced this change in location, I woke up especially refreshed, and was able to continue my shift feeling as though I'd just woken from a full night of unbroken sleep. On that first occasion, at Shoreham Harbour, I kept wondering what had happened, and whether I ought to stop driving and go home to get some rest. But, as I say, I felt fine, and after two or three fares, I didn't exactly forget what had happened, but it receded in my mind until I got home. Then, after opening a beer, I sat to count my money. As I did so, I considered the consequences of sleep-driving. Had I been a hazard? Was I in danger of killing both myself and others? Because I didn't want to face the consequence of answering yes to these questions, I simply put them out of my mind.

The second time it happened, I'd stopped on Hollingdean Lane, and woke up on West Drive, looking out over Queen's Park. The Galaxy was squeezed tightly between a Land Rover Discovery and a Ford Focus. After my initial disorientation at waking up like this, and the surreal moments of trying, in the dark, to work out where I might be, I ignored what had happened and got on with my shift – a curiously easy thing to do at 4.00am.

The third time, however, I was startled awake in Tesco's car park. A man was tapping on my window, looking perplexed.

'Hey, mate,' he said, 'what are you doing here?'

'Sorry,' I told him, 'I just stopped for a few minutes' kip.'

'But, how did you get in?' he asked. 'The barrier's locked down, and I checked the car park earlier to make sure it was empty.'

I didn't know what to say, so I shrugged sleepily and he scratched his head and said, 'Well, I'd better let you out,' and he went off to his little booth, taking out a set of keys, as I started the engine and drove across to the barrier. I smiled at him and gave him a friendly wave, but he didn't respond in any way at all, just looked at me without comprehension as I drove past.

Woman: *What are you and your wife going to do on her birthday?*
Man: *Have a fight.* Saxon Road, Hove, February17th.

4. The incendiary qualities of flour.

I pick a woman up one weekday evening at just after midnight. She is drunk, but not very drunk, and she smiles and chats to me as I drive her from Cobton Drive to Portslade Old Village, via the Sainsbury's petrol station on Hangleton Link Road, where she wants me to stop so that she can buy a Mars bar, because she 'Can't last another minute without chocolate.' I wait in the cab while she goes in and makes her purchase, coming out, smiling expansively, and handing me a Twix as she gets back into the cab. 'For you,' she says. This simple action I find astonishingly moving. How often do passengers think of their driver as another human being? Even when a person is spilling out their life story to a taxi driver, that taxi driver isn't real to them. They're just an ear to be talked into. So,

I wonder if the woman is stoned, but she has none of that compulsiveness that stoned people have when they eat. This is merely recreation, and I smile and enjoy my Twix as I drive, pulling up, sticky-fingered, at the lower end of Southdown Road. 'It's further along,' she tells me. 'Number thirteen?' I say, 'It's just here.' 'No,' she says with a laugh, 'I didn't ask for thirteen, I asked for a hundred and thirty nine.' 'Oh,' I laugh. 'Sorry about that, it's been a long shift.' But I feel a prickle of *something*. I think back to her getting in the cab and I'm sure that she asked for thirteen. But then 'a hundred and thirty nine' . . . well, I guess it would be easy to mishear, especially when tired. Earlier in the evening I had terrible trouble understanding a girl who seemed to be asking for Arlen Close, when in fact she was saying *Hammond* Close indistinctly. I stop off at Budgens and drink a carton of milk to settle my stomach – my guts aren't responding well to my erratic intake of food and the Twix I've just eaten has given me a sugar high that makes me feel dizzy.

The night after the above encounter I slept better, for some reason, and the next day wondered whether I was simply being a little deranged, working so hard and expecting something definable, or categorisable, to happen. The only consolation was that, once more, I'd had no time to feel unhappy or depressed. But now, even more than ever, I realised that one couldn't simply keep this up for ever, working long shifts seven days a week. At some point I was going to have to face up to . . . what?

My future, I suppose.

I still hadn't emailed Graham to tell him how I was getting on with the taxiing, as I'd promised him I would. I couldn't think of anything coherent to say to him, and so I hadn't bothered. At the back of my mind I was expecting to save up enough money to fly out to California and stay with him for a few weeks at the end of my year. That was about the only plan I had, other than to survive my time as a taxi driver and to see whether it suited me or not as a profession.

I continued to work long hours. Sometimes my time would be spent in a series of tedious short journeys with nothing to distinguish one from the other, and sometimes I would be distracted for a while by what you might call a 'story':

It's Thursday night and I get to drive out to Ditchling, on the other side of the downs, to collect a swarthy Spanish baker and bring him back to Hove. I love lifts like this: good fares where you get to drive for a while away from city streets. It is two-thirty when I pick the man up and he is furious. 'Bloody police,' he says in a curious, half-Spanish half-cockney accent. 'Bloody, fuckin' middle-class, Ditchling *police*. They don't stop a respectable white person in the night on the High Street here, but me, *me* . . . I'm respectable, but they stop me each time I work more than eleven at night. Fuckin' pigs. I bloody hate 'em.' I drive him back and we talk about baking. You certainly learn disparate things as a taxi driver . . . I had no idea that flour is pumped into dough machines in large bakeries through highly pressurised pipes. I also had no idea that this could be dangerous, as airborne flour is highly flammable, and so a burst flour pipe can lead to a major explosion. 'You try it, try it at home,' he tells me. 'Take a handful of flour and *bang!* hit your hand – like this – and, whoosh, you have a cloud in the air. And have a friend with a lighter and, whoosh . . . poof! Flames!' I laugh with him, and think perhaps I can surprise people like Lou, or Kat next summer at barbeque time. 'Which burns better,' I ask, 'plain or self-raising?' 'Fine, that's all,' he says, 'it must be fine, very fine-ground flour.' As he says this, I am at the top of Dyke Road. A drizzle has set in so that the lights of Hove are misty in the distance. I start to turn down Woodland Drive, and fail to notice the BMW approaching. The reason I fail to notice is because it must be coming towards me at something over 100 miles an hour (in a 30mph limit) and so it takes me completely by surprise. I brake hard, half sure that there is going to be a major impact. I brace myself for it, and try to pull back onto my side of the road. My passenger lets out a terrified shriek as the Galaxy slews to the right. The BMW driver also brakes hard, but neither of us manages to stop quite in time, and we clack bumpers at maybe four or five miles per hour, with a surprisingly loud crunch in the quiet of the night. I turn the meter off, sit for a moment and turn to my passenger, ready to apologise to him. But after a stunned silence, he lets out a shout of laughter, and continues to shake with merriment as I get out to confront the other driver, who opens his window. I lean down to talk to him. He stinks of alcohol and looks so frightened I almost feel sorry for him, with his dishevelled suit and shaking hands. I regard myself as being about the least intimidating person in the world, but I guess this guy knows how much trouble I can make for him. 'How fast were you going?' I ask. 'And how much have you had to drink?' The bloke doesn't reply. 'I think we'd better call the police, don't you?' 'No,' he says. 'Please.' I go round to the front of the cab to look at the damage. The previously cracked side of my bumper has taken the impact and is now mashed. I go back to him. 'That's hundreds of pounds worth of damage,' I tell him. 'Look,' the guy says, 'I'll pay for it. Don't get anyone else involved.' 'I don't know,' I say. 'I'll have to, won't I? What about insurance and so on.' 'I've got money,' he says, pulling a truly awesome wad of banknotes from his pocket. He peels several fifty pound notes off and looks up at me. 'How much,' he asks as he unpeels note after note, 'how much do you need?' I shrug as he drops a handsome pile onto my palm, and when he sticks out his hand, I hesitate, then shake it and say, 'Okay, okay, but don't drive any further tonight. Where do you live?' 'Lewes,' he says. 'Park up over there, and I'll order you a taxi. And, no,' I add, when he is about to argue, 'this is not up for debate. Either you take a taxi home or I call the police.' I order another cab from the rank, and sit for the five minutes it takes for it to turn up. I want to be sure the BMW man doesn't try to drive off as soon as my back is turned. As I leave and set off down Woodland Drive, I smile and tell the baker that the cab is already booked in the next day to have its bumper replaced. I've made back all the money my own accident cost the previous week. We consider what kind of person carries that amount of cash around on them, and come to the conclusion that, whatever it is, it can't be legal. When I drop the baker off on Bennet Avenue, he hands me a twenty pound note. 'No, no,' I tell him, 'have this one on me.' 'No,' he shakes his head, 'my employer, he pays for this. But, you give me a receipt, okay? This is the best lift I ever have.' When I drop the cab off, I leave £50 in the glove compartment for the day-driver who is going to lose a couple of hours' trade while waiting for the mashed bumper to be changed. At least it's booked in early.

It's almost impossible to put into words how different I felt at the beginning of a shift from the state I'd be in at the end. I would regard myself with horror as I cycled – still knackered – to pick up my taxi at the beginning of the evening. It seemed so absurd to work so hard for such intangible reasons. But, by the end of my shift, I became kind of *locked* into what I was doing, so that it was only numb incapacity that would make me knock off.

When, one evening, I saw that familiar old flicker, that tarry yellow smudge at the edge of buildings, I was almost tearful with gratitude to have regained that particular kind of tiredness. I realised, then, that it would inevitably become more difficult to get into this state as I became increasingly familiar with the city, and as the combination of driving, working out my route, and talking to my customers became less of a constant mental juggling act.

And sure enough, the reappearance of the tarry smudge was a one-off. After that, I didn't even get close to that feeling of vibrant, exhilarating exhaustion of the early days. I just started to become grindingly tired instead. And when, one night, I took a silent youth to his home on Poplar Avenue, I hardly even responded when he said, 'No, it's not here, it's further up the road, mate.'

'You didn't ask for number thirteen, then?' I asked.

'No,' he assured me. 'I asked for forty-two.'

When I dropped him off, he paid me and said, 'Get some sleep, mate, you're a mess.'

I couldn't disagree. I dropped the Galaxy off at four, cycled home and . . . became unconscious.

The following day I felt even worse. The people that I was ferrying home from the psychiatric hospital were in better shape than I was. Later, I collected two particularly drunk women from the Golden Cross after closing time, and almost laughed when they asked to be taken to 'number thirteen Gardner Road'.

'Are you sure you want number *thirteen* Gardner Road?' I asked.

'Yes,' one of them said, 'number thirteen.'

'You're sure? Number *thirteen*?'

'Of course we're fucking sure,' the other one said, 'what is this?'

'Nothing,' I laughed, 'I just seem to have an . . . affinity with the number thirteen.'

'Oh, an *affinity*.'

I drove them home and kept smiling to myself and shaking my head. The women thought I was nuts, and when they asked why I was smiling so much, I laughed and said, 'It's nothing.'

It was a crisp evening and even though there was a late-season twinkling of frost on the cars that I drove past, I could feel the spring approaching. It wouldn't be long before I was driving the first part of my shift in daylight. The snowdrops that Valerie had hoped – and failed – to live long enough to see, had been out for some time. I could see a little clump of them in the garden as I pulled up outside number thirteen Gardner Road.

'Here you are,' I said.

'Not here,' one of the women told me, 'it's on up and round the corner.'

'But this is number thirteen,' I told them. 'You asked *specifically* for number thirteen. I corroborated it with you. Twice.'

'No, we asked for number fifty-seven,' the other one told me, '*fifty*-seven, you mad git.'

They laughed incredulously, and I drove on feeling

suddenly out of my depth and so confused I could hardly concentrate on how much further I needed to go.

'Here,' one of them called, with a sneery laugh, 'just coming up on the right, Mr Taxi Driver. Number fifty-seven, number *fifty-fucking-seven.*'

I didn't feel that the world was shimmering; I didn't feel that it was strangely thrilling – I felt so tired that I could hardly even focus on the money that was handed to me, and I fumbled as I got their change. I didn't get a tip, and the more drunk of the two leaned towards me and said, 'Why are taxi drivers either fat and stupid, or *crazy!*'

I watched them stagger up the path to their door, and thought, *Go home, Stephen.*

When I woke up at one o'clock, I felt that something had changed, something brittle had broken in me. Something had cracked, making a chink to let some light in. I wasn't cut out to be a taxi driver. I thought about my promise to Graham: I had agreed to give up a year of my life, on a mere whim, to someone I hadn't seen for ten years. It was a nonsense. Okay, I could say, quite honestly, that it had pulled me out of my inertia. I was now no longer hanging around, signing on and feeling sorry for myself. I was in a job that – yes, I could admit it – I *hated*, and right now anything would seem better than this half-life in which I'd come to believe that there really had been some weird, dying girl who lived in a disappearing house; in which I had believed the word of one single taxi driver who had tried to scare me in the night for whatever stupid reason, by telling me that I was on the edge of entering, what . . . another world? It was crazy, and I had fallen for it to the extent that even drunkards could tell that I was becoming crazy too.

Enough.

*

I didn't work that night. I had my first night off in over four weeks. I watched some TV, went to that Indian take away on Prestonville Road and got myself a vegetable dansak and phoned Lou to ask when I could see her next. She wasn't free that night, so I arranged to see her a couple of days later at Septimus, an expensive organic vegetarian restaurant on Middle Street. My treat, I told her, adding, 'Have you any idea how much I earned in the last month?' when she said, 'I thought you were broke.' I didn't say that I'd earned it by working over 80 hours a week.

The next day, I made a resolution. I would only drive five nights a week: eight hours a night during the week and ten hours on Fridays and Saturdays. And I would take Sundays and Mondays off. This meant I would be working a total of 44 hours in the Galaxy, which was *quite enough for anyone thank you very much*. And, during the day, I would look for another job. If you counted the three and a half months that I'd spent doing The Knowledge, it meant I had now given nearly six months to this task, and that was enough to have fulfilled the spirit of what had been set for me by Graham. I would email him and explain that he'd been right; what he'd asked me to do had worked – it had got me off my arse and given me a more healthy perspective on my life. I was immensely grateful to him, *but I'd done my time*.

I took the next two days off. Derek, my ex-business partner, with impeccable timing, turned up on the first morning. He looked smug, and told me that his cousin, who was a solicitor, had taken over the legal side of his affairs on a 'no win, no charge' basis. Derek was, naturally, delighted.

'It means there's a good chance that we'll both get our money back,' he told me. 'Andy would never have taken on something like this unless he thought he was onto a winner.'

I invited Derek in and gave him coffee. There was something in the way he projected himself, and all his aspirations, into the future that made me feel breathless, somehow, and sad. It was as if he was saying, 'I'll be happy at some point in the future, when my current plans have come to fruition'. He had put his life on hold. Seeing this in him, made me realise how I'd done the same myself after Downs Electronics had gone to the wall, and the thought gave me an unexpected surge of hope. I was looking to the future, now, but in a completely different way to Derek. It was a shock to realise that this was the case, that I was no longer stuck in an endless replay of the demise of my company.

I wanted to say to Derek, 'Let it go. Leave it to your cousin, and get on with other things.' His conversation was full of simplistic revenge fantasies against those who had done him wrong, and it was both tiresome and tedious to have to listen to his tirade. Even though I knew he was including me in his fantasy of a bright future, and even though he was hoping to get my money back as well as his own, I eventually had to ask him to leave, pleading a non-existent dental appointment.

When he'd gone, I sat on the settee in the sitting room and gazed out of the window. I didn't know what to do with myself. How odd that only a few months ago I'd had so much time on my hands, and it had slipped by so easily, without me apparently doing *anything*. Now, I had that irritating, finger-tapping boredom that prevented me from relaxing.

Eventually, I cycled up to Devil's Dyke, on the downs, and walked along the ridge to the radio masts and the youth hostel on the next hill. It was a walk I'd done many times before, but today I felt bored and listless. It was incredible that I'd been so fit, so recently, from doing The Knowledge, and now I could sense it slipping away because of the extreme sedentariness of my lifestyle.

The downs were beautiful, as usual. Where the watery winter sunshine had managed to penetrate, it had melted the frost, but in the lee of each grassy tussock there was a white, icy shadow that I could hear crunching slightly beneath my boots. The air was clear, and, westwards, I could see along the coast to Worthing and beyond. Back east was Brighton, looking particularly hilly from this angle. No wonder doing The Knowledge had made me fit.

By the time I got home, I was freezing and tired, and as I lay in a hot bath, a kind of creeping lethargy came over me that was wonderful. I lay, looking up at the ceiling and thinking of nothing in particular, and not minding that I wasn't doing anything, and not *wanting* do to anything. Now that I hadn't driven for nearly forty eight hours, I was even more pleased with my decision to give up taxiing. It was only when I was away from the cab that I began to be able to see this decision as the obvious next step.

On Thursday, when *The Argus* had its job section, I bought the paper and spent a couple of hours working through the 750 jobs that were advertised. I phoned for application forms for three – all junior management positions in medium sized businesses in the conurbation – and felt good about what I was doing. Later, I went down for a brisk walk along the seafront and watched the waves for a while, which was restful, though there was a bitter easterly wind coming along the Channel that was whipping a stinging spray up off the sea. I retreated after half an hour or so for warm toast and coffee before setting out to meet Lou.

As I walked down Lansdowne Street, I felt that a chapter was closing in my life. I realised that it might take me some time to find a job that suited me. But I knew that, rather than carrying on as I was, I'd prefer to leave my flat, find myself cheaper accommodation and take more or less any low-paid, low-stress job.

I met Lou for a drink at the Earth & Stars and realised how much I'd missed the Thursday night busy-but-not-frantic bustle in town, and I noticed how ordinary and generally happy people seemed. And it felt as though I had been away for a long time – and that I was finally coming back.

'I never really thought you'd actually *become* a taxi driver,' Lou told me. 'When you mentioned it, it seemed completely mad. And it's exactly the kind of thing that I would expect Graham to suggest, by the way. It doesn't surprise me at all that he's working out in California, smoking dope and being a "strategic engineer" in the luggage business. Of *course* he is. His dad must have pulled strings for him in the industry. Graham was never the kind of person to do anything on his own initiative. Poor Graham. He was born just a little too late to go out there and be a hippy.'

'You say the word hippy as though it was a swear word,' I laughed.

'Actually, I think he'd have preferred hanging out with Jack Kerouac, William Burroughs and Allen Ginsberg to Ken Kesey or Timothy Leary.'

'You mean gay versus straight?' I asked.

'Is that all modern American beat-culture boils down to,' Lou asked, sadly, 'the choice between gay and straight?'

'You're the academic,' I said. 'You're the one who's studied

American culture. You're the one who lectures in it. You tell me.'

She smiled.

'I was just thinking about Graham, that's all,' she said. 'I'm sorry I missed him when he was over. I liked him, you know. You should have phoned me, you bastard, and not kept him all to yourself.'

I shrugged by way of admission to this selfishness, and we left and wandered down to Middle Street and our meal. Septimus was busy when we arrived and we were squeezed into a corner by a pillar. I leaned forward and kissed Lou's cheek.

'I've missed you,' I told her.

'I've missed you, too,' she replied. 'I'm impressed that you decided to work as a taxi driver and that you saw the whole thing through. I'd never thought of you as being particularly flexible or open to change, so I'm impressed that you've proved you are. But you're working too hard; you look dreadful. Drawn and underweight and very pale.'

'I've decided to give it up,' I told her. 'It doesn't suit me. I've already started looking for another job.'

'Good,' she said.

As we ate, I made an attempt to explain a little bit about the unusual significance of the number thirteen. She frankly didn't believe me about the disappearing house – and why should she? I found it almost impossible to believe myself. And as for people seeming to ask me for number thirteen, when in fact they wanted somewhere else . . .

'It's a typical symptom of exhaustion,' Lou told me. 'In your case, you became fixated on a number for whatever reason, say, because you found out that there isn't a number 13 Wish Road, and then, once you became fixated on it, and once you were exhausted enough – and let's face it, you're still exhausted to the point of major ill-health – then, you began to conjure that number out of nowhere. It all seems weird and uncanny to you, but it's just your mind being overstretched so far that it no longer knows what's going on.'

I nodded my agreement and took a sip of wine.

'God, you're so right,' I said. 'Listening to myself speak like this makes it all sound so stupid and implausible. That's what happens when you spend too much time on your own. You lose perspective. You don't have anyone to point out when you're beginning to go off the rails.'

We laughed and clinked glasses and then, as I replaced the glass on the highly polished, pale wood of my table, I saw her. And froze.

'That's her!' I gasped.

'What, who?'

'The nurse,' I said. 'The nurse who helped Valerie when she was too ill to walk by herself. She's at that table over by the window.'

'Nurse?' she said. 'You haven't mentioned a nurse.'

But I was already on my feet and making my way over to her. She was sitting with a man of about her own age, which is to say perhaps forty-five or fifty. He looked smart and stern and I guessed he was her husband, and he looked up, surprised, as I approached them. I stopped by the table and The Nurse did not look at me, even though she must have been aware of my presence so close to her.

'You!' I said, more loudly than I'd intended.

The woman turned at the sound of my voice. She seemed completely unsurprised at this intrusion.

'Yes, you!' I said. 'You know. You know about Thirteen. You know what it is – or what it means.'

She was so calm and so unruffled by my arrival at her table.

Even in my agitation I noticed that she was beautiful. There is no other word I can think of to describe her; she had a mature beauty that some women possess that inspires awe, it is so controlled and so poised. She looked at me, but did not react in any way to what I'd said. It was as though I hadn't spoken.

'Don't pretend you don't know what I'm talking about,' I told her, 'you're The Nurse from 13 Wish Road, you're The Nurse who helped Valerie, or whatever her name is: the girl who died, the girl I used to take to the Cornerstone Community Centre—'

The man looked embarrassed and said, quietly, 'Please . . .'

'Come on,' I said to her, 'come on. Don't ignore me. What happened to that girl, and what happened to the house she lived in? I know you know, you were *there*.'

'Is this gentleman bothering you,' said a voice behind me.

I turned and found the head waiter poised at my side, another waiter behind him ready to give a hand.

The stern man, The Nurse's companion, looked relieved at this intervention and said, 'Yes. Yes, he is rather.'

The head waiter took my elbow but I shook him off. I hadn't realised that I'd been causing a scene, but I didn't care that silence had fallen in the restaurant or that everyone was staring at me.

'Tell me,' I demanded, 'what is Thirteen? You know, *so fucking well TELL ME!*'

As I swore, I was grabbed more forcibly. This time I couldn't shake off the grip on my arm and as I tried to pull away I lost my footing and fell to the floor, the second waiter falling heavily and landing on top of me. He managed, through some deft and astonishingly agile movement, to get my arm in an arm-lock as I lay on the floor. I had fallen in such a way that

I was twisted slightly, looking up at The Nurse's elegant knees and the edge of her dark tweed skirt.

'Tell me!' I hissed up to her.

The waiter held me where I was, pressed against the wooden floor, and The Nurse leaned down to pull her handbag away from where I was lying, and as she did so, she looked me directly in the eyes – calm still – with a calculating, amused, almost smug expression, and, almost without moving her lips, she whispered:

'Thirteen is not a number. It is a state of mind.'

And then she sat up again and turned away and ignored me as I was hauled to my feet and led away.

'It was her,' I told Lou, who joined me at the door after paying our bill. 'She does know about Thirteen.'

'Stephen, you are so embarrassing,' she groaned as she followed me out onto the pavement, hastily tipping the dishevelled waiter £10. 'Of course that poor woman doesn't know anything about Thirteen. She ignored you the whole time, I mean look at her, look!'

I turned and stared through the window and there she was, turned a little away from me, leaning in and saying something to her companion, who laughed and touched her hand gently.

'Stephen,' Lou said to me, 'I love you dearly, but I can't help you with this. You need to see a professional.'

Woman: This is the zone. Enter at your own risk. Stapely Road,
March 19th.

5. Can I give you a lift somewhere?

I felt at a loss. The following day I woke up and thought, *How
can I find her, even if I want to?* The possibility of working so
hard that I might cross some nebulous threshold by dint of
sheer effort looked more and more like what it was – desperation, rather than a genuine, rational strategy.

Lou dropped a card through my door with the name of a
therapist on it, and a short note saying, 'Never do that to me
again, Stephen. I'd love to see you again, soon, but get some
rest first. Come over to my place sometime and let me cook
for you.' I realised immediately that she meant, 'Let's not meet
in public for the time being', and I smiled uncomfortably at
the embarrassment that I'd caused her, and thought, *But I
WASN'T mistaken.*

The Nurse *had* spoken to me.

Later, it felt like the middle of the night already as I drove to my first fare, even though it was only dusk. The clocks would be going forward soon, and then I'd be starting my shifts in daylight. The woman I collected was a publican from an establishment overlooking Shoreham Harbour. She smiled at me – almost slyly, I thought – and asked for 'thirteen Cambridge Road'. I laughed and drove off, wondering what might happen when we got there. I remained silent but alert for our journey and was aware of my interaction with the vehicle as I drove, each gear change seeming oddly meaningful. But she *did* want thirteen Cambridge Road, and nodded when I pulled up, and got out and paid me as usual, and I thought, *Well, some people must want to go to real thirteens occasionally.* And I drove off, disappointed.

It was a usual Friday evening, busy most of the time, but especially between 11.00pm and 2.45am. At 3.00am I was tired – but tired in a normal way – and when I was asked to take a gentleman to Wish Road, I felt that familiar feeling of oddness as I dropped him off and looked at number 11a a few doors along, and I sat in the cab and didn't log back on immediately to get my next fare, but looked instead at the house that was there, with its well-tended rose bushes and tiny lawn. I stopped by the tree under which I used to wait for Valerie, and looked at the dappled orange of the lighting and out into the impenetrable darkness of the park.

And then, I heard the echo of The Nurse's voice, almost as if she was whispering in my ear, '*Thirteen is not a number, it is a state of mind*', and I realised, so clearly that the hairs stood up on my forearms, that *this* was the key to thirteen, this feeling of oddness as I sat and confronted something that contradicted my understanding of reality.

The next night, I found a whisper of it at 3.45am when I

was driving down New Church Road, not far from Wish Road. I saw an animal capering in the road, and so I slowed down and recognised it as a large Rhodesian Ridgeback dog, in a panic for some reason. I stopped to get out and try to calm it. As I did so, I noticed a man lying on the pavement at the foot of Coleman Avenue, in a classic, splayed posture as though waiting for the police to come and draw a white line around his corpse.

I radioed through to ask Sal to call an ambulance. At this point another taxi pulled up, and while the other driver ran to pacify the dog, I went to kneel beside the man, who was, I guessed, in his early seventies, and who groaned slightly as I put my hand on his shoulder. He slowly, achingly, sat up and rubbed his shoulder and said, 'Bugger me, that hurts,' and laughed, and waved at the other driver who was bringing the dog back to his master.

When the ambulance arrived and took the man off to A&E at the Royal Sussex, I agreed to take the dog to the man's sister in Fulking. I'd been thinking of knocking off anyway, and so I logged out of the circuit, and set off towards the Old Shoreham Road. It was a moonlit night and I could see a few dim stars, and could hear the dog making snuffling sounds in the passenger foot well where it was sitting nervously.

In Fulking, the sister wouldn't answer the bell at first, and eventually, when she did, we had one of those conversations conducted through the slit of a door that is on a chain. I completely understood and accepted her fear, and we had a rather bizarre moment when I went to get the dog, and passed the end of the lead through to her, before going back to sit in the cab while she opened her door to let the poor animal in. I told her that I'd sit in the cab for ten minutes while she phoned the hospital.

After about eleven minutes, she came out in her dressing gown. I opened the passenger window and she looked in at me, and smiled tiredly, and said, 'My brother has partly lost the power of speech, but managed to ask me to thank you so much for your help, and indicate that I should pay your fare.'

'It's okay,' I told her, but she thrust a £20 through the window and thanked me again, and said, 'It looks as though he's had a stroke.'

I insisted on giving her £5 change. When I drove off, it occurred to me how life goes on so relentlessly around us. People are being born, and dying, and experiencing everything else that falls within the gamut of human experience, all the time. It gave me a strange sensation, and I thought *I may have witnessed the beginning of the end of a man's life.* One moment he was walking along the road, taking his dog out for a walk. The next, his life was undergoing a fundamental and irreversible change. I was reminded how change arrives without warning, and then nothing is ever the same. And as I had this thought, I remembered Thirteen, and I said to myself, *It is now four-forty in the morning, and I am tired, but not unhappy, and I have a sense like I have never had before that I am ALIVE, and I would love, I would LOVE to meet The Nurse right now, because I think I would be in a position, for the first time in my life, to be able to listen to what she has to say.*

I drove back to Mile Oak to drop the cab off, and I thought of Valerie, and how she hadn't lived to see the snowdrops bloom, and I thought of the man who might never be able to walk his dog again, and I considered myself, and the likelihood that I had years of good health ahead of me, and I thought, *is this the kind of state of mind that The Nurse meant?* And all the way home, I kept looking out for her.

As I got into bed, heavy-lidded and ready for sleep, I thought, *I have to find her. I have to talk to her.*

But how?

Part of me realised that I was beginning to enter a new phase in my relationship with my driving. The job application forms that I'd asked for arrived, but lay untouched on the coffee table in the sitting room. They seemed less pressing, now that I'd seen The Nurse in the flesh, and now that the mystery of Thirteen was beginning to seduce me again. Still, when I was driving, and even while I knew that I was never far from an odd, dream-like state, I also knew that in a taxi you may be only moments away from a scenario so prosaic that dream-states are simply impossible:

I am sitting outside The Dudley Hotel. It is one the first nights of spring, when there is no real chill to the air, but rather an all-pervasive dampness even though it isn't raining. There is a lively wedding reception in progress, and a drunken couple come out, the man first, lurching down the red-carpeted steps towards the cab. The woman, carrying a slice of cake, raises her arm and throws the food at her partner, but she misses him and it hurtles towards me. Even though my window is closed, I involuntarily duck as it bangs against the glass, falling away, leaving a smear of cream and a thin slice of strawberry. As they climb in, she wails, 'You kicked me and called me a cunt, and you're supposed to be my boyfriend!' He ignores her and turns away to look out of the window, and it is only when I say, 'Where can I take you?' that they realise they haven't decided where to go. I sit and listen to them bicker for a while. She wants to go home, and he wants to go out for a curry, and so they – incomprehensibly and a little unwisely, I think, considering how drunk they are – decide to go, instead, to that rough nightclub along Hove esplanade that changes its name on virtually a weekly basis. 'Please,' the woman asks me, 'could you take the taxi right to the door of the club?' The club is actually on the edge of the beach. To get to the door you have to drive carefully up the pedestrian walkway beside the bowling green there, and then down a short, narrow, steeply curved slope that doesn't have a proper turning circle at the end, so that you have to reverse out – a technical nightmare. 'No, it's all right mate,' the boyfriend tells me, 'just drop us off on Kingsway.' 'No, no,' she calls out, 'I want to be taken to the door.' And so they start bickering again, and I realise with a sad pang, that all this woman wants is for a man, just once in her life, to voluntarily do something a little bit extra for her. 'It's all right,' I say, 'I'll take you to the door,' and I drive carefully along and down the slope, even though it takes longer in the Galaxy than it would have done for them to walk. 'I'll pay,' she says, fumbling to get her purse out and inadvertently dropping some coins into her lap. She shrieks with laughter and fishes out a few pounds to pay me. 'Hey, Mr Taxi Driver,' she says, 'do you want to earn some money for a tip?' 'How do you mean?' I ask. 'How do you mean,' she repeats, cruelly imitating me. 'I mean, I've dropped some of my money down my crotch. You can have it if you get it out yourself.' 'You fucking slag,' says her boyfriend, and they begin to wrestle playfully as he sticks his hand up her skirt. 'You slapper,' he shouts, happily, and she laughs. 'I want the driver to get the money out, not you,' she says, pushing him off. 'You want an arsehole like him to put his hand in your panties?' he asks. She pushes her boyfriend hard, and manages to get him back into his seat. 'He's lovely,' she protests. 'Aren't you, Mr Taxi driver?' I look at them and wish I hadn't switched the meter off so quickly. This looks like it might take some time. The woman tries to smooth her skirt as she opens the door. 'Oh fuck,' she says, 'I've dropped the rest of the money.' She leans down to get it off the floor, but bending down clearly makes her dizzy, so she stops. 'Sod it,' she says, 'you can have it as your tip. There must be five pounds down there.' Then she laughs, aghast, and says to me, 'and you were going to put your hands up my crotch. You pervert.' They spend the next minute or so manoeuvring themselves from the taxi (I don't offer to help), and as the woman turns to close the door, she grabs hold of her boyfriend to stop herself from falling over. He leans in to lasciviously lick her neck while she shrieks with pleasure before they stagger off. I carefully reverse up the curved ramp and back down to Kingsway. Between the two bus stops there, I pause to accept my next fare. I can see the door of the club, and as I switch on the internal light to find what coins have been dropped on the floor, I can see them being turned away by the bouncers. On the floor there is 15p.

Incidents like these would make me forget about Thirteen for hours at a time. But, just as surely, and especially later on in my shifts, I would give lifts to people who would make 'that feeling' well up once more:

I pick up a woman who is pensive, almost in slow-motion, and who, as I drive off, says dreamily to me: 'I thought that when I was born, that was a beginning – you know, the start of life. But, actually, being born is the start of death, isn't it?

You come into this world, and every second you live, your death comes closer and closer. At the moment of birth, your death is created too.' I agree with her, and she laughs and says, 'What a bummer, eh?' 'The only thing that's genuinely useless in this world,' I say, 'is worrying about things that can't be changed.' 'But we all do, don't we?' she says. 'Yes,' I agree. 'Sometimes,' she says, 'I think there are two ways of living life. Firstly, you can put your nose to the grindstone and don't ever look up. If you always look at the ground, you'll never be happy, but at least you'll never know that you're unhappy.' She pauses to look out of the window at the bright emptiness of Argos and Kentucky Fried Chicken. 'And secondly?' I ask. 'Yes, secondly,' she says, a little wistfully, 'you can choose to look up and out from yourself. But then, you'll always have to face the fact that you live in a world of suffering.' I look at her in the mirror and she seems fascinated, for some reason, by her fingernails. 'And the advantage of looking up and out?' 'No matter how painful it is,' she tells me, 'you'll always know that you are alive.' She sighs and closes her eyes for some time and we drive in silence. 'And you,' she asks after a while, 'are you happy?' I look at her in the mirror. She is staring at me with such earnestness that I smile. 'I can truthfully say,' I tell her, 'that, right now, I'm not unhappy.' She laughs. 'And you?' I ask. 'I'm dying,' she says, with a light lilt to her voice that is almost sing-song. 'Maybe not now, or for forty or fifty years, or even sixty years if I'm lucky, but I will die, and so will my children, if I have any, and my grandchildren. But how can I have children if I can't stop myself from giving them this terrible gift. It's not something you would do to someone you love, is it? But by giving life to my children, I will also be killing them.' 'You

don't seem to be unhappy about it.' 'Unhappy? No. I'm not.
Isn't that weird? Life comes up to you, just as you're
beginning to think "Hey, this is pretty cool, this life thing",
and then, like the punch-line to a bad joke, life says, "Yes,
but I'm going to take it all away from you." Either you have
to laugh about it, or you'll spend the rest of your life crying.
But, then, that's what most people do, isn't it? Cry about it.
Get fucked-up about it.' I pull up along Walpole Terrace,
and she says, suddenly serious, 'Try not to die. There must
be some way of getting round it, some path we can walk
down, some *other place.*' The way she says 'other place'
makes me shiver. When I ask for the fare, she hands her bag
to me and says, 'Take it out of my purse, would you? I'm not
in a state to do that kind of thing. Money doesn't mean
anything when you're looking at life from the angle that
I'm looking at it.' I take the exact fare – no tip – and hand
her bag back. She pushes the door open, and I say to her,
'Does the number Thirteen mean anything to you?' She
throws her head back and laughs for a long time, steadying
herself on the open door as she gets out and stands for a
moment to look up at the sky 'You're as mad as I am,' she
says and closes the door gently. She comes round to the
driver's window and I open it. 'No,' she whispers,
'the number Thirteen doesn't mean anything to me.
Should it?' 'I don't know,' I say. She turns and walks off,
running her hands over her hips for sensation and laughing
to herself.

After this incident I drove back to Mile Oak to drop the cab
off and, as usual when passing Wish Road at this time of night,
I felt an echo of my experiences there, like a flutter in my
stomach. This city was becoming a patchwork of remembered

experience for me already. Here was Wish Road where I had come to pick up Valerie all those times; now there was the corner on which the old man had collapsed, and the Budgens where the lonely late-night people went; then there was the Dudley Hotel where my cab had been 'caked'; now, Walpole Terrace where I'd dropped off this death-obsessed woman on drugs (acid, I presumed).

In the Budgens, when I stopped to pick up a few things, there were two women in front of me – girls really – and one was saying to the other, 'I'm nineteen, and I've been working behind the bar there for over a year, and now I'm engaged to the manager. And I'm just doing these things. And they're not me. I don't even know what "me" is. In ten years time I'll have three kids and a house on Hangleton Way; I'll probably be shagging someone on the side, and going to the garden centre up at the racecourse on Saturdays . . . and nothing that I can see in the future sounds like me. None of it.'

Her companion hugged her and said, 'You've had one too many vodkas, love. That's all.'

As I pedalled home, I realised that in observing others I was also observing parts of myself. The girl in Budgens had said, 'I don't even know what "me" is', and I had taken that tiny jigsaw piece from her life and applied it to my own. If I did this enough, would I build a meaningful picture?

It is quite possible to change the entire picture of a person with just one, small incident, as in the blue jigsaw piece that you'd assumed all along was sea, when in fact it was sky. There was a woman I used to take to bingo on Portland Road, who had laughed and joked with me each time and whose appearance had always been so radiant. And then, one day, far more drunk than usual, she had sobbed disconsolately as I drove her home and confessed that her life was a mess. The next time I saw her she was back to being radiant – perhaps she'd been too drunk to even remember her previous outpouring of sorrow – and I found her wide smile tragic now, where before it had made me feel lighter.

There was something in all these incidents that made me realise I was beginning to wait, and that observing people in this way was a part of my waiting. Waiting for that one, all-important moment that would start to complete my picture, that would explain Thirteen to me, and let me stop this mad juggling of insufficient detail.

I now found that my working life became, if not actually enjoyable, then oddly serene. I was aware that this could only be a temporary state, because I'd gone into that curious mode of waiting in which all tensions are absolutely balanced, so that they seem to cancel each other out; so that what is left appears to be calmness, when in fact it is something not far from its opposite. But time managed to slip by all the same. A month, six weeks . . .

I drank a lot, for me, at around this time, at home on my own, which I had never done until I became a taxi driver. And I saw nothing of the few friends that I had left. Lou left me alone, and I responded to other offers of meetings in pubs with brief messages that I would 'see you soon'.

I knew I would see The Nurse again and I wanted to be in a position to grab the opportunity when it arose, and I hoped that I would be able to maintain this calm expectancy until I found her because, otherwise, I knew, I would crack into shards and splinters.

By now I'd almost stopped having my odd dream-punctures, because I was working fewer hours and had become more familiar with the city and its routes and short cuts. But, one

Friday in early May, one happened on a night when I'd had a bad shift. It had been one of the first days of early summer when, after a damp and stormy spring, the sun suddenly showed its strength and everything was hot and breathless, even though banks of cloud were looming from the West. Out of habit, I had come out wearing my winter trousers and a thick shirt and had been uncomfortably hot and irritated since the start of my shift. I'd managed to have a series of near misses with other vehicles – none of them my fault, but nerve wracking nevertheless. I'd also had a couple of difficult lifts, such as a man who'd had a stroke and could no longer remember his address, so that we had to drive round and round in circles looking for his house which was 'somewhere near Easthill Park'. He thought I was misleading him and deliberately taking as long as possible in order to get as high a fare as I could. I had to contend with forty minutes of abuse, and only a fiver as a fare (it was all he had on him). Then, I'd managed to box myself in tightly while setting a customer down on a small turning circle at the end of a close off Fox Way: one of those streets that weren't designed for the amount of cars that would one day need to park there. There were several cars clogging the turning circle. With a vehicle as long as a Galaxy, it was impossible to turn round, and so I had to reverse, past cars parked on either side of the too-narrow street, so that at times I would be only inches from clacking wing mirrors on either side. As I pulled out onto the main road, a speeding car squealed past, sounding its horn and making me jump. No wonder, then, that I was more tired than usual by midnight and, for the first time in a couple of months, decided to pull off the Hangleton Link Road for a quick kip in the quiet entrance to the golf club there.

I was woken with a start by someone bashing furiously on

my window. It was the night attendant from the Tesco car park.

'What the hell are you doing here again?' he wanted to know.

I looked around. Sure enough, I was in the empty supermarket car park, looking out at the man I'd met here once before under identical circumstances – a man who was both angry and extremely confused.

'Okay, okay,' I told him, confused myself. 'I'll leave, if you'll just open the barrier.'

He didn't say anything, but pulled a bunch of keys from his pocket and went over to his booth. I started the engine then pulled up behind the barrier. But before the man opened it, he came over to the cab and said, 'Next time you try any of this monkey business, mate, I'm calling the police.'

'Okay,' I said.

As ever, after these dream-punctures, I felt particularly awake and alert. I continued with my shift, feeling the weirdness of the Tesco incident hanging over me, but also aware that its significance was likely to remain mysterious, and that trying to work it out was probably a waste of time.

Some time later in the shift, I accepted a booking for Shoreham Beach, to collect someone from Burger King at the Saltings roundabout services. My previous fare had been a barwoman who smelled of cigarette smoke and lemons and who wanted to be dropped off in one of the curved lanes of Lancing, a place that hadn't fallen within the remit of the Brighton & Hove Knowledge, and so had not yet yielded its secrets to me. I'd thought I knew where I was when I set off again, but got lost a couple of times before I found my way back to the seafront road, and the location of my booking. The place was dark and quiet, and I stopped the cab by the petrol pumps and went to look through the windows of the restaurant to see if I could see a manager in there, locking up at the back. But the whole place was deserted. It was around 3.00am and the wind was getting up, spattering warm skeins of rain across the tarmac. There was a warm edge to the wind, and a muggy humidity, and there was a sudden downpour that only lasted a minute or two, but which left puddles everywhere.

There's something desolate about deserted petrol station forecourts at night. The grim reflections of passing cars in surface water, plus the fact that I was on the lookout for whoever had ordered the taxi, made me feel especially irritable and confused. I knew from experience that, when arriving for a booking like this, you have to give the punter a good five minutes to turn up. Even totally abandoned-looking sites can yield customers from the most unexpected places – unlit doorways, alleys, even debris-strewn waste ground. People wait for taxis in the strangest places. But nobody came, and I scuffed about the concrete for another minute or two, enjoying being out in the night air at least – damp though it was. I eventually went back to the cab and recorded yet another 'no show', and was allocated a job in Rosslyn Road.

I pulled out of the forecourt, and by dint of where I was, and how the cars approaching the roundabout were reflected in the dark windows nearby, I had the odd illusion that the same cars were both approaching and receding at the same time.

At the roundabout at the top of Shoreham High Street an articulated lorry bearing supermarket produce came past – the first sign that tomorrow's day-time traffic would soon be starting – and the detonating sound of air brakes startled me, so that I braked too hard myself, causing the vehicle behind me to sound its horn. As I turned to look out across the roundabout, I smelt a haunting scent of citrus from the previous fare . . . and then I saw her. She was standing by the exit of the short turning circle in front of the Bridge Inn that led immediately off the far side of the roundabout. She was turned away from me, but I had no doubt whatsoever who it was, and without so much as a moment's hesitation I drove onto the turning circle there, pulled up beside her and opened my window.

'Hi,' I said, 'can I give you a lift somewhere?'

Again, she seemed completely unsurprised that I'd spoken to her, and she flashed an inscrutable look at me that was mysterious because it was so unreadable. She was wearing a short, pale jacket and black well-cut jeans.

'No,' she said, 'I'm fine.'

'Please,' I said. 'Perhaps you don't know who I am, but I made a fool of myself the other night at Septimus and I'd like to apologise by giving you a lift – free of charge – anywhere you would like to go.'

She smiled slightly at this, with what might have been a hint of triumph, and said, 'Okay.'

She opened the door and got in directly behind me, which I always dislike because it is difficult to see a passenger who sits there, even in the rear-view mirror. I radioed the office and said, 'Look, I'm sorry but the damp seems to have got to the engine and I've stalled on Shoreham High Street. You'd better send someone else to Rosslyn Road. I'll radio through when I'm up and running again.' Then I logged-out, turned to The Nurse and smiled. I caught her light scent. *Citrus, again.* I noticed, even in this uneven light, her perfect make-up and how well-groomed she was, and I thought, *don't ruin this by being confrontational. Don't mention Thirteen – at least not straight away. Take it easy.*

'Where can I take you?' I asked.

'Well,' she said, 'I'm actually making my way to Queen's Park. It's quite far. I don't want to put you out.'

'That's fine. I'm on my way over to that side of town anyway,' I lied.

I started off along Brighton Road, and thought, *How do I start a conversation with someone whom I've picked up at a house that, maybe, doesn't exist?*

'Nasty evening,' I said, resorting to a comment on the weather as the most obvious conversation starter.

'Yes,' she agreed, and paused for a moment, then carried on with a hint of amusement in her voice, as though she might be mocking me for making small talk. 'Is bad weather good for business?'

'Neither good nor bad,' I told her. 'For everyone that takes a cab because it's raining, there's someone else who *would* have taken a taxi but decides not to go out in the rain.'

There was a short silence, and I craned slightly to see if I could catch sight of her in the mirror, but I could only see her shoulder.

'Forgive me,' she said, 'but you don't seem like the sort of person who would choose to be a taxi driver.' Her voice had a husky quality to it that made everything she said sound as though it might be some kind of *double entendre*.

'A lot of people say that,' I told her. 'People mention it virtually every day.'

'So, what made you decide on taxi driving?'

I laughed. 'I needed work,' I said.

'But you could, surely, have done any number of things?'

'There's nothing wrong with being a taxi driver,' I said. 'It's a good profession.'

'That's true. But isn't it dangerous?'

82

'Yes, it can be.'

'Forgive me,' she said, 'but most taxi drivers you see driving at night tend to be, well . . . the sort of people who look like they could beat the shit out of anyone who might get aggressive.'

'You mean, I don't look like the kind of man who could look after himself?'

She laughed. 'Oh, I'm *sure* you could look after yourself.' She fell silent for a few moments before speaking again. 'I'm just being nosy here,' she said, 'but I'm still wondering why a person like you might want to become a taxi driver.'

'I didn't decide,' I said. 'Someone else made the decision for me.'

'Oh?'

'I was in a bit of a mess a few months ago,' I told her, 'and I didn't know what to do with myself. A friend of mine was staying with me at the time and he suggested I should do this for a while.'

'So, why did *he* think you should be a taxi driver?'

'I don't know.'

'You haven't questioned his motives?'

'No,' I said. 'No, I haven't.'

'That seems strange.'

I stopped at the Wellington Road traffic lights and turned to look at her briefly. She was grinning.

'What would *you* think his motives might be?' I asked.

'How would I know?' she replied.

'I thought, um . . . I thought maybe you might have an instinct about it or something.'

The lights changed and we started off again. Our journey was now well underway, and we hadn't started *talking*.

'This small talk . . .' I said. 'I'm sorry, but I just don't know

83

how to instigate the sort of conversation I want to have.'

'Maybe by asking the sort of questions you want to ask,' she said.

'Tell me, then,' I said as we started along Kingsway, past Hove Lagoon and the covered tennis courts there, 'do you remember that night in Septimus?'

'Yes,' she said.

'Do you remember the question I asked you?'

'Yes.'

'Do you remember what you said to me?'

'Yes.'

'What did you mean when you said that Thirteen was not a number but a state of mind?'

'You know that already,' she said.

'I do?'

'Just think about how you came to notice me this evening.'

'Okay,' I said, 'I'll consider that later. What about the fact that I collected you and Valerie – or whatever she was called – from a house on Wish Road that I now discover was never there.'

'She *was* called Valerie, you know,' The Nurse said, sounding impressed.

'You're evading my question.'

'Oh, Stephen,' she laughed, and her laughter was both soothing and subtly derisive at the same time, 'you *know* all these things.'

I didn't ask her how she knew my name. I was beginning to feel a sense of desperation that our journey would be over before I got anything concrete out of her. 'This is no good,' I told her. 'I need to talk to you for longer than this. Can we stop off for a coffee at Buddies?'

'Buddies?'

'The all-night restaurant down near the Old Ship Hotel.'

'No,' she said, 'I'm sorry, I'm late already.'

As we were passing the Brighton Centre, I could see the flashing blue lights of a police car at the bottom of West Street – perhaps the least surprising place to see a police car at 3.30am on a Saturday night in Brighton.

'How can I find you again?' I asked her.

I heard a siren, and noticed an ambulance approaching fast behind me, so I braked and pulled into the stop by the Odeon cinema and waited as it shrieked past in a fury of light and sound. I took a deep breath, readying myself to speak to The Nurse, thinking that now the cab had stopped, I was in a position to have a proper word with her before I moved off again. After all, the meter wasn't on, she wasn't paying for this. But, from nowhere, it seemed, a group of five sparkling teenagers broke around the cab in a wave of noise and laughter. One of them, a somewhat bedraggled girl with long blonde hair knocked on the window, which I opened to the drizzle that was now turning to serious rain.

'Please, *please*, can you take us home?' she asked.

'No,' I told her, 'I already have a fare.'

I turned to The Nurse, laughing ruefully at this disturbance. But she was gone. The rear door of the cab was open, and a couple of the teenagers were already climbing into the back. I leaned out of the window and craned my neck to see where she might have gone, but there was no sign of her. She must have made a dash for it. From where the taxi was parked, there were several directions she might have taken – down the underpass, up West Street, across and into South Street . . . Or maybe she had simply disappeared into thin air, like 13 Wish Road.

I felt a welling of wordless frustration, and banged my fists on the steering wheel, swearing under my breath. By now, I had five expectant youngsters in my taxi. I closed my eyes and tried to still my heart, then took a long breath. I could hear the wind, picking up and sounding mournful in the night as the first pulse of major rain began to batter against the windscreen.

'Okay,' I sighed, turning to my passengers, 'where do you want to go?'

Woman, to SB: Why am I telling you this? Queen's Road, Brighton, March 12th. Freshfield Road, Kemptown, April 3rd. Hallyburton Road, Hove, April 14th.

6. Secrets revealed.

That night, the night of my frustrating non-conversation with The Nurse – my abject missed opportunity – was the first time I heard the crying. I heard it, in fact, when I was taking that bunch of kids back to Whitehawk. On this occasion, it was a single, quiet sob, which made me start because it was so distinct amidst the laughter. I was at the roundabout at the bottom of Bristol Gardens and Roedean Road when I heard it, and so I stopped for a moment to look round. But there was no sign of distress, and as I hesitated a few seconds longer than I would otherwise have done, to reorientate myself and to overcome the intense momentary sadness that the sob had induced in me, one of the lads laughed even louder than the rest and said, 'Don't stop here too long, mate, you'll lose your hubcaps.'

Later, when I was at home, drinking beer, I sat and looked at the blank screen of the television and wondered, fruitlessly, about my conversation with The Nurse. I'd been feeling that I was in a kind of limbo for weeks, but that feeling was now intensified. I felt not only that I was still in a state of waiting, but also as if I was hanging on to the edge of a precipice by my fingernails, not sure whether to let myself fall or to try, desperately, to pull myself up and away from danger. Weirdly, though, it seemed that if I was to choose to fall, I simply didn't know how to do it.

When I woke the following afternoon, something had changed. Even as I cleaned my teeth I knew that the late-night atmosphere, that strange cloak of hypnotic mystery, was still with me. It made me feel both intensely awake and half asleep at the same time, and the silence in my flat seemed pregnant with appalling, seductive risk. It was a feeling that was to become more and more familiar to me, and which I began to refer to as 'zoning'.

Once I'd eaten some toast and gulped down a cup of coffee, I cycled through the extensive puddles along Portland Road, in the stillness of the rain-washed afternoon.

The cab had just been dropped off on Benfield Way – the engine was still warm, and I could hear it ticking quietly as it cooled – and I jumped in and logged-on, and wondered what my evening would bring. As it happened, town was busy, even for a Saturday. The Seagulls had won an important match and batches of jubilant youths, and complacently satisfied older men, were making their way to and from the various pubs in the city, to drink some more and to celebrate.

For a while I forgot about The Nurse, but always at the back of my mind I was aware that at the periphery of things, at the edge of both my vision and my reason, there lurked something shady that I couldn't quite identify. The city was like some great, slumbering beast that might at any moment rear its head and either swallow me whole, or make gentle love to me, in some curious inhuman way.

That night, I had two consecutive fares that are worth mentioning. The first, a classic example of how accept-and-build conversations can go in surprising directions:

1. At 7.30 I pick up a smartly dressed woman in her seventies from the block of flats at the end of Highlands Road. She is on her way to the Royal Sussex to see a dying friend. As we set off, I notice a couple of Downs Syndrome adults walking along the pavement with a chaperone. 'Oh, Downs Syndrome' says the woman for no apparent reason. 'Sometimes, in the early evening,' I tell her, 'I give lifts to parents with Downs Syndrome children. The kids always seem so cheerful, it's heartening.' 'I have a Downs Syndrome daughter,' the woman says. 'Is she a happy person?' I ask. 'Yes. She was born when I was in my forties. She's been in care for years and years.' The woman has a string of pearls, and I can see her stroking them with her liver-spotted hands. 'My husband,' she says, with a sigh that sounds almost wistful, 'my husband couldn't give our daughter love when he discovered she had Downs Syndrome. It was a loveless marriage.' I stop at the traffic lights on the Old Shoreham Road, by Hove Recreation Ground, and look in the mirror at the woman. She looks poised as she gazes out beyond me at the road ahead. 'Do you mean,' I say, 'that it was always loveless, or that it became loveless after your daughter was born?' 'It was always loveless,' she tells me. 'And abusive, too.' As I drive

down by the station, she tells me how her husband used to knock her to the ground and spit on her. 'I left him eventually,' she says. 'I can't think why I didn't do it before.' As we come up Edward Street and approach the hospital, she murmurs, 'Why am I *telling* you this?' As I pull in at the front of the hospital, she says, 'Can I book you to bring me home again in about an hour?' 'I can certainly book you a taxi for an hour's time, but I can't guarantee it'll be me that picks you up.' 'Oh, please,' she pleads, 'I'd much rather it was you.' 'I'll try,' I tell her. An hour later I am dropping someone off in Lancing, so I don't see her again.

2. I give a lift to three lads of perhaps seventeen or eighteen, one of whom seems sullen, or perhaps unhappy, though he does smile briefly when I turn to ask them where they want to go. Curiously, it is only when he smiles that I realise he is in psychological pain. I gather from their conversation that they used to be at school together and have met up for a reunion drink. We stop to let the quiet lad off on Hampstead Road, along by Preston Park station, and as I set off up the hill to Dyke Road, one of the remaining boys says, *sotto voce*, 'Did you see his pair of bracelets?' 'What?' 'His bracelets.' 'He wasn't wearing bracelets, you daft twat.' The first lad leans towards his friend and whispers so loudly that I wonder why he's bothered lowering his voice, 'Bracelets are the scars left behind when you've tried to top yourself.'

Something about that sad, quiet boy remained with me for the rest of the evening, and I knew then that I was skirting the edge of Thirteen, somehow; that I was on the verge of zoning.

At 2.30am I was taking four lads back to Lancing. They

were all well-dressed and well-spoken, and I assumed they were pupils from Lancing College, the fancy public school there, whose monstrous chapel sits in gothic splendour on the skyline as you leave the conurbation. They were amphetamine-bright and rowdily talkative, and at one point the lad in the front passenger seat turned to the others and said, 'You know when you shag a bird, and you've got your hands round her neck, and she's gurgling as though you're strangling her, but afterwards she says she loved it . . . ?'

The stunned silence that greeted this question made the hairs on the back of my neck stand up, and when eventually one of the boys in the back said, 'Um, no . . .' I had the sense that this electric embarrassment, this sudden wariness – this instant reassessment of a friend – was some kind of metaphor for sudden and unexpected change of many kinds. And thinking this made me feel suddenly connected to what The Nurse had said to me, so that I almost wanted to stop, turf the boys out of the cab then and there, and drive straight over to 13 Wish Road, to see if it had reappeared.

But I continued to ply my Saturday night trade, with a growing conviction that something was about to happen, whether I went searching for it or not. I kept an eye out for The Nurse, but there was no sign of her. I did deliberately take a detour down Wish Road at one point, but number 11a was disappointingly there . . .

On Kingsway, at the bottom of Wish Road, there were road works and some temporary traffic lights. I was driving to pick up a fare on Grand Avenue and while I was waiting, passengerless, I noticed that someone was looking towards me from the back window of the white Ford Mondeo ahead of me, and with a jolt I realised that it was Valerie. As the lights changed I waved to her, but although she was facing me, she wasn't looking directly at me, and she didn't notice that I was trying to attract her attention. Her face, still drawn and ill-looking, was listless somehow, and needy. She was staring fixedly, motionlessly out of the rear window – sightless, almost, it seemed. Her hand was held up slightly, as though holding something in her palm for me to see. I wondered, briefly, if she was being abducted.

The only thing I could think to do was catch up with the Mondeo and try to overtake it. I put my foot down, and sped recklessly up to it, sounding my horn and waving across. But Valerie was still craning round, and as I sounded my horn again, all I could see was the back of her head. There was a traffic light in a couple of hundred metres, and I decided I would jump from the cab when I stopped, and try to attract her attention that way. But, just then, as I started to brake, I noticed the strobing blue light of an approaching police car.

'Fuck,' I said aloud, braking further and pulling over.

When I stopped, I could see the Mondeo at the lights, and the distant, still-motionless silhouette of Valerie as she looked down the road towards me. One of the policemen came round to my side and I opened the window.

'Do you realise how fast you were going, sir?' the policeman asked.

Behind the policeman, I could see the Mondeo move off from the lights, its red rear lights diminishing as it passed the King Alfred Centre. I said the first thing that came into my mind.

'Bloody fare-dodgers,' I said. 'The woman in the back of that Mondeo owed me a tenner.'

The policeman turned round and looked at the passing traffic. 'Even so,' he said, turning back to me and leaning down so that he could look at me more closely, 'you were doing forty-seven miles an hour in a thirty mile an hour limit.'

'I'm sorry,' I told him, 'all I wanted was to get my money back. When someone does a runner on you, you just want to go after them.'

He nodded briefly, then said, 'Wait here,' and went back to talk to his colleague.

I waited, not particularly caring what was going to happen. After a short time, the policeman came back to me and said, 'Under the circumstances we've decided to let you off. I know what a bastard it is when someone does a runner. But still, be more careful in future or you may well find yourself in trouble.'

'Thanks,' I said.

He patted the roof briefly and sauntered back to his vehicle. I waited while they drove off, and waved as they passed, trying to look sheepish and contrite, but actually feeling exhilarated. Being a taxi driver does occasionally have its advantages, especially where the police are concerned. I sat on for a minute or two, feeling pensive and weird, before continuing to pick up my next fare. I was zoning, I knew, but had no idea what to do with the altered state that I was undeniably inhabiting.

At home after my shift I opened the bottle of vodka that I'd bought some time before because it was Lou's favoured drink, realising only as I did so that I hadn't yet had her round to see the flat. I sat drinking vodka and orange juice as I counted my money, and something fell into place inside me, and I thought, *I'm doing this wrong.* It occurred to me that it was only when I'd tried cajoling The Nurse into stopping and having a coffee with me that she'd disappeared. It was only when I'd raced after the car in which Valerie had been sitting, that the police had turned up to stop me.

But what was I supposed to do? Wait for them to come to me?

When I got up the following afternoon it was Sunday, so I had two days off before returning to my cab, and I felt curiously energised. I realised that in some strange way I was in the process of falling under a spell, which was why I hadn't got in touch with Lou, or anyone else who might break that spell. And so I continued with my solitary existence and spent those two days sorting out some things in the flat that I should have done as soon as I moved in, such as purchasing a shade and a less bright bulb for the light in the sitting room. I bought a throw for the dingy sofa, and a couple of lamps to give some background lighting. I also gave the wall round the window a lick of paint where it had some old damp stains. The result was a transformation. I couldn't believe it had needed so little to make it look so much better.

I cleaned the place thoroughly for the first time since I'd moved in, throwing away fast food cartons, empty beer cans, discarded magazines, before vacuuming or scrubbing every surface. At the end of the afternoon on Monday I stood in the doorway to the sitting room, surveying the results of my efforts, and, with a lurch of something that might almost be described as (why am I so wary of using this word?) happiness, I thought, *I'm no longer depressed.* The realisation came as a complete surprise. When had it happened? I couldn't place the moment.

I got out all my old CDs. I hadn't listened to music like this since my – to put it euphemistically – change of circumstances. It was incredibly relaxing and I found myself smiling as I listened through some of my older stuff – Modern Life is Rubbish, and A Storm in Heaven, as well as my stalwart P J Harveys. When I got into bed that night, I fell almost immediately into a calm, refreshing, dreamless sleep.

On waking I knew that I was still zoning.

Even so, it occurred to me, yet again, that Lou might be right: that I'd probably imagined everything – right from the beginning, when I first collected Valerie from 13 Wish Road – that I was delusional and, perhaps, slightly mad. Zoning was simply a delusional state. But this madness, or whatever it was, felt a great deal healthier than my previous unhappiness, and I realised that I simply *didn't care* whether it was 'real' or not. Maybe that was the maddest thing of all, that I was going mad and that I wanted to embrace my madness.

The world felt subtly different again, as though I'd changed the prescription in my glasses and everything had become suddenly sharper, but at the same time further away. I found that my driving was unaffected by this odd sense of visual perception. However, I also discovered that I'd lost the full spatial awareness of my own body, which meant, for example, that when I went up steps to ring doorbells it was easy to stumble because the steps were taller than they'd looked as I approached them.

I have sometimes felt a little like this when I've over-caffeinated myself. I don't drink caffeinated drinks often, but once, in the very early days of taxiing when I found myself feeling sleepy, I stopped off for a double espresso and spent the next two and a half hours feeling edgily overfocussed, as though something terrible was about to happen. Now, I had that same sense of premonition, but it was calm rather than edgy. But how could I grasp this state of mind, how could I use it?

Tuesday is one of those unpredictable nights – it can either be deadly quiet, or brisk all evening. On this occasion it was quiet. While waiting for jobs, I would close my eyes and do gentle breathing exercises that I'd learned seven or eight years before when I'd attended a course in meditation. I'd been going out for a short time with a somewhat wistful girl who was into it, and when we parted, I'd stopped. Now, I was pleased to have recourse to this simple and effective exercise.

Later, it was as though my fares were an unwanted imposition. I wanted to sink into this new internal territory without the need for such trivial things as conversation – especially the kind of conversation you often have in taxis. Still, sometimes people are so unusual that a journey can become totally surreal:

It is a warm evening in mid-May and I'm driving a couple of drunk people from The Aldrington on Portland Road to Moulsecoomb, a journey of several miles. Part way, one of my fares declares that she's a post-operative transsexual and bursts into tears because she reckons no-one finds her attractive. Her female companion tries to calm her down, but this – tragically unconvincing – woman looks at me and says, in a voice too deep to sound anything but male, 'Do you think I'm attractive?' I can think of more than one person I know who would have described her as 'pig ugly', but that has nothing to do with her gender. 'Yes,' I say. She leans forward and tugs at my elbow. 'Will you be . . . the first?' she asks. I say thank you, genuine emotion catching me unawares so that a tear springs to my eye, but I don't know whether this is empathy or pity. I tell her I'm too busy to spare the time to take her feminine virginity, and she turns to her friend and sobs that everyone gives her the brush off; no one wants to fuck her. The friend strokes my leg plaintively. 'Please,' she says, 'my friend would really appreciate it.' She reaches down suddenly and grabs my crotch. 'Well,' she laughs with what amounts to a cackle, 'at least he's got the equipment for it!' I push her hand away, and try to look disapproving, but can't help laughing with her instead. 'No one will make love to me,' the transsexual wails from the back seat, distraught. 'No one. I'm ugly, I'm just ugly. Please, please, Mr Driver, please take me home and make love to me.' We stop at some lights and I turn and look her straight in the eyes, and say, 'I'm so sorry, I'm working and genuinely can't spare the time, but I'm sure you'll find someone before long, if you want to.' I drive on and there is silence for the first time. As we pull into their close, I see flames. 'Oh, my god, what's going on!' the woman next to me cries. It turns out to be some kind of arson attack on the next door neighbour's multiple rabbit hutches, which are fully ablaze as I stop the cab. A woman from the house in question is desperately uncoiling a hose as she hurries over the back lawn, water spouting in arcs as she unwinds it from its holder. A man is throwing a bucket of water onto the flames. My passengers show no sympathy once they realise what is going on. 'Fuckin' bastard,' says the transsexual, without further explanation. They ignore their neighbours and invite me in for a drink. I decline, but – at their request – give them both a friendly goodnight kiss on the cheek. They get out, but don't walk away. As I reverse, they stand in the glare of my headlights, flames and smoke towering up behind them, and they wave goodnight to me – sad, jerky crab-like movements – and I feel a further welling of emotion as I lean forward to accept my next fare. As I am about to reverse onto Newick Road, I see the transsexual giving the finger to the man with the burning rabbit hutches. I hear him shouting something, but can't hear what it is. As I turn to set off back to the Lewes Road, glancing back at the flames, I hear the sob I heard a few days before. It is so quiet that I go still, straining to hear it more clearly if it should come again. It is accompanied by a kind of muted chest-heave, so that I know it is part of a protracted bout of crying. But it is so quiet, I can't be absolutely sure I've heard it.

Those flames haunted me, and not just because of the rabbits that must have died. There was something in the colour of the flames – that sharp, bright orange, and the billows of smoke twisting upwards. And perhaps the fact that I'd heard that piteous sob, just then, made the image remain with me so surely.

Given the state of mind this incident induced in me, it was almost inevitable that I would come across Valerie again – or at least someone from Thirteen. This time I had a passenger in my cab. I was at the bottom of North Street, waiting at the lights, about to go up St James Street. Valerie was waiting, alone, at the pedestrian crossing on her way up the Old Steine. Even though I had been looking out for someone significant, it was still a shock to see her, dressed in a pale blue summer skirt. The light pleats caught in the breeze so that she was surrounded by billowing movement. I immediately opened my window to call out to her, but there was no need – she'd seen me already.

The green man flashed on at the crossing and Valerie set out across the road. My cab was first at the lights, and instead of walking in front of it, she came straight towards me, inclining her head at me in recognition. I noticed that she didn't seem to be ill at all. She was radiant, in fact, looking impossibly young and healthy. I smiled at her as she came up to me.

'Stephen,' she said, and held her hand out to me. I thought she wanted to shake my hand, but as I opened the window still further so that I could reach out, I realised she wanted to give me something.

'When are you going to come and see me?' she asked. 'I've been expecting you for ages.'

I stared at her, trying to see in her serious, radiant expression, some further meaning than the inviting look that was etched there, and I felt the light touch of something in the palm of my hand. But I didn't look down. I held her gaze.

'Meet you where?' I asked, urgently.

She smiled, slightly, as if distracted by a distant noise, and turned to walk on, 'Oh,' she said, looking back at me over her shoulder, 'Thirteen. Of course.'

I was about to say something further, but the lights were changing. I looked down at what was in the palm of my hand. A snowdrop.

'Beautiful woman,' said my passenger as we set off up St James Street. 'I can see why you're so keen to meet up with her.'

As soon as I'd dropped my fare off, I drove straight over to Lou's. I rang her bell in a state of breathless excitement. It was only after the third ring that an upstairs window opened and a man leaned out.

'Who the fuck? . . . Oh . . . it's you, Stephen . . .' He tried to think of something to say. Failed. 'I'll get Lou.'

The window closed and I didn't hear anything more for a couple of frustrating minutes. Then, through the bubbled glass of the door, I could see a blurry image coming down the stairs. When Lou opened the door, she looked dreadful, and it was only then that I remembered how late it was.

'Stephen,' she sighed, 'come in. Do you know that it's half past three?'

'Oh,' I said, 'I'm sorry. It's like the middle of the afternoon to me.'

She held the door and I sidled past in the narrow hall. Once she'd closed the door, I followed her into the kitchen where she put the kettle on. I looked at the snowdrop, then, with its three pale, veined petals hanging lantern-like from the stalk and with its green-fringed skirt beneath. So delicate.

'What is it?' Lou asked.

'I've seen her,' I said.

'Seen who?'

'Valerie.'

'Valerie?'

'Let's sit down,' I said. 'I'll have to explain.'

I couldn't tell whether Lou was bored as I talked about Valerie, The Nurse and Thirteen, or if she was just struggling to stay awake, but she didn't react in any way to the story that I was telling her, and when I presented the snowdrop as my *piece de resistance*, she looked aghast and said, 'Is that *all*?'

I laughed, expecting this, and said, 'It's the middle of May, Lou. Yesterday, the weather was *hot*, as you know. It's ages since there have been any snowdrops. And no one grows them commercially. Where do you think it's from? Air freight from the Andes? No, this is my first piece of real evidence.'

'Stephen,' she told me, 'I agree, it *is* odd that you've been given a snowdrop like this, in the middle of the night by a woman who happened to be wandering around with one in her hand, but maybe you can grow them at any time of year if you know how to do it, and if you have the right greenhouse, or something.'

'What, you mean like a *refrigerated* greenhouse or something?' I said.

I picked up the flower and looked at the delicate green

veins that ran up the lower part of each petal, and at the odd nacreous wings that the petals made, like the delicate carapace of some angelic insect.

'Okay, okay,' I said, 'I'm sorry I bothered you. I'll leave now.'

At the doorstep, Lou hugged me and said, 'It is odd, Stephen, and I can see why you're so excited. But there'll be some mundane explanation for it. It hasn't come from another world or anything like that. Don't get worked up about it. Please be careful. Don't make a fool of yourself. Not again.'

I left and got back into the cab. As the door clunked closed behind me heavily, I suddenly remembered what Valerie had said to me in reply to my question about where to meet her. *Thirteen. Of course!*

Why had I gone to see Lou?

I had to get to Wish Road. Now.

I was currently on Belle Vue Gardens, which meant a journey right across the city. I looked at my watch. It was almost four – nearly fifty minutes since I'd seen Valerie.

Please let Thirteen be there, I thought as I drove, conscious of my speed and the very real possibility of being stopped by the police again, or caught by a speed camera, if I went anything like as fast as I was inclined to. I don't need to go on particularly about the subjective nature of the passage of time, but that journey was a killer. I drove along New Church Road at thirty-six miles an hour, and it felt as though it'd be quicker to walk. As I turned into Wish Road, my sense of anticipation gave me a stab of genuine pain in my chest.

It was there.

Or rather, a house was there that was conspicuously not number 11a, but neither was it the house where I'd collected Valerie so regularly. This place was a bay fronted, brick built Edwardian semi. Slightly neglected, as the previous number

13 had been, but otherwise not similar at all. The garden was the same, however, with the same gate, brass numbers and untamed privet. It was only the building itself that had changed. Considering it was so ordinary looking, it was amazing, the shiver of emotion that shook my body. What did it mean, that this was a 'new' house?

I parked directly outside. The air was fresh and slightly salty, and I could see, in the street lighting from across the road, the new foliage on the trees that flanked the park. I opened the gate, which squeaked slightly. The wooden gatepost had the number 13 on it, in small dirty brass letters; nothing special – in fact, the sort you'd get at any DIY store. I don't know what I'd expected, but it was almost *too* ordinary. The curtains in the sitting room were open, and the room was dimly lit, but it was impossible to see in because of the privet that was raggedly unkempt in front of the windows. I could see through the glass above the front door that there was a light on in the hall.

The path was made of concrete paving stones, some of them cracked, and I stopped for a moment to catch my breath before going up the red-tiled steps to the arched doorway. I hesitated for only a moment before ringing the bell, which was oddly similar to the one on that other house – small, round and white, with the word 'press' printed in black across it. It had a dirty brass surround to it that had probably never been polished. Pressing it like that was such a familiar thing to do. I had done exactly this many times before, to collect Valerie and take her to her class at the Cornerstone. But on those occasions I hadn't realised the significance of what I was doing. I hadn't realised that I'd been standing on a doorstep that didn't, in some important way, exist. As a flicker at the back of my mind, I wondered how many other moments in my life that had seemed utterly normal at the time, might have been, in fact, very, very strange.

After only a few seconds I heard someone approaching, and I didn't have the time to get any more nervous before the door was opened by a large man wearing chinos and a dark shirt. Although he was smartly dressed, he was clearly some sort of security person.

'Hi,' I said, 'I've come to see Valerie.'

'Piss off,' the man said. 'No one comes here to see Valerie.'

'She invited me,' I told the man, 'I've just seen her, about an hour ago, and she asked me to come round.'

'You're not welcome here,' he said. 'Now, bugger off.'

'Wait,' I said, 'just go and ask her, okay? Tell her that Stephen's here. Stephen Bardot, the taxi driver.'

'There's no one living here called Valerie,' he said. 'Never has been.'

'Yes there is. You've just mentioned her yourself. I've often picked her up here. Can I at least leave a note for her?'

He had me up against the wall in moments. His face was so close to mine that I could feel the spittle on my cheek as he shouted.

'When I said you weren't welcome,' he yelled, 'I fucking *meant* it. I don't know how you've managed to get here, but let me give you a word of advice. Don't come back.'

He calmed down slightly and loosed his grip. There was no way that I could struggle – he was a wall of muscle.

'This isn't the place for your sort,' he said. 'Now get lost.'

'Please,' I said, 'can't I just *talk* to someone?'

He managed to grab my shoulders, spin me round and have my arm twisted up behind my back in one fluid movement. He half-pushed, half-dragged me down the path and onto the pavement, then flung me against the cab so that my head caught the edge of the door with a sickening thud. Then he pulled me forward and punched me in the face so that my neck gave a dull crack. Another thump and my head caught the edge of the roof. The next punch contacted between my forehead and the bridge of my nose and I went backwards over the edge of the bonnet, landing face-down on the road. There was a brief silence before I heard the man walking round to where I was lying.

'If you don't understand words, mate,' he said, 'perhaps you'll understand that.'

I listened to the steady, diminishing footsteps as he walked off, and I felt the warmth of the blood from my nose. I lay for a few seconds with my cheek against the cool tarmac before I could bring myself to move. I was in a welter of pain, but my mind was completely sharp, and I felt a pang that was half way between fear and panic as I glanced down at the pool of blood, looking black in the orange street lighting, in which my cheek was resting.

I sat up slowly, then pulled myself up using the taxi's bumper. After that first gush, the blood flow diminished to a steady drip-drip-drip that I could feel beginning to make my sweatshirt clammy against my stomach. I let myself into the Galaxy, started the engine and set off to A&E. It felt as if my nose was broken, and that other parts of my face and head might need attention, too.

I was on my way along Kings Road, passing the foot of Preston Street, when I saw her. The Nurse. She was standing at the foot of the war memorial, wearing a short, tweed coat, under which I could see the dark blue of her nurse's uniform. She was also carrying a Gladstone bag, and she waved me to stop as I came through the lights.

I pulled in, and as soon as I stopped she opened the passenger door and jumped in.

'My God,' she said, 'what a mess. Quick, drive us back to your flat.'

'I'm on my way to A&E,' I said, sounding nasal from my various swellings.

'No, no, it's okay,' she told me, patting her valise. 'I've got everything I need in here.'

I hesitated. I'm not sure why. It's not that I didn't instinctively trust her. It was just that, well . . . I was in such a state, I reckoned casualty was where I ought to be.

'Look,' she told me, 'I've got far more experience of this than most people you're likely to see up at the hospital.'

'Okay, okay,' I said, turning up West Street, deserted now at 5.00am. Churchill Square, too, was eerily empty and bereft. I would have sped home at top speed had it not been for the traffic-calming humps along Western Road. I doubt a policeman would have detained me once he'd seen what state I was in, especially given that I had a nurse with me. Still, my suspension had a tough time of it, and every time we went over the bumps, my face throbbed agonisingly with the jolt.

There was, miraculously, a single parking space quite near the bottom of Lansdowne Street, and so I parked – badly – and we made our way up to the flat. The Nurse handed me a tissue, which I held gently against my nose as I walked. Once we were inside, she instructed me to lay a towel over the end of the sofa, and to lie back on it as comfortably as possible. She moved one of the lamps closer, so she had better light. Then she checked me over.

'Hmm,' she said, after gently pressing her fingertips all round my nose, 'it's not broken. Luckily. You took the blows on your forehead and cheekbone mostly. You'll need a dressing on both, and some non-invasive stitches just above your eyebrow. I can give you a tetanus jab, right now, and a decent tranquilliser so that you'll get some sleep.'

She gave me the injection, then checked me for other injuries: a shallow cut on the back of my head, bruising on my ribs, and a pulled muscle in my shoulder from having my arm twisted so sharply. My neck was also stiff and painful, but mobile.

'There's some nasty bruising and a lot of swelling,' she told me, 'so you'll look a bit scary for a while. But you'll recover far more quickly than you might imagine. Just take it easy for two or three days before you even think of getting back into your cab, that's all. Now, I'll give you a pill that'll make you sleep. I'll just go and get a glass of water for you. Is the kitchen through here?'

'Yes,' I told her, and she left, smoothing her blue skirt and looking, I thought, more like an actress playing a nurse, than an actual nurse.

I lay immobile while I waited for her to return. I felt as though my whole body was injured – there was no specific site of pain, just a general feeling of batteredness. The Nurse came back with a mug and handed me a small yellow pill, which I took and swallowed down with some water.

'How come you were out so late, and with all this … medical stuff?' I asked.

'Oh,' she laughed, 'you'd be surprised what I get up to. Nursing is just one of my many talents. I'm not often called out like this these days, so perhaps you could say you were lucky.'

I lay back and looked at the ceiling.

'You know what happened to me?' I asked her.

'You were beaten up,' she said.

'By someone at 13 Wish Road,' I told her. 'I was trying to visit Valerie, but it was a different house, and I came up against this . . . bruiser instead.'

The Nurse looked at me, as though I might be a wayward child, or a bad student.

'But you knew it could be dangerous to visit Thirteen,' she told me. 'You've been warned against it, haven't you, by one of your taxiing colleagues. And yet you've still sought it out?'

'But I've seen you at Wish Road; I've seen Valerie at Wish Road.'

'Outside the house,' she said. 'You've never actually crossed the threshold, have you?'

I considered this statement for a moment.

'Even so, Valerie invited me to visit her, so why wasn't she there?'

'Maybe,' The Nurse said, quietly, 'maybe she would have been there if you'd genuinely expected it.'

She smiled at me, and patted my knee and said, 'Look, what you need is to lighten up. You should come and see me when I'm off duty and we'll relax together, okay? I may be middle-aged, but I get invited to some fairly impressive parties.'

I laughed, which made me wince with pain.

'That's all right for you to say,' I gasped, 'but how am I going to do that? I don't know where to find you.'

She shrugged at that and said, 'You found me tonight, didn't you?'

She busied herself with packing up her bag.

'I'm sorry,' I told her, 'this is a bit too much for me right now. I feel like shit, and you're just talking in riddles.'

She stood and picked up her bag, then looked down at me.

'I've got to go, but you must come and see me sometime. I've been expecting you.'

'That's what Valerie said, and just as cryptically.'

She laughed, a laugh of genuine pleasure, and said, 'Valerie's a nice girl, and you really should get to know her. Or maybe I should say you need to get to know her. But I can think of one or two other people you should meet as well, just so that you can learn to let your hair down. Perhaps in my capacity as a medical expert I'll prescribe you a bit of fun. We'll see. In the meantime I'll introduce you to my brother. I don't particularly want to, but at some point, I suppose I'll have to. He was quite impressed by that little scene you made of yourself at Septimus. I was quite impressed too, you know. It showed a real, healthy curiosity.' She laughed. 'What did your friend think of it all?'

'Lou? She was freaked out, to say the least, and still thinks I've gone mad,' I said.

'I'm not surprised,' she told me. 'This is not an experience that you can share.'

'But why don't you want me to meet your brother?' I asked.

'He . . . well, let's just say that I refer to him as Seymour *no-fun* Bentham. I think I need say no more than that.'

'So don't introduce me to him.'

'We have an agreement. It actually works quite well, even if I do find it irritating at times.'

As she said this I was finding it more and more difficult to keep my eyes open, and there was a slight blurring to my vision.

'Now,' she said, 'you get to bed or you'll fall asleep on the sofa, which is not a good idea for someone in your condition.'

I half rolled off the settee and steadied myself on one of the arms as I got up, feeling more and more groggy. The Nurse took my elbow and steered me through to the bedroom.

'Can you undress,' she asked, smiling, 'or shall I help you?'

I pulled at my sweatshirt and only half managed to get it off, so nodded to her and she kissed me on the cheek just above my dressing, and pulled the sweatshirt gently over my head. After that, she helped me with my jeans. In her role as a nurse, this seemed completely appropriate, though there was a moment, as she undid my flies, when we both smirked. When I fell back onto the bed, still wearing my boxers, socks and T-shirt, she pulled the duvet over me and left. Sleep enveloped me just as surely as the folds of the duvet.

Woman: Fuck you!
SB: Pardon?
Woman: Yes, FUCK YOU!
SB: (About to reply, realises she's talking into her mobile phone.)
St James Street, Brighton, May 27th.

7. Ignorance is the condition for all learning.

I woke up after a dreamless sleep. The first thing I noticed, even before I opened my eyes, or remembered any of the events from the evening before, was a feeling of wellbeing: a lightness in my body, and an energy and alertness. I put my hand to my cheek, and found the skin there smooth and undamaged. This caused me to sit up, suddenly alert, and look at myself in the small mirror on the battered pine bedside table. There was no trace of cuts, swellings or dressings. Nothing. My skin was completely undamaged. The shock of this made me go still inside. I looked at my watch. It was 5.30pm. I'd been asleep for nearly twelve hours. I should have dropped the cab off for Bruce, the day driver, by 6.00am at the latest . . . Over eleven hours earlier.

I ran through to the kitchen, where Bruce's number was pinned to the notice board, and called him on his mobile.

'Look,' I said, when he answered, 'about the cab. I'm sorry about it being so late—'

'I didn't pick it up until 7.45,' he told me. 'It was there by the time I needed it, so don't worry about it.'

What could I say? The fact that the Galaxy seemed to have driven itself back to Mile Oak while I slept seemed no more bizarre than any number of other events that had happened since I'd encountered Thirteen. I mumbled something to Bruce, then went back to the bedroom to get dressed. As I did so I thought of my beating the previous evening and sub-sequently being looked after by The Nurse. I could remember it all clearly – meeting her, driving back to the flat, being tended by her . . . But there was something else, too, that I seemed to have forgotten, as though it had all happened in a dream, the bare facts of which were the least important or meaningful.

Once dressed, I padded back through to the kitchen, which looked particularly shabby today for some reason, and got some coffee going. Then I got Lou on her mobile.

'Hi,' I told her, 'I'm phoning to apologise for getting you up in the middle of the night.'

'That's okay,' she said, 'but you know how nervous Colin is about night-time disturbances after we were burgled last year. If you buy us a drink or two next time we're out together and let him take the piss out of you, he'll be fine.'

'You know that snowdrop I showed you . . . ?' I asked.

'Yes,' she said, 'I've been thinking about that. All I can say is that, yes, it is genuinely odd that someone handed you a snowdrop in the middle of the night. But it's just a co-incidence, Stephen, that's all. Loads of flowers are being grown all year round these days.'

'You're probably right,' I said. 'Look, I've got to go and pick up the cab. But I wanted to call you first.'

I ended the call and thought, *So at least the snowdrop episode happened.* Lou had seen it, so I had independent evidence. But what was all this about injuries that disappeared by morning? I went to pour myself some coffee and get some breakfast, then took my cereal through to the sitting room.

I saw the note immediately, on a scrap of my own paper. It read:

Dear Stephen,

I've thought about it and decided that the best thing is for you to formally meet my brother. I'll book a table at Septimus for this Thursday (22nd May) at 8.00pm. Please, come as my guest. I'll book the table in your name. See you then.

Helena Caburn (The Nurse!)

I sat and sipped a second coffee, reading and re-reading the note, and wondered how I was going to last for two days without going mad with curiosity. The more I considered the note, the more isolated I realised I'd become. I mean, there was no one I could talk to about this. My interaction with Lou had proved this – and she'd been more sympathetic than most people might have been. Also, when I'd seen her, I felt that I'd only mentioned Thirteen in the briefest of ways. As The Nurse – Helena – had remarked so poignantly to me night before, as far as Thirteen went, I was on my own . . .

I cycled over to get my cab. Although I was aware that I was still zoning, I somehow knew to wait until it was dark before going to Wish Road. I plied my trade for a while, then drove up to Mill Hill, on the edge of the Downs, to the car park where radio-controlled planes are often flown. Here I could look out over the river Adur and Lancing College to one side, and the conurbation on the other. I watched as the dusk gathered, slowly – incredibly slowly, it seemed – and gloomily under the grey canopy of cloud. It was a dull, creeping shade, devoid of the colour that can make twilight so spectacular. But darkness fell all the same, and gradually the city began to shimmer under its myriad lights. Only when the horizon – the surgically sharp line between sea and sky – finally disappeared, did I make my way back down and into the city once more.

As I drove, I considered how I knew I was zoning. What quality of awareness, or what mental state was it? I couldn't put it into words, but even as I pulled into Wish Road, I knew Thirteen would be there. And it was. Just as it had been two days earlier. And again, the house itself was different. A bay-fronted semi of ochre brick this time. Shabby again, in the same way that the others had been, with old paint and disintegrating window frames.

Instead of parking under my usual tree, I drove about a hundred yards further up the road and walked back down as casually as possible. Once there, rather than walking up to the front door, I crept across the small lawn to the overgrown privet bushes in front of the sitting room windows. As I did so, I could see that, in one of the first floor rooms, the window was open a few inches. It was dark inside the room and I could hear a muted, disconsolate sobbing, and I thought, *Ah, THAT'S where the crying comes from.*

I crawled between the bushes and crouched down, trying to find a more or less comfortable position. I knelt and steadied myself by holding onto the stem of the thickest bush, and waited there for a minute or so while my pulse calmed, then I carefully peered into the room.

It was dim inside. There was a diffused light, out of sight to one side, and a couple of candles on the mantelpiece flanking a rather trashy gold-framed mirror. The room was a little old fashioned, probably untouched since the Seventies. The wall-paper was brown and vinyl-looking with floral patterns. Standing with his back to me and wearing a dark blue suit was a man I didn't recognise. He was too slim to be the man who'd assaulted me the previous evening. Sitting on a wooden dining chair in front of him was another man. I couldn't see much of him because he was obscured, partly by a Swiss cheese plant on a low table, and partly by the man who was standing between me and him. The seated man's shoulders were taut against the chair so it was clear that his hands were tied together behind the chair's back. He was inert, his head hanging down, unconscious.

I didn't absorb any more detail because the only object that held my attention was the knife that the suited man was holding in his right hand. I was cramped, kneeling in the way I was, but I remained still, breathless. Watching. A shaft of light fell across the room as the door opened. I couldn't see who it was, but could hear a murmur of voices and the suited man bent forward and cut the bonds of the seated man. What happened next was a little confused, but the man in the seat seemed to be coming round and managed to stop himself from falling as he slumped forward, free of his bonds. As he righted himself, I heard voices more clearly. The man in the chair, still looking down, shook his head – whether to clear his head or to refute what was being said, it was impossible to tell. I heard a woman bark the command, 'Do it. Just do it!' and then laughter. The suited man leaned forward and stuck the knife into the seated man's side. The seated man became instantly rigid, kicking his legs out and falling sideways onto the floor. I could see the shoulder of the woman who'd shouted as she came into view, walking towards the window – she was wearing a dark blue jacket. I didn't see any more of her than that as I had to duck down and remain like that for some time, wondering if I'd been seen.

But no one looked out or came to the door.

I remained crouched where I was, stunned by what I'd seen. However, I was becoming more and more cramped and uncomfortable and so eventually I had to move. I risked another look, flexing my legs as I did so – an incredible relief. I leaned back a little, away from the window, to be more discreet, and peered carefully into the room once more.

The suited man was there still, standing with the knife in his hand. In front of him was the man he'd stabbed, unconscious and tied up in the chair yet again. I carried on watching and, when I saw the shaft of light as someone came into the room, I realised that I wasn't seeing something new, but a rerun of what had happened only a couple of minutes before. There was the sound of conversation, then I saw the man having his bonds cut. There were the raised voices, the command of 'Do it. Just do it!' accompanied by laughter, and then the stabbing. This time, it was completely unreal. For a start, I knew it wasn't happening in real time. This was something I'd already witnessed, and whether it had been real or not then, now it was . . . what? A replay?

I ducked down again and backed out from the bushes. I didn't want to see this again. It was not what I'd hoped for. Keeping low, I crept back across the lawn. As I did so, there was a tap at one of the upstairs windows. My heart lurched, and I involuntarily looked up. There was someone looking at me from the window above the door, hardly visible in the darkness. Given the reflections on the glass it was almost impossible to tell, but it seemed to be a child of maybe eight or nine. I couldn't tell which gender they were, but they were beckoning. I could see that the child was distressed; was presumably the one who'd been sobbing. I looked up helplessly. What could I do? There was at least one armed man in there who was, as I had witnessed, perfectly happy to commit murder.

As I stood, gazing up at the kid in the window, I saw a light being switched on in the downstairs hallway, so I turned and ran from the garden, across Wish Road and into the seaward entrance of the park, stopping a few metres in and stepping back into the bushes where I wouldn't be seen. Then I looked back across the road.

But where 13 Wish Road had been, 11a now stood, utterly quiet and still.

I arrived at Septimus at exactly eight o'clock. I'd been nervous all day. After Thirteen had disappeared on Tuesday evening, I'd done the rest of my shift, followed by a full shift on Wednesday. But there hadn't been so much as a whisper of anything out of the ordinary. Now, as I walked down to the restaurant, I knew that I was nowhere near zoning, and so I arrived wondering if perhaps The Nurse wasn't going to be there.

The waiter who greeted me was the one who'd frog-marched me out of the place when I was last there. Thankfully, he didn't recognise me, and asked if I had a table booked.

'Yes, you should have one in the name of Stephen Bardot,' I said.

'Ah, yes,' he said, 'your guests are already here. Please. This way.'

I followed him through to the larger dining area towards the back of the restaurant and there, beneath a false window glowing with discreet lighting, sat The Nurse and her dining companion from my last visit: Seymour, her brother. His full head of dark hair, greying only slightly at the temples, was carefully combed and parted. He was wearing a green tweed suit and looked even more stern, if that was possible, than the last time I'd seen him.

'Stephen,' The Nurse said, smiling broadly and standing to greet me and give me a friendly kiss on the cheek. 'Let me introduce you to Seymour. Seymour Bentham.'

He stood too and shook my hand firmly. I noticed that he was wearing a gold and onyx identity ring on his little finger. For some reason – and this later puzzled me, since they were so outwardly dissimilar – he reminded me of Graham, my erstwhile childhood prankster, and sometime guru of what-to-do-next-in-life. Seymour smiled and said, 'Helena and I were just talking about you. Please, sit down and we'll order you a drink.'

I sat while The Nurse summoned the waiter and ordered me a Harvey Wallbanger. I looked at her and laughed. She was wearing a dark, low cut dress in a kind of silky material that had shiny black leaves printed on it. Her full cleavage was evident. Her earrings were strands of diamonds that fell to her shoulders. Her curled hair fell in gentle waves around her face, and her make-up was subtle, making her look glamorous and powerful, like an off duty executive or – and this was a little shocking – a high class madame.

'You laugh?' she said.

'It's just that I always think of you as "The Nurse",' I told her. 'It seems so inappropriate now, when you're looking so—'

'So call me Helena,' she smiled, turning to her brother and saying, 'poor boy, I told you, he's hopelessly formal.'

Seymour smiled at this, and caught my eye with a kind of precise, clinical look, as though he wanted me to know that he was about to tell a joke, rather than to indicate that he was actually amused.

'Nothing wrong with being formal,' he said.

'Nothing wrong with being formal, *necessarily*,' she said as the waiter arrived with my cocktail. Helena was drinking a Martini, while Seymour appeared to have whiskey.

I raised my glass and Helena did the same, clinking it against mine with, I don't know, a sort of extraordinary intimacy. Seymour slightly inclined his head towards me, without a trace of a smile, and Helena laughed aloud and shook her head.

'Oh, Sey, we've got to get Stephen out of his shell, not put him back into it.'

I sipped my Harvey Wallbanger – a favourite cocktail of mine. How had Helena known? I didn't really care. I was simply pleased to be here in this restaurant with her, in circumstances where, for an hour or two – and for the first time – I didn't have to worry about her disappearing on me. It made me feel comfortable with her. She certainly had an informal air about her that was seductive. I began to wish that we were alone together, without her alarming brother.

We chatted a little about me, about my past and how I'd come to be a taxi driver. I wanted to skirt quickly over all that, partly because I'd told Helena something of it in my cab when I gave her a lift, but also because I wanted to talk about them, rather than me. But Helena was interested in the Graham episode.

'So,' Helena asked, 'why do you think Graham told you to become a taxi driver?'

'I guess he knew how weird it could be, and how different in terms of life experience.'

'Do you suppose he knew you'd find Thirteen?'

'I wonder,' I said. 'Maybe I should ask him. I told him I'd keep in touch, but I haven't.'

We paused while our starter arrived – a large open mushroom on a rosti base, for me, in a rich dark caper and soy sauce. This was accompanied by an organic 'biodynamic' wine that I'd eyed on the menu when I'd been here with Lou, but had decided against as it was so expensive. It was excellent.

'And what about you?' I asked Helena. 'What do you do? You're obviously not a nurse all the time.'

Helena looked at Seymour, who looked back at her with a hooded – but warning – look, I thought, and Helena smiled to herself.

'I'm, umm, retired,' she said. 'Both Seymour and I have private incomes. I only work occasionally, and only then for interest's sake. The rest of the time I like to spend on, well, what you might call . . . cultural pursuits.'

'She means the word "cultural" in the loosest possible way,' said Seymour.

'I seek intoxication,' she said, raising her glass to me. 'Of all kinds.'

She sipped her drink and turned her attention to her food – some kind of warm basil salad – and we were silent for a few seconds.

'And what do you do with your time?' I asked Seymour.

He looked at me with a hard, full stare. His dark eyes flashed with intelligence.

'I educate myself,' he said, 'so that I can watch the world with informed clarity.'

'What he really means is that he's a dry academic,' Helena said. 'We pursue our interests separately. We only get together at times like this, and spar a little, in a friendly sort of way. Don't we?'

He paused and then said, carefully, 'I think it does us both a lot of credit that we have remained friends when our outlook on life is so radically different.'

'The attraction of opposites?' I asked.

'If you like,' he said.

'Seymour is so moderate it sometimes makes me want to smack him,' she laughed. 'See, he's still on his first glass of wine. I keep hoping that one day he'll come with me to one of my parties. Then he'd realise that dry study is not all there is to life.'

'I don't disapprove, in principle, of what you do,' he said, 'or how you enjoy yourself. I just subscribe to the belief that hedonistic pleasure can only be positive when indulged in with caution.'

Helena laughed again, and I realised what a musical, what a genuinely friendly laugh she had.

'But caution is precisely what you must jettison in order to enjoy hedonistic pleasure,' she said, then looked at me with a conspiring glance. 'But, Stephen, don't take him seriously. Hedonism isn't the only thing I'm interested in. Seymour likes to tease me about it, that's all. There are many kinds of intoxication that far transcend hedonistic pleasure. Seymour just goes on about it because he thinks I'm too indulgent sometimes. What he doesn't take into account is all the other things I get up to. Like nursing, for example, which is a purely practical and useful occupation, and not hedonistic in the least. After all, I patched you up pretty well, didn't I?'

I looked at her, at her slight, questioning frown.

'I don't know,' I said, 'did you patch me up? There was no sign of it in the morning.'

She laughed again, delightedly, and said, 'That's what I want to hear. Genuine, delicious perplexity mixed with brittle curiosity.'

She took another sip of wine, and laughed, yet again, and patted Seymour's hand, looking at him with affection and concern.

'Baudelaire,' she said, turning to me, 'do you know his poem about intoxication?'

'No,' I said.

She looked across the now-crowded restaurant, bringing the words to mind. 'It doesn't translate brilliantly, but still . . .'

She closed her eyes for a moment.

'"Be always drunken,"' she murmured, catching the rhythm of the words. '"Nothing else matters: that is the only question."'

She opened her eyes and looked at me and raised her voice. '"If you would not feel the dreadful burden of Time weighing on your shoulders and crushing you onto the earth, be drunken continually.

'"Drunken with what? With wine, with poetry—"'

'"—or with virtue,"' Seymour added, '"as you will."'

They laughed together, slightly mocking each other.

'"And if sometimes,"' Helena continued, '"on the stairs of a palace, or on the green edge of a ditch, or in the dull solitude of your own room, you should awake and the drunkenness be half or wholly slipped away from you . . ."'

She ran her finger round the rim of her glass and nodded slightly towards me as I sat, entranced by the mesmeric quality of her recitation.

' ". . . ask of the wind, or of the wave, or of the star, or of the bird, or of the clock, of whatever flies, or sighs, or rocks, or sings, or speaks, ask what hour it is; and the wind, wave, star, bird, clock, will answer you: 'It is the hour to be drunken! Be drunken continually! With wine, with poetry—" '

' "—or with virtue," ' murmured Seymour.

' "—as you will." '

She laughed, and raised her glass to me, and we clinked, and Seymour raised his glass too and they looked at each other with genuine affection, and with something else, too. A history, perhaps, of pain and compromise, and maybe argument or healed wounds that would always remain, despite forgiveness. A lifetime clearly lay between them, and I had a sense that their affection was coloured by a mutual disapproval that was very real, yet too weak to break their bonds.

We sat silent for some time after that. I don't actually remember much of the rest of the meal. I felt that I ought to be asking questions about Thirteen, but knew instinctively that Seymour wouldn't answer me, and that Helena would laugh and parry my queries. Only once, as we sat sipping liqueurs, did I find myself asking something that slipped into my mind so suddenly that I gave voice to it without thinking.

'But,' I asked, leaning in to the table earnestly, 'are either of you real?'

I looked directly at Helena.

'You seem so real now,' I added, 'but you also seemed completely real the other night when you patched me up after I'd been beaten up. And my wounds have disappeared.'

Helena laughed so loudly at this that she attracted attention from other tables. Seymour looked suddenly furious, as though I had broken the spell, in some way, that had kept us together and he signalled to the waiter that he wanted the bill. Helena took a packet of cigarettes out of her bag and put one to her lips. I picked up the wallet of matches in the ash tray and struck one for her and, as the flame flared, she said quietly, 'Don't you recognise me, Stephen?'

There was something about the flame, flickering between us, that made me catch my breath, that made my heart beat harder.

She said, 'We've met once, before all . . . this.'

I thought carefully, but no solid memory presented itself.

'No,' I said slowly. 'I don't remember.'

Seymour stood up, with an irritated look.

'I'm sorry that I allowed myself to be persuaded by Helena to come here tonight to meet you,' he said. 'Our meeting has served no purpose whatsoever. I have only one piece of advice for you, which I know you will ignore, but I'll give it anyway.'

He paused for emphasis, and looked so arrogant that I suddenly despised him.

'Don't visit Thirteen again,' he said, then folded his napkin and placed it carefully on the table. I looked at him now, and he avoided my stare, and I thought, This is one piece of advice that I shall take great pleasure in ignoring.

'Now,' he said to Helena, 'seeing as this was your idea, I presume you're paying?'

'Of course,' she said.

'In that case, I'll leave.'

He stood up and held out his hand.

'Goodbye, Stephen. I don't mean this unpleasantly, but I sincerely hope we shall never meet again.'

'But Seymour,' Helena said, 'you haven't answered Stephen's question.'

'Oh?' he said.

'Stephen asked if we were real.'

Seymour looked contemptuously at me for a moment, as if I were a schoolboy asking a silly question of the headmaster.

'Of *course* we're real,' he spat, then turned and left.

Helena watched him go, a half-sad, half-satisfied look on her face, then she turned to me and shrugged.

'Oh well, and I'd so hoped you might get on together.'

She said this with such utter insincerity that I was forced to question why she might have invited him along at all.

'What did you mean,' I asked, 'when you said that we've met before?'

'Oh, that doesn't matter,' she said. 'If you don't remember, let's leave it at that.'

I looked over to where Seymour was being helped into his coat. I saw him handing a note to the waiter and leaving the restaurant.

'What did I do to offend him?' I asked. 'I don't feel he gave me a chance.'

'Maybe,' she agreed. 'I suppose it was stupid of me to imagine that the three of us might get on. But, you see,' she added, 'it was you who made tonight inevitable, by pursuing me in the way you did.'

'*Pursuing?*' I asked.

'Well, whatever. You wanted to see me again, to find out more about Thirteen. Like it or not, Seymour is a part of it.'

She placed some cash on the plate that had been put in front of her, and when the waiter came to collect it, she smiled at him and said, 'Hello, David. My friend Stephen was asking me about whether or not I'm . . . um . . . real.'

The waiter looked nonplussed.

'I think what he means,' she said, 'is that he's not convinced that I'm a genuine Brighton resident. What would you say to that?'

'Oh,' he said, with something close to innuendo in his voice that I couldn't quite decipher, 'you're always dining here, Helena. You and your brother, so you do have a connection with the city, whether you live here or not. It's always a pleasure to see you.'

'Thank you, David,' she said, and raised her eyebrows to me.

'Now,' she said, 'I think it's time to go.'

We stood, and I felt awkward, not wanting the evening to end just yet, but aware that I had no control over that side of things. David brought Helena her coat, and she shrugged herself into it with such grace that I felt a little breathless. When we left, she paused on the pavement and I said, 'So, when am I going to see you again?'

'Stephen,' she smiled, 'that sounded almost like a pass.'

I laughed and said nothing. She took my arm.

'As to "when am I going to see you again?",' she said, 'I'm afraid I haven't finished with you yet this evening. Not by a long way.'

I felt a thrill pass up my spine. The westerly breeze gusted up Middle Street and caught my hair, tousling it and making me feel brash and energetic. Helena raised her arm to a passing taxi, which stopped for us, and we got in.

'Eastern Terrace,' she said, and the taxi pulled out and we set off down to the seafront and along by Brighton Pier, whose strings of lights seemed appropriately dynamic as we passed by and up Marine Parade.

The house that we stopped outside was set back slightly

from the seafront. It was in the middle of the terrace and from the steps we could look out to sea and either back along the seafront towards the pier and the city centre, or eastwards to the marina and the cliffs towards Rottingdean. What was unusual about the place was that it was a single dwelling – wide-fronted and on five floors. As we walked up the shallow, broad steps from the pavement, the door opened and a man in a black suit came out to greet us. He gestured for us to go in, and said, 'Hello madam,' to Helena, who shook his hand and smiled, saying, 'Hello Gordon,' then allowed him to take her coat. He nodded to me, with a brief twitch of his neck as I handed him my jacket, and as soon as we came into the hallway, he left us there and went off down a passageway to the side.

Two words sprang to mind as I stood there with Helena: 'vast' and 'magnificent'. The hallway was tiled in black and white marble, with a curved wooden staircase in front of us. A massive, glittering chandelier hung above us, blazing with golden light. In the distance I could hear the pulse of music. Helena touched my elbow to indicate that we should carry on into the building, and we started up the staircase.

'Formal,' she whispered to me, 'this is all so formal.'

I looked at her, and realised that my back had become rigid with tension, and when she laughed, I laughed with her, and began to relax. She started to walk faster up the stairs. I began to take them two at a time to keep up with her, and so she broke into a run. I could feel that she was trying to lighten my mood and release my tension and so I ran too, catching up with her, and overtaking her at the top of the stairs. She grabbed me round the waist as she came up behind me, and hugged me, laughing, and we looked around the galleried landing. I leaned over the banister and gazed down into the stairwell, and then back at the four closed doors that surrounded us. Helena looked at me, questioningly. It was from the door to my left that the thump of music came, so I nodded my head in that direction, and we walked over, and I opened it. And we went in.

The first thing I noticed was the lighting: dim, fluctuating. I realised that there were projections coming from one end of the room, but I was distracted by the softness of the carpet. I noticed Helena kicking off her shoes and bent down to remove my own. The music wasn't particularly loud, and so I could easily hear her say to me, 'Socks, Stephen, and your socks.' I nodded and pulled my socks off and let my toes sink into the dark softness of the pile.

When I looked up again, I could see that there were quite a few people here – maybe twenty or thirty. There were different coloured lights sweeping the walls, and in the corner there was a DJ playing minimalist, dark music, heavy on the bass. To one side, and rather incongruously, a cello player was accompanying him – a young woman, dressed in a black skirt and white blouse, who took the haunting rhythms that he was playing and mesmerically overlaid them with a kind of wistful melody.

I turned to Helena, but she had wandered off to a makeshift bar near the huge, floor-to-ceiling windows. I stepped to one side and leaned against the wall, looking at the projections. On the back wall of the room there was black and white footage of waves breaking on a rocky coast. I'm not sure what had been done to it, but it seemed to be in negative with highlights in incandescent purple. The other projection was again in black-and-white, but stills this time that would fade from one image to the next from time to time. Right now, it was fading from a view of piles of autumn leaves receding along a well tended, tree-lined path, to a seventies concrete car park.

Helena handed me a drink and I sipped it – Harvey Wallbanger again. I wasn't drunk yet, and I wanted to remain sober enough to experience this party so, after taking a further gulp, I put the glass on a table at my side, and looked around me. Although the beat of the music was slow, people were dancing, with large expansive movements. Of course, they had plenty of space; the room was huge and there was no furniture except for the short curve of the bar and a couple of long, low tables against the walls. It might have been the music, or the fact that I was here with Helena, when I'd worried that I might never see her again, but I felt fantastic, caught by an exhilaration that made me suddenly breathless. I experienced a rush that caused a light-headed warmth, leaving me ready for anything. I was pleased to be here and incredibly grateful to Helena for making it happen.

I turned and noticed that Helena had moved away and was talking to someone over by the window. They were both looking out into the night. I stayed where I was, and closed my eyes briefly to let the music take hold. When I opened them, and looked at the cello player, I noticed that it was Valerie. I crossed over to her and she looked up at me and nodded.

'I can't talk now,' she called to me as she drew her bow over the strings, 'but later?'

'Definitely,' I said and walked away, then turned to look at her. She leaned over her instrument with earnest effort, with that curious dreaminess that she'd had the last time I saw her, at the bottom of North Street. But there was something troubling about her appearance, too, and it took me a while to realise what it was. She was younger. I realised, too, that when she'd given me the snowdrop, this had also been true. When I'd been taking her to her positive thinking classes

I'd assumed she was in her late twenties. When she'd dropped the snowdrop into my palm, she couldn't have looked more than nineteen. Now, she seemed to be barely fifteen. I turned and saw that Helena was approaching. She picked up my cocktail and brought it over to me.

I was feeling a little strange, having seen Valerie like this, so I accepted the drink and took a couple more swift gulps. Helena held out her arms to me and so I downed the rest, then took her in a loose embrace and we danced for a while. It was a wonderful moment of connection. Warm. Empathetic. Was there a hint of eroticism, too? I couldn't tell.

'You're getting the hang of this,' she told me. 'Are you pleased I brought you here?'

'Incredibly,' I said. 'It's wonderful. But who are these other people?'

She looked around, then back to me.

'Various other inhabitants of Thirteen,' she said. 'Go and talk to them if you like. They won't bite.'

The black-and-white still against the wall was now a view of Tintagel castle in Cornwall, which I recognised, having visited it with my parents as a child.

I smiled at a woman with dark maroon lipstick, and even darker shadowed eyes. She wore a black rubber waistcoat, skirt and boots with fetishistically high heels and, as I looked at her, she smiled back at me – not in a friendly way, but as if I were a camera and she was posing for her portrait. Helena disengaged from me in an 'I'll leave you to it' sort of way, kissed me briefly, and wandered off. The woman in black came closer and pouted slightly and said, 'Hi, Stephen. Helena said you'd be along at some point. Look, I could give you some *tips* about your dress-sense if you'd like. I think it could do with some work.'

She looked down at herself, and her fetish gear, with approval. I laughed.

'You mean I look terminally boring?'

'Not terminal, no,' she said, 'but we should talk. Call me.'

She handed me her card, but it was a little too dark to read it and so I put it in my pocket. I was about to reply, but she had turned away from me and was already wandering out of earshot. I turned to see where Helena was, but couldn't see her, so went over to the bar, where a smart barmaid was serving drinks. As I approached her, she was mixing a cocktail with aplomb, and she looked up and said, 'Good evening, Stephen.' And she handed me the drink. 'A Harvey Wallbanger.'

She was maybe twenty, with dark blond hair that tumbled over her shoulders and she eyed me with a certain knowing look – not exactly flirty, but certainly intimate. I smiled at her and she laughed, which made me laugh, too. It was a wonderful shared moment. I looked at my drink, and then at her.

'You haven't got anything a little more—'

'Unusual?' the barmaid said.

'Yes.'

As the music continued its hypnotic journey, I put my drink back on the bar and watched with admiration her skill and dexterity as she mixed me a cocktail made from peach schnapps with amaretto, apricot juice and a dash of absinthe. As I took the glass out of her hand, a voice said at my side, 'I'll have the Wallbanger.' I turned. The man who had spoken was perhaps ten years older than me, wearing a slim black suit, with a roll-necked top and an ankh pendant. His hair was longish and pulled back in a pony tail. The barmaid handed him the drink and he took my elbow and steered me over to the window.

'Look, Stephen,' he said to me, 'Helena tells me you're isolated. Or at least that you *feel* isolated. There's no need for that, you know. There are plenty of people here – including me – who would be happy to be your friend. I'll introduce you round later if you want. Just ask, okay?'

As he said this, the woman in the fetish gear was passing, so he beckoned her over and said, 'Charlotte, come over and say hello to Stephen.'

'We've met, Kenton,' she said, and kissed me briefly on the mouth.

'I was just saying to Stephen that I'd introduce him around,' said Kenton. 'If he wants to meet people, that is.'

'But he's so shy,' she said, 'aren't you Stephen?'

'Yes,' I said, 'I am. Though tonight that doesn't seem to matter.'

She smiled and unzipped the rubber skirt that she was wearing and removed it, revealing dark panties and suspenders. I wondered if I was supposed to respond to this, but she didn't give me a chance.

'Oh, well,' she said. 'See you later.'

'Bye,' I said to her receding back. I turned to Kenton.

'Wow,' I said.

'Charlotte's someone I'd advise caution over,' said Kenton. 'Some women can fuck your life up as surely as . . . well . . . let's just say, some women can fuck you up and no mistake. And not just Charlotte.' He looked around to see if anyone was close by, and leaned in to me. 'Please,' he said, 'come and see me. I think I could give you some perspective on . . .Thirteen.'

I looked at him questioningly and he raised his eyebrows and touched me on the elbow to emphasise his point.

'Why, what is it that you think I ought to know? And why can't you tell me now?'

'It's a question of perspective. If I said something to you such as . . . well, such as what I just said about Charlotte a moment ago, it doesn't particularly mean anything, does it, because you've never met her before? We'd have to get together so that I could tell you something about her. Her past, and how she came to be as she is. Maybe I could tell you a little about Helena, too. I've known her for a long time.'

He looked around to check that she wasn't nearby, then leaned in conspiratorially.

'In strictest confidence, of course.'

'Yes, I'd like to do that,' I told him.

I'm not sure if the volume was turned up at this point, but I suddenly became intensely aware of the music, of its insistent beat, and felt myself nodding involuntarily to it as I looked around. Over Kenton's shoulder I saw a woman I hadn't noticed before – about my age, wearing pale jeans and a tight, short blue T-shirt that showed her midriff. She had dishevelled brown hair and a slightly angular face.

'Ah,' said the man, looking over his shoulder in the direction of my gaze, 'I see you've already chosen someone you want to be introduced to. Well, I'm hardly surprised. Follow me.'

I felt a little breathless as I followed Kenton, and not at all sure that I *did* want to be introduced to this beautiful stranger. I felt, really, that I wanted to watch Valerie playing her cello, and the DJ creating this seamless soundscape, and the slow swirl of the people around me. It was a long time since I'd felt such extraordinarily complete contentment, and part of me wanted to sit in the corner and wallow in it. But then, I realised, this was my shyness asserting itself. I knew that I'd wanted to enter Thirteen with such yearning, that to be passive now I'd got here would be to waste what might be my only opportunity to connect with this extraordinary place.

'Phoenix,' Kenton said, and the woman turned and noticed me, and said, 'Stephen, hi,' and leaned forward and kissed me on the cheek as though she'd known me for years. I could smell a vague scent from her; clean and light - a hint of cinnamon with that characteristic Thirteen citrus edge, plus a soap smell, too. I could feel the softness of her lips against my cheek as she kissed me, and the slight dampness of her lip gloss.

'Okay,' the man said, sadly, 'I'll leave you two together. Though we really should continue this conversation at some point, Stephen. I think you would genuinely benefit from what I have to tell you. Do you want a drink, Phoenix?'

'Thanks, Kenton,' Phoenix said. 'I'll have my usual.'

As Kenton walked over to the bar, Phoenix leaned in to me and said, 'How long have you been here? I've only just arrived.'

Her voice was clear, strong and steady, and I noticed her eyes were icy blue and scintillating, and I said, 'A while.'

'So,' she asked, 'do you think you might be ready to leave soon?'

'Oh,' I said, surprised, 'why?'

'To go back to your place, of course.'

She looked at me, then, frankly.

'To fuck,' she added.

I felt bewildered for a moment. This was happening a little fast.

'Don't worry,' she told me, 'I don't mind staying here long enough to enjoy my drink. I'll ask you again later.'

Kenton came over with Phoenix's drink, and she raised her glass to me and chinked it against mine.

'Harvey Wallbanger,' she said and downed the whole drink in four measured gulps before smiling a delightfully wicked smile and saying, 'Come on, let's dance for a while, okay?'

Her embrace was firmer than Helena's, and I felt no particular hurry to make a decision about whether to leave with her. I just wanted to have this moment of contact: to feel the neatness of her body as it moved with mine; to watch her vague concentration; to feel her breasts against my chest. I wanted, in fact, to simply experience Thirteen without it exerting itself on me in a disturbing way. Here, in this room, I felt alive and connected. To what, I wasn't sure, but right now that didn't matter.

I noticed that there was a balcony. Someone had opened the middle window so that it was possible to step outside, and so I pulled Phoenix over with me and we came out into the cool of the night. The music was quieter out here, and the traffic below seemed purposeful, somehow, as it passed along Marine Parade. The distant pier was sparkling in the night, and out to sea I could see the occasional cluster of a ship's lights. Phoenix leaned in against me and we stood like that, silent, for some time, until I put my arm round her shoulder and she leaned her head against my chest. I felt a constriction of some kind, as I looked down at the top of her head, as though this much pleasure might cause me some kind of seizure. I breathed deeply, and smiled, and thought, this is perfect. This moment is perfect.

Phoenix broke away from me, and said, 'Let's go back and dance.'

I nodded and we went inside. The current black-and-white still was of a bonfire, and a black shadow passed over me briefly as I looked at it, and Phoenix pulled me a little tighter and made a noise in my ear that could have been a gasp, or just as easily a sob. I could suddenly feel my body as an aggregate of my past, and I was aware of the way I was moving – slowly, hesitantly, gracelessly, I thought; hindered, perhaps by some nameless debris that prevented Phoenix's extra-ordinary sensual beauty from eliciting a sexual response in me. Like a work of art that inspires awe, she was too perfect to give rise to an animal response. And she didn't need to. This was enough.

How long we danced like that I'm not sure, but at some point she sighed in my ear, a spontaneous sound that ended almost with a snarl, that broke the awe that I felt towards her, and suddenly I wanted nothing more than to rush home with her, right then. And she noticed this change in me, and responded to it by sticking her tongue in my ear. She stopped, suddenly, pushed me away from her and held me at arm's length, smiling that wicked grin, and said nothing, but took my hand and led me from the room. As I left, I glanced back, and saw Valerie, still playing the cello, but she looked tiny now, the cello huge in her grasp, almost impossible to play. She was a child of eight or nine. I wanted for a moment to stop and wonder at this, but I was pulled from the room. The chandelier in the hallway must have been on a dimmer switch, because the light in the gallery was dusky, now, and we ran down the shadowed curve of the staircase to the hallway, where Gordon, who'd let us in, was already waiting with our coats.

Outside, we managed to flag down a passing taxi, and as we were driven back to Lansdowne Street, I was suddenly aware of how many significant moments happen in taxis. Anything that comes with a sense of urgency: birth, death, marriage, disaster, crisis, or simply a moment of sexual urgency like this one – all these things frequently entail taxi journeys. As we approached the flat, though, I began to get the first flutterings of panic about taking my clothes off, though I tried to put the thought to one side.

I tipped the taxi driver well, and Phoenix and I made our way down the narrow, steep steps to the basement.

'It's a bit basic, I'm afraid,' I told her.

She shrugged and laughed and said, 'It's not the flat I've come to look at.'

I unlocked the door, and almost before we were inside, we were in a mad embrace. I kicked the door shut and we staggered through to the bedroom and fell on the bed, where I peeled her T-shirt off in one swift movement, Phoenix holding her arms above her head to help me. I stopped then, utterly enthralled by what was revealed. I don't want to fall into exaggeration or cliché – but she really was mesmerisingly beautiful.

I wasn't ready to take my own shirt off, and actually said, 'No, please wait a moment' when she started to unbutton it. She stopped and looked at me questioningly, and I sighed. What was it about this evening that stopped me from recoiling? That stopped me pulling back, as I'd always done before? The continuing sublime quality of my mood, perhaps, and the strange other-worldly quality of Thirteen. I'd needed the pause to prepare myself, but Phoenix was so gentle that it was impossible to resist her. Of course, she saw the scars immediately. She didn't say anything, just traced her fingers over the longest one, the one that twisted round my waist and across my back. I closed my eyes, and she leaned forward and found my lips with her own. She hadn't made my scars disappear, and she hadn't made them unimportant, but she had stopped them being an obstacle to our intimacy – perhaps the first time this had ever happened for me.

During the act of sex, however, at the back of my mind, I was aware that I knew nothing of this person, and although a part of me fought to simply exist in the moment; part of me was also wondering what I would think of all this if, after- wards, she turned out to be unpleasant. This preoccupation lasted for some time, but, eventually something took over in me. Maybe it was just a hormonal thing, but for the first time ever (and what a strange thought *that* was), I found myself fully giving myself up to the sexual experience. It was a revelation, to be so utterly engrossed in something that the quiet watcher inside me was silenced at last. No insecure little voice giving a commentary on what was happening. And it wasn't just that I'd never let go during sex, it was that *I'd never truly let go in any experience I'd ever had.* To have lost myself – even for a moment, just once – was to prove to myself that I'd never done so before.

It occurred to me that only this evening, Helena had described me as hopelessly formal and in need of being brought out of my shell, and I thought, *I like this. I could get used to this . . .*

At about four o'clock, lying in a loose embrace, I found myself drifting off to sleep, and as I did so, I felt Phoenix stirring beside me. I opened my eyes and saw that she was getting out of bed.

'What's the matter?' I asked.

She looked at me with a sleepy, hooded look.

'I have to go,' she said. 'I won't be here in the morning.'

'Of course you won't if you leave now.'

She looked at me with something that might have been pity.

'You know what I mean,' she said.

138

I looked at her, naked in front of me, and I sighed, and nodded. She was from Thirteen. Of course she wouldn't be here in the morning.

'Okay,' I said, a mournful beat already making itself felt in my chest, 'and I won't ask when – or if – we'll meet again. Though, if there's any chance of getting together, I'd like to.'

She smiled and leaned down to kiss me and said, 'Goodnight Stephen, sleep well.'

Woman: I'm so hungry I could eat £650 worth of mild cheddar cheese. Fox Way, Mile Oak. June 3rd.

8. The simple pleasure of relaxing with friends.

It's my last fare of the night. I pick up a couple from a party at the bottom of Downland Drive. They are maybe nine-teen or twenty. The boy is tall and pale; the girl has long dark hair, a high forehead, and wide, laughing eyes. She is stunningly beautiful. They are both drunk, laughing. They whisper something, then kiss and laugh at a private joke. The boy says, 'Shaftesbury Road, mate,' and I start off. 'Wait, wait,' the girl cries, 'stop, I've left my bag behind.' I pull in and she opens the door, but before she jumps from the taxi, she leans over and kisses the boy on the lips. 'Back soon,' she says. I watch her in my rear view mirror as she runs to the house where the party is. The young man looks at me, and he is so happy that I feel a constriction in my chest. I'm not sure whether it's empathy or envy. 'Hey,' he says to me. 'What do you think of her?' 'She's beautiful,' I say truthfully, 'and lively.' 'I only met her a week ago,' he tells me, 'and she's . . . she's *wonderful*.' He leans back in his seat and lets his head fall back, so that he is looking up at the sky through the sunroof. He sighs, unable to fully comprehend his happiness. I see the girl making her way back to the cab. The loose movements of her body are casual and confident. It's clear that she feels the same way about him. Once she's in, and we're on our way, he says, 'Hey, mister, can I ask you a favour?' 'Yes,' I say. 'Can we sing you a song?' he asks. I laugh, infected by their happiness. 'Of course.' 'Okay, okay,' the girl says, 'what do you want to hear?' 'Anything you want to sing,' I tell them. 'Sing me a song you like to sing.' 'No, no,' the boy says, 'you choose. We'll know it.' 'All right,' I say trying to think of an old classic, 'how about The Beatles? Sing me a Beatles' song.' And so I drive down Neville Road while this young couple on the back seat serenade me with 'Day Tripper', 'Baby You Can Drive My Car', 'Michelle', then 'Got To Get You Into My Life', which they sing loudly, badly, almost shouting, clutching each other and swaying bliss-fully in each other's arms. When we get to Shaftesbury Road the fare is £7.40. The boy hands me a tenner and says, 'Keep the change, mate. You're the nicest taxi driver I've ever met.' The girl, who has already got out, leans back into the cab, as if she wants to give me a kiss, but I'm too far from her. 'Have a nice life,' she tells me. 'Have a *beautiful* life.' I laugh, charmed, and say, 'I'll try.' She looks suddenly earnest, totally serious. 'Please do,' she tells me.

When I woke up in the morning, I knew I was still zoning. It was bizarre, feeling like this in broad daylight after a full night's sleep. It was four o'clock in the afternoon and the sun was shining, though there were a few clouds about so it wasn't all that warm. When I made my way up onto the street I noticed the breeze, and I knew that I was going to see Helena. I *knew* it. I have rarely felt such complete certainty before, and it was a strange feeling because I also knew that I had no reason to feel certainty at all where Thirteen was concerned. And yet I did.

I phoned Lou, knowing that she didn't have her mobile switched on when she was at work, but wanting to leave a happy message for her. Then I went down to the seafront, and sat on the shore – a few people were sunbathing in the lee of the groynes, but the breeze was cool and otherwise too fresh for naked flesh. I sat and looked at the sea. The waves caught the sun, dazzlingly, just before crashing onto the stones. That roaring sound – not when the water rushes forwards, but as the water retreats, pulling the stones down with it, sucking down a cascade of pebbles – was deep, almost sub-aural, and made me feel something in my stomach: a melancholy shadow of some kind that edged my happiness and which I couldn't define.

I heard a crunching of pebbles beside me, and I looked up to see Helena. She stood three or four feet from me. We were separate, but close enough. Valerie was on the far side of Helena. I didn't say anything for a moment, just closed my eyes and turned my face to the sky, so that I could see the glow of the sunshine through my eyelids, and I felt a quiet elation stirring in me. I knew it. I *knew* if I got it right, that Thirteen would come to me rather than the other way round.

I opened my eyes, and looked at Helena.

She looked back. Her eyes were hidden behind sunglasses.

She was wearing jeans and a light-coloured blouse. Her body language was totally relaxed, and she smiled.

'Well done,' she said, as though I'd passed some important test.

I looked back at the sea, at the West Pier, at the surfers in their wetsuits making their way out to catch the best waves, and I said, 'I love this.'

Valerie leaned forward and said, 'Hello Stephen.'

'Hi,' I said. She looked about sixteen or seventeen today.

'This,' said Helena, 'this tableau, this moment, is intoxication of the highest order.'

'Yes,' I agreed.

She smiled and said, 'Now that we're in the mood, let's intoxicate ourselves a little further, shall we? There's a café – The Boardwalk – overlooking the sea down near the pier, that serves some tolerably good wine. What do you think?'

'Let's go,' I said, and laughed. I could hardly believe that *she had come to me.*

'I may as well have a drink,' I said. 'I don't suppose I'll be taxiing tonight.'

'No,' Helena laughed, 'no, I don't suppose you will.'

We wandered along the seafront, past the vendors by the West Pier, who sold jewellery, sarongs and second hand books, then on past the small sailing boats whose masts clinked in the breeze. I turned to Valerie.

'The snowdrop that you gave me when I last saw you,' I said, 'where did you get it?'

She pondered this for a moment, then, ignoring my question, said, 'I gave it to you because it represented . . . something. Between us. Didn't you think it was appropriate?'

'Yes,' I said. 'Actually, *totally* appropriate, somehow. But of what?'

144

She glanced at me with that Thirteen look, that 'You know this already' look, which caused me to experience a sudden, brief, but intense pang of anger. I took a breath and closed my eyes for a moment. *Okay*, I thought, *don't take things too fast. You've managed to interact with Thirteen at your own instigation. Don't expect them to answer all your questions too.*

'Never mind,' I said to Valerie. 'But thank you for the flower. Do you remember that you told me how much you loved snowdrops, when I was taking you to the Cornerstone Community Centre?'

'Yes,' she said, 'of course. Conversations like that are never lost.'

I wondered about that for a moment as we wove our way through the crowds by The Beach and The Fortune of War.

'I thought you were dead,' I told her. 'When you stopped taking taxis like that, after you got more and more ill. Of course, at that point I didn't know you were from Thirteen.'

There were some mats, spread out on the edge of the shingle, by the rusting sculpture that curves upwards in a skewed horseshoe. Henna tattoos, hair wraps and some pieces of jewellery were on display. Valerie stopped to have a look, and said something light and jokey to one of the dreadlocked vendors, who laughed.

Helena touched my elbow, and stopped, too. She seemed radiant, somehow, as she surveyed the beach and gazed out to the horizon. The sea was dotted with sailing boats, one with its spinnaker up, racing past a more sedate dinghy. I stood beside her and we didn't speak. I was intensely aware of the importance of this moment, of how it was somehow defined by being utterly informal. I knew that if I tried to force either of them to answer my questions, they would become inaccessible to me, in one way or another.

'The sea looks wonderful,' I said.

'Mmm,' Helena murmured.

The wind stirred my shirt and I was intensely aware of my body as I stood there, which felt oddly okay and sensual, and which I enjoyed without any self-consciousness. Valerie turned to me and held out her clenched hand.

'Here,' she said. 'For you.'

I held out my own hand, palm upwards, and she dropped a multi-coloured woven wristband into it.

'A friendship band,' she said. 'Something that won't wither in just a day or two. Here, let me tie it on for you.'

I held out my wrist and she knotted it for me.

'I'll buy you one, too,' I said, and went over to where the vendor sat, smiling up at us. He was wearing a white T-shirt and an embroidered waistcoat, and with his fine, adolescent beard and clear complexion he looked almost as young as Valerie. I chose a band in yellow and blue, and then, impulsively, a jade-coloured stone ring for Helena.

When I handed the ring to Helena, she nodded her head slightly but didn't say anything. Then I tied Valerie's friendship band to her delicate wrist, and she laughed delightedly.

'You've been elusive to say the least,' I told them, 'and you've caused me considerable confusion. But you have also made me realise that there is more to this world than me and my own suffering. Whatever may happen in the future, I want you to know that I'm grateful to you for that.'

'Thank you, Stephen,' said Helena.

We began walking towards Brighton Pier, and I said, 'I won't ask questions, either. So don't desert me.'

Helena held out her hand to look at the ring that she was now wearing. Her pale blue blouse had gold patterns embroidered onto it and she looked, I thought, supremely elemental.

At The Boardwalk we managed to find a table in the open-air seating area that looked out towards the West Pier. We were away from the thoroughfare here and so were undisturbed by the promenaders. We'd hardly sat down when the waiter came over to us, smiling as he recognised Helena.

'Hello there,' he said to her, 'how are you?'

'Hello Michael,' she said. 'Can we have a bottle of the usual?'

He nodded, almost bowed, in fact, with an extraordinary deference, and went off to do her bidding.

'It's the most expensive on the list, but actually, it's well worth it,' Helena told us.

Although I wasn't facing directly towards the sea, the sound of the breaking of waves was a constant backdrop to our conversation. We talked about a wide variety of things in that careless way that comes with being relaxed with people you don't know very well. It's strange that I remember almost nothing, now, of what those things were. The wine we drank was excellent, and the impression that I'm left with is one of having *bonded* in some way, the three of us. I also got the impression that Helena had nursed Valerie back to health, in the genuine medical sense. When I remembered how ill Valerie had been the last few times I'd given her a lift, I realised what a transformation had taken place, and I understood that Helena was responsible for this. And although I didn't know Valerie in any meaningful sense, I was grateful to Helena for what she'd done, and not just for Valerie's sake, but for mine, too, in taking me to the party where I'd met Phoenix.

As I thought of Phoenix I felt a kind of shiver up my spine. *Well*, I thought, *how can someone NOT be grateful for being taken to a place where a person like that can turn up?* I wondered

147

if that had been Helena's intention – that I should meet Phoenix. I recalled that it was only *last night* that I'd slept with her. It seemed incredible.

As I thought this, I looked out across the beach, and there she was. Walking towards us past the Honey Club. As I looked towards her, she noticed me and waved, smiling suddenly.

'This,' said Helena, 'is our cue to leave.'

'No,' I told her, 'please stay.'

'Really,' she told me, 'I do have to go. I have other things to get on with.'

Valerie stood and looked at me and said, 'See you soon, Stephen. Come round when you're free. We need to talk. Just the two of us.'

Helena leaned over and kissed me quickly on the lips, and then turned and, taking Valerie's elbow, led her away to pay the bill. Valerie waved at me and held her wrist up to show off the friendship bracelet that I'd bought her, and she laughed, and then the two of them made their way from the seating area, just as Phoenix arrived. Helena gave her a hug and whispered something that made her laugh.

As Phoenix came up to my table, I stood. She looked even better in daylight, when the brilliance of the light accentuated the flawlessness of her complexion. Her pale blue eyes seemed drenched with sunlight. She kissed me on the cheek and sat down opposite me. As she did so, the waiter arrived with another bottle of wine and a fresh glass for Phoenix, and said, 'Courtesy of your friend.'

I thanked him, and poured us both a glass of excellent Bordeaux.

'I didn't expect to see you again so soon,' I said. 'Were you out for a walk?'

'I just had an . . . intuition . . . that I might bump into you along here,' she told me, and smiled and took a gulp of her wine, nodding at her glass with appreciation. 'Mmm,' she said, 'Helena always knows how to pick the best. Cheers.'

We clinked glasses and then Phoenix leaned over the table and gave me another light, but lingering, kiss. I noticed other people at the café noticing us, and I thought, Yes, *she IS beautiful*.

'I'm sorry you left like that last night,' I told her.

'Yes, so am I, but you know how things are...'

'I suppose so,' I said. 'Helena and Valerie have gone off just as enigmatically as they arrived. Just as you did last night. I guess it's inevitable with people from Thirteen.'

'In a way,' Phoenix said. 'But don't think it's because we're indifferent to you. Precisely the opposite in fact, in some fundamentally important ways.'

I looked at her and raised my eyebrows slightly, questioning. I didn't want to ask direct questions, but hoped to encourage openness. I suppose I was already a little drunk on this superlative wine, and so I relaxed into Phoenix's company. She didn't respond to my look, but laughed instead and topped up my glass.

I couldn't think of anything to say and so remained silent for some time, looking out over the uncluttered horizon and at Phoenix, who sat utterly relaxed and alert. Even though Thirteen had been incredibly disruptive, I was, once again, amazed at how grateful I felt for this moment. Not because I was sitting at a table drinking wine with a beautiful woman with whom I had slept – or at least not *just* because of this – but because I had been pulled into a new kind of existence by what I had come across in Thirteen. When I thought about it, I realised I could no longer remember clearly the last time I'd felt depressed or unhappy. In fact, I could no longer remember what those states of mind felt like. Such was the transformation.

'I wish taxi driving wasn't such a crucial part of gaining access to Thirteen,' I said to Phoenix. 'Or maybe I should say, if only exhaustion wasn't so crucial to gaining access to Thirteen—'

'Look at Thirteen as being a key,' she said. 'Doors may be very difficult to open, until you have the key, and then access is simple. Whenever you want it.'

'Okay,' I said, and nodded. 'I take your point. But I don't suppose you're going to tell me how to find the key? Or maybe you'd just say I've already got the key, if only I could see it.'

She laughed but didn't say anything. I paused as the breeze ruffled my hair and caught Phoenix's blouse, pressing it against her to briefly reveal the curve of her breasts.

'Last night was amazing,' I said. 'Going for dinner at Septimus and meeting Helena and Seymour, then on to the party at Eastern Terrace, and meeting you. But I've also seen terrible violence in Thirteen, and I've been beaten up so badly I needed stitches – albeit stitches that vanished by morning. But that doesn't mean my wounds didn't hurt me. It doesn't mean that my memory of being hurt is any less difficult to deal with than it would be if it had really happened.'

'It did really happen,' said Phoenix. 'The outward effects just disappeared.'

I looked carefully at her, and asked, 'Why?'

Phoenix looked at me, pensively, warily, and I said, 'Look, I'm sorry, you don't have to answer that. I know that in some way I'm being "given" this experience of Thirteen, and that questioning the experience somehow inhibits the experience. But you can't blame me for being curious.'

'Okay,' she said.

'By the way,' I said, 'you obviously know Helena quite well. She was extremely friendly when you turned up. But what about Seymour? Don't answer if that's not a valid question but—'

'Seymour's worth persevering with,' Phoenix told me. 'He comes over as a bit dry, but you'd be surprised by him if you knew him better.'

'In what way?'

Phoenix laughed, with an extraordinary and genuine happiness, almost with glee, and said, 'Stephen, *Stephen*, if you need to learn one thing, just one thing, it's that you must give yourself up to experience without questioning it all the time.'

She picked up the bottle of wine and poured a glassful for each of us, and as she did so, her expression became intensely serious, almost sad.

'Answer me this,' she said. 'Think carefully and answer me truthfully. When have you ever – and I mean *ever* – when have you ever experienced *anything* for itself alone, without questioning it?'

I looked out at the fleeting, pale clouds over the horizon, at the definite, perfectly etched line where the sea appeared to meet the sky, and I felt suddenly crushed. I looked at Phoenix and said, 'Only once. It's only ever happened once in my life.'

'And when was that?'

'Last night,' I told her. 'At the party at Eastern Terrace, and especially later when we were making love.'

She registered this, and said, 'And how did it make you feel?'

I tried to think, to remember the experience as objectively as I could.

'It made me feel,' I said, slowly, 'that I'd learned something of devastating importance. It made me feel that I might have gone my whole life and never realised that there is this extra dimension of involvement. It's kind of tragic—'

'Only if you never have that experience.'

'But how rare is it? As far as I know it hasn't happened to anyone that I've known.'

'But it happened to you.'

'Yes,' I acknowledged, 'it happened to me.'

She closed her eyes for a few seconds and when she opened them, she was kind of *smouldering*. Not sexually – though there was something of that – but with a sort of desperate need to communicate.

'Just live, Stephen. It seems to be the hardest thing to do, but once you have the key it's easy – the easiest thing of all.'

I found my breath suddenly stifled in my chest as she looked at me, and I opened my mouth to speak, but no words came out, until eventually I managed to whisper, 'I don't know how.'

I saw her eyes fill with tears and she pushed her chair back and stood, and looked at me with a concern that was so personal, so intimate, that I shall never forget it. And she said, 'I can't make you understand anything, Stephen. I can't make you understand what I'm saying. But maybe I can *do* something to help you.'

I stood with her, and she put her arm round my waist in a gesture of concern and said, 'Let's go back to your flat where we can have some privacy.'

As we walked off, the crowded seafront felt almost private. I still felt a little drunk and the wine made me expansive, somehow. I'd had an intention all along of at least making an effort not to question what was happening, and after Phoenix's words, I was even more committed to not doing anything that might get in the way. It fitted my idea of what was happening – being happily drunk in the afternoon and making my way back to make love with this beautiful, enigmatic woman.

The sun was slipping from the sky as we came to Hove lawns, and the breeze was taking on a light chill, and I was looking forward to getting back to the flat. As we walked up Lansdowne Street, the road was in shadow, though the sky was palest blue and clear.

The flat was still warm from the sun of the afternoon, and Phoenix stopped in the hall and gave me a deep, lingering kiss. And I remembered that last night I'd been concerned that I didn't know her; that it might ruin my experience if I discovered that I disliked her. Well, now I knew I did like her. That, in fact, I could easily fall in love with her. She had that quality, so apparent in Helena, of nurturing friendliness. Of genuine positive regard. It was about the most attractive quality in a person, and for Phoenix to have it as well as her physical beauty made me feel, I don't know, kind of *amazed* at what was happening.

I responded to her kiss and pulled her through to the bedroom where we undressed quickly and I pulled her into a firm embrace. What were the words I'd used to myself the previous night, when I had seen her body? Mesmerisingly beautiful. Yes, this was absolutely true, and I lost myself in that hazy connection with her flesh, with her smile, with her intensity.

I was, I suppose, only a few seconds from orgasm when I heard the smashing of glass: a great shattering sound from the sitting room, followed by silence. I was jolted, both by the sound and by a sense of threat. I pulled away from Phoenix and jumped from the bed, grabbing a towel to wrap round my waist as I dashed through to the sitting room.

Two of the three panes of the bay window had been shattered. The bricks lay on the carpet surrounded by shards of splintered glass. I could hear receding laughter from outside, and I ran to the front door and then up onto the pavement, just in time to see two boys dash round the corner at the bottom of the street. I considered running after them, but they had quite a head start, and I was barefoot with only a skimpy towel round my waist.

I was surprised that they were so young. I'm not good at guessing children's ages, and these boys were already a couple of hundred metres away, but I don't suppose they were more than ten or eleven. I took a deep breath, and then returned to the flat to have a look at the damage. I considered phoning the police, but decided to think about it later, maybe after I'd finished making love with Phoenix . . .

Once inside, I went through to the bedroom.

There was no one there.

I did a quick search of the flat – which took about thirty seconds. No Phoenix. I had only been up on the pavement. She couldn't have got past without me seeing.

'Shit,' I breathed. It was another of those moments, when something I wanted to hold onto had been snatched away from me.

'Fucking *Thirteen*,' I hissed, and punched the wall. The pain from my grazed knuckles jolted me and allowed a familiar wash of frustration and deflation to course through me. I went through to the sitting room and sat on the edge of the settee looking down at the glass, and at the bricks sitting there in the debris. What had Phoenix said? That I should just live? Just live! How the hell could I do that if people kept disappearing all the time? Jesus!

I went through to the bedroom and got dressed, then went

back and started to clear up the glass. I realised that I was furious, and didn't know who to blame. Had Phoenix known that this was going to happen? Had she somehow orchestrated it? Or had she responded to a circumstance beyond her control? It seemed incredibly suspicious that the glass had shattered when it had. Not before, not afterwards, but at the climax of our lovemaking.

By the time I'd cleared up all the fine shards of glass from the carpet and fixed a bed sheet up over the broken panes – using a small, barely serviceable stapler that for some reason I still had from my days of working in an office – it was dark. There was no point calling out an emergency glazier. I would be able to replace the glass myself the following morning from the DIY merchant in North Road. I busied myself accurately measuring the frames, then went down to Grubbs and bought myself a burger and chips, which I brought home and ate in silence. I was feeling extremely sober by this stage, and so opened a can of beer to drink while I ate, then had another. And another.

At 10.00pm I decided I had to do something. I could feel that I was still, at least peripherally, zoning, and wanted to make use of it. Okay, the 'I'm not going to ask questions' strategy hadn't worked. Now I would try another tactic. I'd go out once more in search of Thirteen – in search of explanation. I wondered briefly if it was a bad idea to leave the flat so vulnerable to burglary, but realised that I owned so little of value – either material or sentimental – that it didn't really matter if anyone came in and took it.

I left the light on, and the television at low volume, and walked down to the sea. The breeze had stilled and the night was calm, and I walked down along the esplanade, by the

West Pier, and past the café where we'd drunk our wine, and I felt a kind of belligerent anger at Phoenix, and Helena and Valerie.

After I'd passed Brighton Pier, I wandered along by the Volks Tavern, up the arcade steps and onto Marine Parade, where taxis came past plying their Friday evening trade, making me realise that what I was doing here was costing me money – more money than I could afford. But I was focussed on what I was doing, and didn't want to be distracted. I wanted to be certain that I'd have access to Thirteen. Although I could feel that I was edging in and out of the zone, I knew the crux of it was to have absolute confidence that I would find it.

When I got to Eastern Terrace, I went straight to the house where Helena and I had been to the party; where I'd met Phoenix. I took the steps two at a time and rang the doorbell. Nothing happened. No one came to the door. I rang the bell again and waited. After a while I knelt and pushed the letter box open and shouted, 'Answer the door! I know you're in there.'

I had to wait a long time before I heard anything, but I wasn't going to be put off. I stood and waited, and waited ... then rang the bell again, then again. Eventually, I heard footsteps approaching from deep within the building, and the door opened. It was the man who had welcomed Helena and myself the previous night.

'Hello,' I said, 'Gordon, isn't it? I've come to see Helena.'

'I'm sorry, sir, she's not here this evening,' he said to me, and started to close the door on me. I responded by pushing myself inside.

Although the interior was certainly that of the same building I'd been in the night before, it was decorated differently. Where the flooring had been black and white marble tiles, now it was covered in dark, plain carpet. There was no chandelier. The sweeping stairs that had been plain wood now had red carpet, held down by brass stair rods.

Gordon looked nonplussed that I was now inside, but he didn't do anything. Just looked at me, politely. I ran up the staircase and onto the landing, then went straight to the door behind which had been last night's party. I went in. It was dark, but I was immediately aware that the floor was no longer soft with thick-pile carpet. My shoes clacked onto parquet. The huge floor-to-ceiling windows let in a certain amount of glow from the street lighting outside, and in this light I could see that I had stumbled into an empty room.

I went over to the window and looked out. I could see the lights of the pier a mile or so away, and the traffic along the seafront. This was, but at the same time was not, the room I'd been in the night before. Did it surprise me? Not at all. But Phoenix's proposal that Thirteen would be there if I believed it to be there now begged the question: what *part* of Thirteen did I have access to? Obviously, at this moment, not a part with Phoenix or Helena in it.

I was startled by the lights being turned on behind me – over-bright, even in this huge room, from a large, Art Deco multi-bulb unit. I turned, and saw the bouncer who'd beaten me up at 13 Wish Road. I closed my eyes, briefly. He stayed by the door and didn't say anything. He didn't have to; I knew exactly what he was capable of.

'Okay, okay,' I said, 'I'll leave. You don't have to throw me out. I can see that I'm not going to get to see anyone I'd hoped to see.'

I walked towards him, and he stepped back slightly to let me past, his face completely impassive but chilling. He turned

157

and followed me out of the room, and down the staircase. I could see Gordon standing at the back of the hall, watching me. When I came to the door, which was open, the man said to me, in a not-unfriendly voice, 'Don't even try to come here when you're not invited. You'll just get hurt. It may sound strange, and maybe you won't believe me, but I genuinely don't want to hurt you.'

I sighed, and shook his proffered hand.

'But,' he added with a half smile, 'that doesn't mean I won't, if I have to.'

I nodded, and walked down onto Marine Parade, and set off for home. The moon had risen, a nail-paring, so delicate and sharp, and I remembered someone having said something to me once about the contradiction of the moon – that even when its crescent is sharp, the roundness of it is still there. It is both sharp and round at the same time.

A taxi was passing and so I flagged it down. The driver said something friendly to me, but I replied in a monosyllable and remained silent for the journey.

SB to Indian woman in sari: Where can I take you?
Woman: Mecca!
SB is puzzled for a moment before he realises she means the bingo hall on Middle Street. Amberley Drive, June 14th.

9. She's so fucking gorgeous.

I get a fare up on Poynings Drive. It is about 1.00am and I get out and go up to ring the bell. Before I get to the door, a boy of about sixteen or seventeen opens it and leans out and says, 'Hi. I'll be quick. Just wait, okay?' 'Okay,' I say and go back and sit in the cab. I wait for ten minutes, the clock ticking at a little over 20p per minute, so that the fare is already £5. I can see the boy's shadow as he moves around in the house, but it is difficult to see what is going on. I get out of the taxi, and go up to the front door, and ring the bell. The boy comes downstairs and opens the door, and says, 'Shhhh! I'll only be five minutes.' Then he goes off again. I go back to the cab and wait. When the fare has reached £8, I get out of the taxi again. It is prime time, and I am losing out here. A driver earns far less when the meter is idling than when plying trade. I go up and ring the bell again. The boy comes to the door, and says, 'Shhhh!' I say, 'Look, it's already £8 on the meter. How long are you going to be?' He says, 'I'm nearly done,' and goes off again. A couple of minutes later he opens the door and comes out with two suitcases, a weekend holdall and several carrier bags, and I think, *He's running away!* I don't know why I hadn't realised this before. I help him put his luggage in the back of the cab, and we both get in. The fare is now £9.20. I say, 'Where can I take you?' He looks at me, and I suddenly realise that he has no idea where he wants to go. No idea at all. He looks at me in despair, and says, 'Just drive.' As we set off, he says, 'Look, I only have eleven pounds. Take me as far as that will go.' It is already £9.40 on the meter, so I say, 'It'll only get you to the bottom of the road.' We carry on and, as we get to the traffic lights at the bottom of Clarke Avenue, the meter hits £11, and he says, 'Okay, okay, stop here.' I pull in, and look at him. Here is a boy, sitting with all his worldly possessions, at 1.30am, only 400 yards from the home he is running away from. He hands me the £11 and says, with a kind of sad, desperate heartiness, 'I'll get out here, it's okay. Thanks, mate.' I take the note and the coin and say, 'Look, if there's anywhere I can take you, I will. Isn't there anyone you know who might take you in?' He shakes his head. 'A friend?' I ask. He shakes his head. 'A relative?' He shakes his head again and says, 'I'll get out here,' and opens the door. I help him take his luggage out, which he gathers around him, and stands, looking down at his belongings, and I feel choked, I mean really choked. But what can I do? 'Look,' I say, 'can I take you home?' 'No, no,' he replies, startled, 'don't worry. I'll be okay.' I hesitate, then thrust the £11 into his hand and say, 'Here, you might need this.' He doesn't want to take it, but after he's refused a second time I let it drop to the pavement, and get back into the cab. As I lean forward and press the button on the computer to accept my next job, I can see him bending down to pick it up. The job is in Mile Oak. I drive off and wave to the boy, and open the window and call, 'Good luck,' to him. I pass that way about an hour later and there is no sign of him.

When I got back to the flat from Eastern Terrace, after my unsuccessful attempt to find Helena again, I paid the driver and started down the stairs to my basement. As I did so, I stopped dead. The windows were unbroken. My response to this was not relief, but a familiar confusion. I heard a shout from down the road and, looking up, saw Phoenix walking up the street towards me. I waited for her, and as she approached she gave a half-wave, half-salute.

'What was *that* all about?' she asked. 'What happened?'

'I was hoping you might tell me,' I said, gesturing down the stairs. 'Look, the windows aren't even broken.'

'No.'

I stared at her.

'Did you do this?' I asked. 'I mean, did you make this happen?'

Phoenix shook her head.

'No,' she told me. 'No ... Look, Stephen, something weird's going on here that I don't understand.'

'Something that *you* don't understand?' I said. 'Okay, let's go inside and talk about it.'

She followed me down to the flat, and once we were inside,

I said, 'Do you want a coffee?' and she said, 'I'd love one.'

I went into the kitchen and she reclined against the door frame, and said, 'So, what was that breaking glass we heard?'

'It was two kids throwing bricks,' I told her. 'Disappearing bricks. Of course.'

'Who were they?'

'I don't know.'

Phoenix came up behind me and slipped her hands around my waist as I was spooning coffee into two mugs. She leaned in and kissed my neck.

'I went to Eastern Terrace,' I said, 'to where the party was last night, to look for Helena, or Valerie, or you – or anyone from Thirteen. Or at least anyone useful from Thirteen.'

'Don't you know how to find Valerie?' she asked, surprised. 'Don't you know where she lives?'

'I only know that she's from Thirteen. Nothing more specific than that.'

She pulled away from me slightly and asked, 'How well do you know her?'

'Hardly at all. I saw her quite often before I knew that she was from Thirteen – I gave her regular lifts in my taxi. But we never had what I would describe as a proper conversation. Since then, I've only had one actual conversation with her, at the café where I met you this afternoon – and that was in the presence of Helena, so it wasn't particularly personal. She and Helena got up and left as you arrived, without saying anything about where they were going or how I could find them again.'

I thought about it. 'She's told me to visit her, and that we "need to talk", whatever that means.'

Phoenix stepped back. She seemed concerned, perhaps even suspicious. 'Don't you know *anything* about her? Who she is and what your connection with her is?'

'No,' I said, 'I have no idea. I'm interested, but there doesn't seem to have been the right moment. Certainly not this afternoon.'

'What about the others last night? People like Kenton, and Charlotte?'

'They're the same,' I said. 'They've offered to talk to me, and I would like to meet them, but it seems like I specifically shouldn't ask any questions about Thirteen. The couple of times I tried, even in a subtle way, my questions were parried or blocked, or Thirteen has been snatched from me like it was when we were in bed together earlier.'

Phoenix frowned. 'But, why were you at the party last night?' she asked, perplexed. 'I was under the impression that you were there specifically to see Valerie – an impression that seemed to be corroborated when I saw you with her and Helena this afternoon.'

'Helena took me along to the party after we'd had dinner at Septimus.'

'I don't understand this at all. Why would she have done that if you weren't friends with the people who were there?'

I felt her sense of confusion. What was this? 'Maybe you can tell me why this matters?'

'I would never have spoken to you if I'd known you weren't a bona fide guest,' she told me, still confused.

I was about to say something when she laughed mirthlessly.

'Of course. Of *course!*'

I wasn't prepared for the look she gave me then – of recognition and disgust combined.

'God, I've slept with an impostor. You haven't even been *invited* to Thirteen, have you? Not properly. You're one of those *tourists*.' She spat the word as though it was the worst

163

insult she could think of. 'One of those tourists who some-times hang around with Helena. Shit, I should have known.'

I looked at her, at her narrowed, dark eyes, her beautiful face.

'Okay, okay,' she said. 'Look, let's just forget about last night and this afternoon. Jesus! This is *not* what I expected.'

She turned and went out into the corridor.

'What's the matter?' I asked. 'Why won't you stay?'

'You're lucky it was me you brought home with you last night,' she said. 'Another person wouldn't have been anything like as understanding.'

'This is *understanding*?'

She shook her head then opened the front door and slipped out, closing it firmly behind her. I was left in the short, narrow corridor, feeling gutted, and breathless. There were two newly made cups of coffee, not to mention a whole set of hopeful emotions, back there in the kitchen. What had I done? What had I *done*?

I looked at my wrist and saw that the friendship bracelet Valerie had given me was still there. I didn't know what this meant.

The following evening, I kept playing the scene with Phoenix over and over. So, I'd been an impostor at the party because I didn't know Valerie . . . If I could somehow get to know her, would I be allowed back? Would I get to see Phoenix again? Did I want to see Phoenix again? All I knew was that for some reason, which was far from clear, the next thing I had to do was go and find Valerie – to see if I could – what? – become her friend?

It was Saturday, and as busy as ever. After a brief lull between nine-thirty and ten, I worked straight through until

4.45am, finishing off with a half-hour drive out to Angmering, on the far side of Worthing – a handsome fare. I logged off the circuit before returning, and enjoyed the journey home along the deserted coast road. At the traffic lights at the foot of Hangleton Link Road, there was a milk float clinking its way round from Boundary Road, and the sight of it gave me a strange sense that my whole life had become inverted. It also made me realise that I was *still* zoning.

Of course I drove straight over to Wish Road. All evening, I'd been debating whether or not I should do this. In the end, you can say no a hundred times, but you only have to say yes once. I knew Thirteen would be there, but was beginning to wonder if I had the energy left to cope with any further perplexity, or hostility at turning up to places without being 'invited'. I was sick of being perfunctorily ejected, or otherwise rejected.

Still, I parked in the usual place and crossed the road. There were no lights on at all, but I could see the weathered brass numbers on the post as I opened the gate. The house that stood there was the same house from which I'd collected Valerie all those times. The dull, fake-leaded windows were so familiar they were comforting. I went straight up to the front door, but instead of ringing the bell, I put my ear to the wood panelling and listened.

Silence.

I tried the handle, and found to my surprise that the door was unlocked, so I pushed it gently and it swung open onto a dark hallway. I stepped inside and closed the door behind me. As I stood there, wondering what to do, my eyes gradually became accustomed to the muted street lighting that was coming through the glass panel above the door. I could see a grandfather clock, ticking slowly to my left, and to my right, one of those large, round convex mirrors that give a wide-angle view in which everything is distorted. I glanced at the mirror and felt an eerie sense of *déjà vu* as I saw myself darkly reflected there.

I didn't have a chance to explore further as, just then, something hard hit the back of my head and I was knocked from my feet. I blacked out before I hit the floor.

When I came to, the first thing I noticed was that I had a blinding headache, particularly above my right eye, and that I had difficulty focusing – on my thoughts as well as my vision. I blinked and could feel some swelling of my eyelid. The second thing I noticed was that I was sitting on a chair with my hands tied behind my back. My arms were completely numb – I couldn't move my fingers at all. I looked up. The mantelpiece had a couple of candles on it, flickering gently and providing as much light as the small, dim side lamp on the table beside me. I recognised the mirror immediately, a gaudy, fake Victorian one with an over-ornate gold plaster frame. Reflected in it I could see the leaves of a large rubber plant. It had been a Swiss cheese plant last time, I remembered. Even so, despite the fact that this was not exactly the same as the scene I'd watched previously whilst crouching outside in the garden, I knew immediately what was happening. As my bonds were cut, I closed my eyes firmly and tried to gather my thoughts, as my arms fell, numbly, to my sides and I put my foot forward to stop myself from falling to the floor. Just then the door opened and someone came in. I was blurry and time didn't seem to be passing in a particularly linear way. I glanced up at the window and thought I saw a movement in the dark-ness outside, but was distracted by a murmur of conversation behind me. I felt suddenly nauseous, and everything wavered for a moment, as though I was about to pass out once more.

From previous experience, I knew that I had some control over my interaction with Thirteen, even if only in a small way, and I desperately tried, then, to imagine my way out of what was happening. When I heard the woman's voice demand 'Do it. Just do it!' I opened my eyes and, in spite of my sluggishness, was about to lurch forwards, when I felt the knife being plunged into my side.

The pain was searing, the blade seemingly fiery-hot, and, as I toppled from the chair, I had an immediate and intense sensation of clarity. The pain had focussed me, and I wriggled slightly as I lay, trying to get some movement back into my arms. I could feel the warmth of blood against my side, and an odd silence in the room. I would have thought it was empty if I hadn't been able to see the legs of the man who'd stabbed me, from the corner of my eye, as he stood motionless close by. The pile of the carpet was coarse against my cheek, and I could hear myself sob, just once, for a moment, finding myself unable to get up.

Then I realised that the numbness in my arms was lifting, and I put my right hand to my side and felt the terrible gash there, which I tried to hold closed as best I could. I managed to scramble a little and, by twisting slightly, I pivoted myself round on my shoulder and up onto my knees. My breathing was fast and shallow. I couldn't bring myself to look at the wound in my side, which was making me double over with pain, and which was making my right leg drag behind me. Still, I managed to get to my feet. The person who had stabbed me remained impassively in front of me, but the person who had said 'Do it. Just do it!' wasn't in sight. I managed to lurch from the room and out of the house. I could feel the wetness of blood as it soaked my trouser leg, and I fought off panic as I stumbled across the road to the cab.

Once in, I had the awful business of trying to get the Galaxy started using my left hand. Using my right foot was hard, too, and I kept feeling waves of dull, but sickening, pain every time I extended my right leg. I drove off, using only my left arm to steer, which meant that I had to let go of the steering wheel to change gear. Already, I was desperately looking out for Helena in her guise as The Nurse. I saw a vehicle in my rear view mirror, approaching in the distance, and was afraid, for a moment, that it was a police car, but it was only another taxi.

I made a real mess of getting onto Kingsway, slewing out onto the seafront road. Fortunately it was quiet and when I arrived at the traffic lights outside the King Alfred Centre, I didn't slow down, but went straight through on red. Even as I did so, I heard the siren from up Hove Street, and could see the blue flashing lights. There was no way that I could avoid the police, and so I tried to pull over, but miscalculated and crunched up onto the pavement and stopped, only inches before hitting a wall.

As soon as the cab had stopped, my head fell forward onto the steering wheel. There was a kind of odd silence then, for a few moments, before I was aware of the door opening, and a voice gasping 'Jesus!' before I passed out.

When I came round, I was lying in a hospital bed. There was a nurse a few feet away with her back to me. I wondered whether I should attract her attention, but realised that I was sedated and so I lay and felt a kind of muffled relief that I wasn't in pain. The next thing I registered was surprise that I was in hospital at all. The last time I'd been physically injured while in Thirteen, I'd met The Nurse and been patched up by her. The 'real' world hadn't been involved. But here I was – I could see the other beds around me, the curtains pulled back at the side of my bed, the grey lino of the floor. I was just thinking how weak and thirsty I felt, when I noticed the drip hanging by the bed, and the tube going into my arm.

The next couple of hours are still somewhat confused. As soon as the nurse – as opposed to The Nurse – noticed me, she smiled and came over, asking how I was, then went to get the doctor, who came, accompanied by a policeman. I came to the sudden, dark realisation that, even though I was truthful by nature, there was almost nothing I could tell him about what had happened to me.

Before the policeman was allowed to question me, the doctor explained that I was lucky that the knife had sliced my side, rather than being plunged deeply into it. This meant that no internal organs were affected, though I would have quite a long scar.

'You already have heavy scarring in that area,' he told me, 'so we'll have a go at treating your old scars at the same time as your new one. Technology has vastly improved in that department over the last fifteen years.'

Fortunately, when the policeman spoke to me, I discovered that the police had already established several important facts. Firstly, that the stabbing had occurred outside 11a Wish Road. Secondly, that I had been hit on the head from behind at more or less the same time as being stabbed. This second fact was useful for me in that I could say that I had no knowledge of being assaulted, and no knowledge of who had done it. The third and most important detail was that, at the time of the assault, I had been logged-off the circuit, and so was not on my way to pick up a fare. What then, I was asked, was I doing on Wish Road? I had no answer to that. But then the policeman asked if I was gay, and when I said no, he narrowed his eyes slightly as though he disbelieved me.

This is how I discovered that the toilet on Wish Road was a trysting-place for gay men, and that at least occasional cruising happened in the park. Well, it let me off having to explain what I'd been doing there, as assumptions on that score had clearly already been made.

I stayed in hospital all that day. In the evening, Mark, the cab's owner, came and visited me. He was deeply concerned and upset, and not just because he might have lost one of his drivers. I was touched.

'Kin 'ell, mate,' he said when he saw me. 'You all right?'

I nodded, and told him that the swelling round my eye looked worse than it was. I asked him if he'd got his cab back.

'The police brought it over this morning, after they'd finished with it. You'd left the keys in the ignition. Fuckin' mess, though. It took my wife nearly three hours to get all the blood off the upholstery. Bled like a stuck pig, you did. Good thing Bruce didn't need the cab today.' He smiled, wanly.

'I should have brought you some chocs,' he said, 'but I thought you'd be better off with a mouthful of this? Whatcha think?' He pulled out a quarter bottle of whisky. I nodded and he looked around, opened the bottle and handed it to me. I took a swig, gasped, took another one, then handed it back. He took a gulp himself, then put the bottle in his pocket.

'Every taxi driver's nightmare,' he said, 'getting knifed, or sommat like that. But the police said it was a homophobic attack.' He looked around, then leaned in closer to me. 'Now, look,' he said, 'I don't give a toss if you do that sort of thing, but hanging about in parks, when you don't know who could jump you . . .' He shook his head. 'I don't mind you doing whatever you like in the back of my cab. You can do as much shagging as you want to, so long as you don't stain the seats—'

He stopped, looked at me, suddenly realising what he'd said and ducked his head in embarrassment.

'I'm not . . .' I began, but realised I would have to come up with another plausible scenario if I was going to contradict this one, and so I started to laugh. He laughed too.

'Yeah . . .' he said, 'well . . .'

He gave us both another swig of whisky and asked how long it would be before I'd be back to driving.

'I'll be out of here tomorrow, I think,' I said, 'but I've got to take it easy for a week, and then only gentle exercise for another week after that, so I guess it'll be a fortnight at least.'

We talked a little about business, I finished the whisky and then Mark went off to start work. As I lay there, alone, I was now more aware of the pain in my side, and the stitches there. The dressing was bulky, and any real movement felt unwise. I simply didn't know what to make of this. What I didn't understand was: why hadn't my wounds vanished once I'd left Thirteen?

I knew that certain things had made the crossover from Thirteen – the snowdrop, for example. Lou had seen that. My friendship bracelet, which I was still wearing. And now, of course, these injuries. But I still didn't understand why they'd disappeared last time, and not this time. It made no sense.

The next day, as a nurse was finishing putting on my new dressing, Lou turned up, tearful, holding a copy of *The Argus*.

'*Stephen*,' she cried, 'I can't believe it! I've only just read it in the paper. It's on the front page.'

She sat down beside me and took my hand.

'Are you all right? You look pale. Except for that black eye.'

'I'm fine,' I told her. 'A bit . . . exhausted—'

'I'm not surprised,' she said. 'Have they found the culprits yet?

'Not as far as I know,' I told her.

She tried to smile. Failed.

'I didn't even know you did that kind of thing. You know . . . in parks.'

'I don't,' I told her.

'Oh,' she said, then fell silent for a moment. I could see realisation dawning on her.

'My God,' she said, 'this hasn't got anything to do with this Thirteen business, has it?'

I looked at her and sighed and said, 'Yes, it has.'

She looked as if she was about to start crying again, and squeezed my hand.

'You know, I talked to Colin about all this. Well, he wanted an explanation of why you turned up in the middle of the night like that. So I told him everything you'd said.' She smiled then, at the memory. 'He thought the snowdrop business was more unusual than I did. When he was at work, he looked up about them on the Net to amuse me, and because he was intrigued. Actually, I think I have something about them in my bag.'

She leaned down and rummaged briefly, and sat up with a piece of scrap paper.

'"Snowdrop",' she read, '"*galanthus nivalis*. It hybridises so easily that there are thousands of varieties. Being the first flower of spring, there are Christian and superstitious associations with new beginnings, purity and hope for the future". Then there is the sinister side of the flower,' she added. '"It is sometimes said that a snowdrop represents a corpse in its shroud. A snowdrop must never be brought into a house".' Here she glanced at me. '"They are bad luck for women who want to lose their virginity" . . . Well,' she said, then folded the paper and put it in her bag, and added, 'but what happened, Stephen, if it wasn't a homophobic attack, what was it?'

'I don't know,' I said. 'I just don't know. Not yet. But I saw it happening, a few weeks ago – only I didn't know it was me who was being stabbed.'

'You mean you had a kind of premonition?'

'Something like that.'

'Oh, Stephen,' she said, 'can't you somehow *disengage* from this? I don't know what's going on, if this is all in your head, or if it's weirder than that. But if you carry on like this you're going to get yourself killed.'

I closed my eyes and nodded. She was right.

'I thought,' I said, 'that visiting Thirteen was some kind of wonderful adventure. And it was in parts. But it's also been confusing. And increasingly dangerous.'

Then I remembered Phoenix; the night I'd slept with her. I remembered that feeling of losing myself in an experience, totally, for the first time ever. Was there some kind of similarity here, between Thirteen and my taxiing? Perhaps I could look at it this way: I paid for my cab, and my petrol, and my weekly dues to my rank, but even with my high outgoings, I still made a profit. Was Thirteen the same – you had to pay out, make an investment, to get any reward? The difference was that you had to pay in a different currency.

'Look,' I told Lou, 'the thing is that I've learned something about myself from all this. I realise that, before this, I never fully engaged with life. Not really.'

Lou looked down at the drip coming from my arm.

'There are ways of engaging with life that don't mean ending up somewhere like this,' she said.

I looked at her. Her straightforwardness, her normalness, grounded me.

'You're right,' I told her. 'You are so right.'

I felt a sudden, familiar wash of hostility towards Helena and Phoenix. I know Helena had warned me that Thirteen could be dangerous. But she must also have been aware of how curiosity works, how compelling it can be. I now felt even more certain that Phoenix had been 'sent' as bait, to lure me into temptation. Helena had wanted me to be captured, captivated, and extreme physical beauty had been her tactic. Well, I thought, it was a tactic that was no longer going to work.

'I guess I have to decide how to get some balance back into my life,' I said. 'I now realise that the first thing I need to do is stop being a taxi driver. I should have done that the first time, but I couldn't give up pursuing Thirteen. And then the second thing is to look around for something else to do that leaves me space in which to really become myself. Whatever that means.'

Lou looked relieved at this and said, 'Look, I could find out if there's any work up on campus if you like. I mean, in admin or something. You'd be a great administrator.'

I nodded.

'Maybe,' I said. 'Or perhaps I'm ready to consider studying. When I talked to Graham about it, it seemed glamorous and impossible, as though I was saying I might decide to become a research chemist, or a famous surgeon. Worthy, but not rooted in reality. Now, I suppose I'm beginning to feel I might be ready to learn. When I think of how it felt to do The Knowledge, how my brain felt as if it was waking up; being exercised for the first time . . .'

Just then, a nurse arrived.

'Hi there,' she said, 'it's time to remove that drip of yours.'

Lou smiled and said, 'Okay, let's finish this conversation

when you get out of here.' She said goodbye and promised to visit me at my flat, 'Which, I have to remind you, I still haven't seen yet.'

I promised to invite her over. She left, and I felt lighter, somehow, more sure of myself, and happy in the knowledge that Thirteen was just too dangerous a place for me.

For my own sanity – as well as my safety – I would simply walk away from it.

When the time came for me to be discharged, I was told that my details had been sent on to my GP and that I should go and see him the next day. I was also given a timetable of appointments for a course of scar-reduction treatment. This would mostly consist of a series of injections into the scar tissue along with the application of porous, adhesive gel pads. It all sounded a bit phoney, but at least it was free.

I took a taxi home and wondered if I would ever drive a cab again. As we were passing Waitrose, I asked the taxi driver to stop there. I paid him, and got out. Once inside the supermarket, I explained to the check-out manager that I couldn't lift anything and was assigned a friendly young assistant who followed me around with a trolley while I bought provisions for the coming week.

Back at home, I made myself comfortable and waited for my food to be delivered. I felt oddly calm. Of course, the psychological trauma that I'd experienced was nothing like an 'ordinary' public mugging, in that I didn't have any sense that the streets of Brighton had suddenly become more dangerous. The danger lurked elsewhere.

The following day was a revelation to me. My doctor was incredibly sympathetic. I liked him, but hardly ever saw him.

I'd been on his books for over a decade, but had only been to him half a dozen times, if that. He'd seen my story in the paper, though, and was aghast on my behalf at what had happened to me. He checked my dressing, and went through some of the details of the scar-reduction programme that I was going to undertake. I mentioned to him that I'd decided to give up taxiing as soon as possible, but needed to find another job first.

'I'll sign you off sick,' he said without hesitation. 'Of course you can't go back to driving after what you've been through. I can get you sickness benefit for a couple of months at least, and then we can talk about strategies after that, if necessary.'

We discussed the possibility of post-trauma counselling, but I was clear that I didn't want any, at least for the time being. And that was that.

I phoned Mark and said I wouldn't be driving his cab again. He was totally unsurprised, and said, 'I reckoned you'd decide that. Don't worry. There's three or four drivers coming through. But take some advice from me, mate. Don't let your licence lapse. It costs hardly anything to keep your licence up. If you don't, you'll have to do The Knowledge again. Who knows when you might want to get back behind the wheel.'

I said I'd think about it.

'Any time you're interested,' he said, 'I'll be able to fit you in somewhere.'

And that was that.

It was less than a year since I'd last claimed benefit. It seemed so much longer. I sat at home and thought to myself, *I am no longer a taxi driver.*

It felt wonderful.

But what next?

I decided to try to put that question aside for the duration of my convalescence. I would make an effort to relax as much as possible.

Moving, but especially any kind of turning, was problematic, and so I crept about the flat, and watched a lot of daytime television. Lou came round with Colin and they cooked me a meal, and the three of us had an evening together that had nothing weird about it at all. Thirteen wasn't mentioned. Lou was thrilled that I'd been signed off sick and said, 'Now you can take your time looking for another job.'

I re-read some of my favourite novels and amazed myself at how much I'd missed them while I'd been running my dad's company. What had I thought? That I'd grown out of these things? Literature. Culture . . . I went to The Duke of York's cinema four times in that second week – a perfect place to go if you need to keep yourself immobile for periods of time – and I thought, 'I'm coming alive.'

I had a number of outpatient visits to the hospital, to check my progress, and for injections into my scar tissue. My side and a portion of my back were covered in special, impregnated silicone dressings that constricted my movement, making me even more aware of my present and previous scarring. This was no bad thing, I guess, as otherwise I'm sure I'd have ended up lifting heavy objects before I was ready.

As soon as I got into a settled routine in which I wasn't constantly reminded of my injury, Thirteen started to become something of a blur. It wasn't that I forgot about it – after the stabbing, how could I? It was just that it became, in some curious way, only a shadow at the back of my mind that I didn't consider. Perhaps this was because of the sense of relief I felt at being 'back to normal'. I realised I hadn't felt settled like this since before I'd lost the company – since before I'd taken over as director, in fact.

There was a part of me, however – and it was difficult to acknowledge this – that understood that this new sense of being settled was a deeper and more profound state of stability than I'd ever previously felt, and this stability was largely due to what I'd experienced and learned about myself while interacting with Thirteen. Even though I now felt hostile towards Helena, I had to accept that I'd learned some important things from both her and Phoenix. Before I'd suffered my numbing depression – which was now completely absent – I'd taken my life completely for granted. Maybe once you've had a brush with danger, whether real or imagined, 'ordinary' life takes on a prized edge that feels suddenly both precious and delightful. Even wandering up Western Road to Taj or Waitrose to get my groceries was something that could now give me simple pleasure.

I put this new sense of happiness down to the fact that I'd now given up taxiing, and to a consequent positive attitude about what I might do in the future. Thirteen, though in many ways so close, was now in the past, and I was keen to forget about it. I was fully aware that it represented the possibility of further trouble – even catastrophe – if I didn't put it behind me, and though there was a mixed bag of emotions concerning it, which included gratitude, I still wanted to have as little to do with it as possible. After all, how much more did I want to be hurt by it? What could it teach me that might compensate for nearly losing my life?

I got hold of prospectuses for both Sussex and Brighton Universities and considered my academic choices. My 'A' Levels were in maths, history and geography, so the possibilities for undergraduate study were wide, even if I restricted myself to studying here in Brighton.

*

As I returned to what I thought of as my 'normal' self, I got back in touch with another friend from my teens, Katherine. I hadn't seen her since I'd made the decision to be a taxi driver, and it was a genuine pleasure to meet up with her again. The last time she'd seen me I'd been depressed and now I wasn't. She could see that change for the better in me, and was happy that I'd pulled through a bad patch. I didn't mention Thirteen to her. There was no need. That had all happened in the parentheses of our friendship.

She was surprised to see me in such good shape because she'd heard about the stabbing and had imagined that I might be devastated by it. Instead, we just ended up laughing about how victims can become semi-celebrities instead, where everyone who knows you, however peripherally, suddenly knows you for this one, big fact. There was, of course, the irony of being seen as someone who had been 'queerbashed' (about which Kat and her girlfriend made relentless 'we didn't know you were one of us' fun of me). Also, people do look at you slightly differently if they know you've nearly been murdered. It's an odd minority to be a member of.

As a duty call, I got in touch with Derek, to ask him how things were going. He was disconsolate. His cousin had got nowhere with the legal actions that Derek had instigated, and the whole process of trying to get his money back had been abandoned. He'd spent thousands on other solicitors before he'd turned to his cousin, so the fact that his cousin hadn't charged a fee was only small comfort. He'd spent a year hoping for success, and in that time had continued spending money at his previous executive level. Now, he confessed to me, his wife was looking for a job. He was going to have to put his kids into non-fee paying schools. He was selling his Mercedes. He was ruined.

I tried to be as sympathetic as possible, and remembered how gutted I'd been in the weeks after I'd lost my business. It reminded me of how difficult it is to let these things go. If I hadn't met Graham like that, and become a taxi driver, I might still have been wallowing now.

We talked a little about what Derek might do with himself, and I mentioned taxi driving. He laughed unpleasantly, and said he'd been shocked that I'd even considered doing something like that, and that he would *never* stoop so low. As he said this, it suddenly became clear to me that, for Derek, it was his loss of status that was the most difficult thing for him to cope with. Driving a Mercedes and sending his kids to private school were what defined him. Of course, he was older than me, and ambitious in a way that I'd never been, and I was suddenly grateful for this simplicity in myself – a quality that I'd never been aware of, but which I could now see as precious.

I said goodbye, and made some mention of the possibility of meeting up, but we both knew this would never happen. I wished Derek luck with his future ventures, and ended the call feeling sad for him. I had been through my rough patch, and the future for me was an unthreatening place. My needs were so basic: I had no dependents, no material aspirations, attached no status to what I was doing. I realised, in fact, that the friends who had been impressed by my money – when I had money – were the friends that I was not sorry to lose; were the friends that I hadn't thought, even for a moment, of contacting again.

I went back to my new, simple life and got on with appreciating it.

On one of those pale, sunny evenings in July, I met Kat and her girlfriend, Clare, for a drink outside The Beach. We sat at a chrome table looking out over the darkening sea. I felt light, and happy, and pleased to be living in Brighton. People were wandering along the esplanade, and I thought, *Most of these people have paid to come to Brighton. And I LIVE here.* It was a great feeling.

Kat was tall and energetic in her movements, purposeful and powerful. Clare was wispy, with an odd sleepy quality about her, and a lazy way of speaking that could sometimes come over as apathy. But she could catch people out with her incisive, pithy comments at unexpected moments. They'd been together for eight years, and were obviously happy with each other.

Kat was talking about the job she had in a media consultancy, and the frenetic but happy atmosphere she worked in, and I was about to reply to her, when I noticed Helena walking towards me along the edge of the beach. She was wearing a light maroon dress that caught the wind as she walked, and she looked as elemental as ever, her hair long, straight and free. I had opened my mouth to speak, but the words died there.

Kat leaned over and gestured towards my empty glass. 'Same again?' she asked.

I nodded mutely.

Clare got up too and said, 'I'll come with you. I need a pee.'

As they walked off, Helena arrived. I quickly looked away, suddenly furious that she'd turned up to spoil my evening. I stared at the ground, and could see her feet, at the periphery of my vision, as she stopped. She was wearing leather sandals that were finely tooled and edged with gold. Her nails were painted a deep ruby red. I didn't look at her.

'Hello,' she said.

I didn't reply.

'Hello, Stephen.'

I looked up and saw that enigmatic smile on her face. I ignored her and then, as she hadn't moved, I said, 'Go away. I have nothing to say to you.'

She looked beyond me, up into the sky, her fine throat exposed, then back again at me.

'I thought,' she said, 'you might have said something more appropriate, such as "thank you".'

I choked with anger, and was about to speak, when I thought, *Don't engage with this. She wants me to engage. Ignore her.*

I turned my chair away from her, folded my arms and closed my eyes, staying like that for some time, until I felt a tap on my shoulder, and Clare saying, 'Are you alright, Stephen? You seem angry, or something.'

I opened my eyes, and looked round. Helena was perhaps a hundred metres away now, disappearing into the crowd.

'I'm fine,' I said, looking out to sea as Clare sat down beside me, glancing across with concern. I made an effort and smiled at her, and she relaxed. I guess I must have looked pretty strange, sitting so adamantly with my eyes closed.

The horizon was melting into darkness as Kat arrived with the drinks, and we clinked glasses. But the pleasure had gone from my evening. I drank my pint quickly, then made my excuses and went home. Why, oh why had I thought I would be left alone? I had no doubt that if I'd decided to acknowledge Helena, I would have become caught up in Thirteen again, pulled back into it, irrevocably, and who knows what would have happened then? My stabbing seemed like a mere preliminary: a first dose of the pain that could be meted out to me if I allowed myself to be sucked into that world again.

Woman, into mobile phone: Yes darling. Alright, I'll see you later, sweet pea. Bye. Bye . . . Yes, I love you too.
Turns off phone.
Woman (bitterly): Cunt! Station Road, Portslade, June 25th.

10. A sultry week.

I collect a guy with a miniature Schnauzer. I'm okay about taking dogs in the cab, and the man gets in and seems very friendly. I ask him how old the dog is, and whether or not that breed makes good pets (they do), and then we get to talking about how long dogs get left alone when their owners are out at work. 'My house has quite a large garden,' the man says to me, 'and Twilo is small enough to get in and out of the cat flap, so he can roam around as much as he likes. But, you know, one of the things I find interesting is that when I come home from work and pick up the chain to take him for a walk, he goes bananas with pleasure. So, I put the chain round his neck, and he's happy. What I'm actually doing is putting a

183

restraint on him. But what I see as a restraint, *he* sees as freedom.'

At the weekend I went down to the Prince Albert to be somewhere busy and loud, and I thought perhaps I'd go on to a club if I felt like it. I still had money left from my taxiing to supplement my sickness benefit, so I could afford it.

When I went into the bar, I recognised four or five people in there and had the bizarre realisation that it was only a little over eighteen months since my company had gone bankrupt. Many of the people that I had socialised with at that time were still coming out here just as they had done when I was last a regular . . . To them, only a relatively short time had passed. I could hardly believe it. When I went to the bar, a guy on one of stools next to me turned and said, 'Hey, Stephen, I heard about your . . . accident. Are you all right?'

'Fine,' I told him, trying – and failing – to place his name, 'I'm fine.'

'You're looking well,' the person said and turned back to his friends.

I nodded, and ordered myself a pint.

A little later, a guy called Russell turned up; someone I'd never talked to much, who had been a friend of a friend, but whom I'd liked back when I was, what . . . my previous self? We ended up chatting. It was bizarre that it was so easy, to come out like this and meet someone to talk to. I thought back to how I'd been dropped by all my 'fast' friends after I'd lost my job and realised, for the first time, that this had been as much my fault as theirs. I'd stopped going out as much as they'd stopped inviting me. And not just when I became broke. I'd run dad's company for nearly seven years before the company went bust, but it was only in the first two or three that I'd really gone out. After that, I'd simmered down to pubbing once or twice a month, and perhaps the odd meal in a restaurant. Looking back on it from this perspective, I found it almost impossible to imagine what I'd actually done with my time.

Russell remembered the friends I'd hung around with, and wasn't particularly complimentary about them. It turned out he'd been a friend of a friend of a friend of someone I'd quite liked, and we laughed about this, and he said, 'Hey, weren't you that guy who got stabbed?'

This question made me sigh. Not because I minded it, but because, as an identifying fact, it seemed so unrepresentative of who I was. But I nodded, and he said, 'Of course, I never made the connection until now, because the paper said you were a gay taxi driver.'

I explained – at least as much as I could – and told him I was currently signed off sick.

'I'm not surprised,' he told me. 'My girlfriend's an air stewardess. She was mugged in Detroit once and it took her over three years before she could fly again. They had to give her a ground job, which she hated. But she got back to flying in the end.'

It was wonderful being out with a friendly companion. I found myself laughing easily with him, and telling him some of my taxi stories.

A couple of Russell's friends turned up and he introduced me, and it became clear that I was welcome to come on to a club night at the Concorde 2 with them later on if I wanted to.

All three of them, it turned out, worked in a home for 'disturbed' children. Dealing with tantrums – and worse – all day sounded like a nightmare to me, and I couldn't imagine

Russell doing such work. He was so slight of build, and mild-mannered with it. But, he assured me, he found he enjoyed doing something genuinely useful.

'And I do make a difference,' he said. 'To some of them.'

By the time we went on to the Concorde, I was feeling half drunk and mellow. It was the first time since well before my company had gone bust that I'd found myself in this situation – going out for the evening with a group of friendly people that I didn't know very well. It was wonderful. The Concorde was already busy when we got there and I even danced a bit, which surprised me, especially the fact that I enjoyed it. It was too loud for much conversation but that didn't matter. Russell and I ended up swapping phone numbers and agreeing to meet up for a drink with his girlfriend the following week at the Great Eastern, and so I knew that something positive was happening to me.

Later on, after dancing for a while to some music of a completely unidentified variety, I decided to take a break and go and buy a round of drinks. I was standing at the bar, leaning forward with my ten pound note in my hand, trying to catch the barman's attention. Someone came and stood beside me, and turned to look at me so conspicuously that I had to look back to see who it was.

Phoenix.

I froze. I should have known, or at least have considered the possibility, that this might happen. But I hadn't. It was a complete, and unwelcome, surprise. She smiled her wicked smile, and I pulled away from the bar and stepped back, away from her. She followed me.

'Stephen,' she said. 'Hi.'

I turned away from her without acknowledging her presence and walked over to the far edge of the dance floor, by

186

the emergency exit. Phoenix followed me, and grabbed my elbow as I started to push my way through the crowd, away from her.

'Stephen,' she shouted. 'Stop. Talk to me.'

I turned to face her, leaning in close so that I didn't have to shout too loudly for her to hear me.

'You're not even real,' I told her.

'Of course I am.'

'Do you have a national insurance number?' I asked her. 'Do you have a postal address? Are you registered to vote?'

She laughed.

'Is *that* what you think makes a person real?'

'Right,' I said. 'This conversation is pointless. I have two things to say to you. Firstly, it was you who fucked off and didn't want to have anything to do with me. You called me "an impostor" if I remember rightly. Secondly, if you think I have any intention of having anything to do with Thirteen again after what I've been through, then you're mad. I was stabbed, Phoenix, *stabbed*. I had to have twenty-one stitches in my side. If the knife had gone straight in, rather than obliquely, I'd be dead. Go and tell Helena that I want to be left alone.'

Phoenix responded by smiling at me and taking off her blouse. She had her tight T-shirt on underneath. She stood, only a metre or two away from me, and started dancing, and smiling at me as she did so. Russell, who was dancing with some friends on the far side of Phoenix, noticed what was going on and came over to me.

'Who is *that*?' he asked.

'Yes, yes, I know,' I said. 'She's the most gorgeous woman you've ever seen. Let me introduce you.'

I grabbed Russell's elbow and pulled him over to Phoenix. I

leaned in to her and shouted, 'Phoenix, I want to you to meet Russell. Russell, Phoenix.'

They shook hands, and I left them to it and went off to the bar in the next room. I only bought a drink for myself, though, as I didn't want to have to approach Russell while he was talking to Phoenix. When I came back into the main dance area and stood at the back, I noticed, to my surprise, that they were deep in conversation, standing against the back wall, where there was a stall selling fluorescent T-shirts and other club paraphernalia. Russell would look over at me from time to time, and it made me wonder what they might be talking about.

I danced again but my heart was no longer in it. Phoenix's presence made me feel hostile. I ended up leaning against the wall as far away from Russell and Phoenix as I could get. At least I'd set a firm date to meet Russell again, so if I slipped away it wouldn't matter. But after a while Russell made his way over to me, smiling. When he got to me, he said, 'Phoenix is not only gorgeous, she's lovely with it.'

I shrugged but said nothing.

'She really likes you, too,' Russell told me. 'She wouldn't be specific, but it sounds like there's been a misunderstanding of some kind.'

He leaned in closely, earnestly.

'Look, I hardly know you,' he said to me, 'and I don't know what Phoenix did, but don't push her away like this. She likes you. She's in *love* with you, for God's sake.'

'Some people do things that you just can't forgive,' I said.

Russell absorbed that for a few moments and then nodded to himself.

'Okay, okay,' he told me. 'But if someone that gorgeous was in love with me, I'd be . . .'

He stopped, lost for words, realising that he was being superficial, then looked at me and laughed.

'I'm sorry,' he said, 'you're right. But she's so *fucking* gorgeous. I bet she's great in bed, too.'

I looked down. 'Yes, I know, she *is* gorgeous,' I said. 'It's true. I don't blame you for feeling overwhelmed. That's what she did to me when I first met her.'

I was about to say something else when I noticed that Phoenix was making her way towards us. 'Oh-oh, I think this may be my cue to leave,' I said. 'Look, thanks for talking to me this evening and inviting me along here. Maybe I'll explain more about all this when I see you next week.'

I said goodbye, then made for the exit. Outside in the lobby I stopped briefly at the coat check. There was no queue, so I managed to get my jacket straight away, and I ran out onto Madeira Drive. Once there, there was still no sign of Phoenix, and I managed to hail a getaway taxi to take me home. I was lucky. It was 1.30am, during the lull after the pubs and restaurants have closed, and before people start to leave the clubs, when it is moderately easy – even at weekends – to get a cab. As I sat in the back, looking up at The Grand and The Metropole on one side, and out at the black, and therefore uncluttered, seascape of the English Channel on the other, I thought of Phoenix. Of the effect she'd had on Russell. Of the effect she'd had on me the first time I'd seen her, and how, in spite of that, I was pleased she hadn't followed me out of the club.

Back at Lansdowne Street, I paid the driver and got out. I was a little drunk. Even in this urban setting, I could see some stars as I looked up. I could see Cygnus clearly, and hear the distant murmur of the sea. I shrugged to myself, pleased that I had dealt with Phoenix so perfunctorily and so decisively.

There was a balmy quality to the night, and a restlessness in the air and I decided to go down to look at the sea. I was neither tired nor sleepy, but felt a curious sense of invigoration instead. Perhaps this was because I had finally started to open up after my self-imposed exile. Perhaps it was because I'd had an evening in which I'd begun to make a new friend. I was glad that I'd managed to stop Phoenix from ruining it.

The tide was low, and the breeze south-westerly, so that long breakers were rolling in in the dark. I took my shoes and socks off, rolled up my jeans and wandered out across the mud flats that stretch from the bottom of the steep shingle banks that make up Brighton beach. Once in the water, the rushing of the waves cut me off from the night-time noises of the city. The sea itself – cool but not cold – was wonderfully refreshing, and when I felt my jeans getting wet as the water splashed up over my knees, I didn't care. In fact, the only reason why I didn't decide to swim was because it would have taken so long to wade out to water that was deep enough.

I turned and looked across at the perfect regency façade of Brunswick Terrace, which not only seemed intensely beautiful, but also to define something wordless and unstated in my mind about the human desire to make beautiful structures, where nature – as in the waves that were rolling in around me – can just *be* beautiful. It was a fleeting thought, and then I waded back out of the water and sat to put my shoes back on, looking out at that wonderful, dark openness.

I wandered back up to Lansdowne Street. There was more traffic along Western Road now, almost all of it in one direction – taxis taking clubbers home from the city centre. I smiled to myself in genuine relief that I was not one of those drivers, and walked on up past the silent antiques showroom on the corner, and into the narrowness of Lansdowne Street.

The building in which I lived was about a third of the way up, and I paused to take a full breath of fresh sea air before turning to descend the steep, narrow steps to my door.

It was only then that I saw Phoenix, sitting hunched on the bottom step. She looked up at me as I came down, and stood and gestured in an open way, almost as if she was opening her arms for an embrace that I might walk into. I stopped and glared at her. Damn her beautiful face.

'Stephen?'

'No,' I said. 'No, don't say *anything*, Phoenix. I'm not going to interact with you in any way. Not even to tell you why I won't interact with you. I know that Helena wants me to re-engage with Thirteen, but I'm not going to. Even saying this is doing more than I should.' And with that I edged past her to the door, shrugging off her attempt at a hug. I opened the door as little as I could to squeeze inside, and as I did so, she pushed in behind me.

'No, Phoenix,' I told her, 'go away.'

'I just want to come in and talk to you,' she said. 'Please. It's nothing to do with Helena. I just wanted to apologise to you.'

'Apologise?'

She stood, looking imploringly at me, half in, half out of the door.

'Yes,' she told me. 'I was wrong to have said what I did about you being an impostor. I realise it's not true. Please let me come in and talk to you. This has got nothing to do with Helena . . .'

I clearly looked unconvinced because she said, 'No, really. Stephen, I *need* you . . .'

I laughed. 'That is so insincere, Phoenix. Go away. If Helena thinks she can drag me back into Thirteen by waving a bit of bait in front of me – no matter how beautiful – then she has underestimated me. Tell her from me that, in some mad, perverse way, I'm actually glad to have met her, but that's about as complimentary as I'm capable of being.'

I turned away from her, and tried to close the door. When I realised that I couldn't, I pushed her back. Maybe that was my big mistake, because just as I pushed her, she pushed her body forward and, grabbing me by the shoulders, pulled herself into the hallway.

'No, Stephen,' she said, grunting with exertion, 'I don't think you can hear me properly. I said I *need* you. You can't just close the door on me because it's inconvenient that I've turned up on your doorstep like this.'

She walked past me and into the sitting room. I closed the front door and tried to use these moments to collect my thoughts, so that I could confront her with some kind of rational statement.

'No,' she said as I came into the sitting room. 'Don't try to tell me that I'm not welcome here. I've been here before, remember, Stephen. And you wanted me to be here. Don't pretend to me that you didn't.'

I felt calm as I faced her.

'You know you're not welcome here,' I told her. 'Don't try that "you wanted me once, so you still want me now" routine, Phoenix, it's absurd. I *don't* want you. Now go back to Thirteen and tell Helena she'll have to try a lot harder than this if she wants me to show any kind of interest in re-establishing contact with her. Now, I'm off to bed. You can let yourself out.'

I turned to go, but Phoenix jumped forward and, with her full weight and both fists, punched me in the chest. The blow made me stagger back against the wall, and I stood for a few moments, winded, my lungs empty, making pathetic noises as

I tried to breathe in. I had no time to recover before she punched me hard in the face, and I felt a crack as my head connected with the wall again. I was dazed for a few moments, and yet again I felt the warmth of my blood as it bloomed across my upper lip and started to drip down onto my white T-shirt. Just then she kicked me in the balls and I doubled over and fell to my knees, whereupon she kicked the side of my head.

All my instincts told me not to hit back, to just resist what was happening. But my anger erupted, white hot, in response to this totally unprovoked violence. And she was strong, too, and uninhibited.

'I had nothing to do with you at the Concorde,' I shouted, 'precisely because I wanted to avoid this kind of confrontation—'

'Well, you can't,' Phoenix shouted back equally loudly, equally angrily. She came at me again with her fists, but I pre-empted her by lunging and head butting her in the stomach, so that she fell back, with me on top of her. I grabbed at her arms, trying to pin them to her sides, but as we went down, heavily, against the radiator in the window, my weight fully on top of her, her head connected with the corner of it with a sickening crack, and she suddenly went limp. I slumped against her, breathing hard, dazed myself, and lay against her for a few moments before I pulled away.

I could see the blood on the dirty-white enamel of the radiator, and a there were a few of her hairs stuck to the sharp edge, looking dark against the paint. I looked down at her, at her beautiful, immobile face and leaned forward to grab her. She was out cold, and so I took her hand to feel for a pulse. There wasn't one. Of course there wasn't one. I leaned back on my heels and looked down at her and felt a kind of hard nugget of emotion constricting my chest. I sobbed, one quiet strangulated sound, and then punched the edge of the sofa. I looked up at the ceiling.

'Fuck you,' I hissed. 'Fuck all of you. What do you *want* from me?'

And I seemed to go utterly quiet inside as I sat and looked at Phoenix, and considered her supine form and the blood in which she was sitting.

'Haven't I been scarred enough?' I whispered.

This was crazy.

'I don't know if you can hear me, Helena,' I said. 'I suspect that in some way, you can. But I'm too tired for this. I just don't care any more. I'm going to bed.'

I leaned forward and wiped a stray lock of hair from Phoenix's pale forehead. 'Goodbye Phoenix,' I whispered.

I got up and left. I went through to the bedroom and fell onto the bed, genuinely exhausted, and lost consciousness without further thought.

When I woke up, sunshine was streaming through my window. I felt light, and cleansed somehow. Then, memory flooded back. I sat up abruptly and swung my legs from the bed and leaned forward to look at myself in the mirror by the bed. My face seemed slightly flushed, I thought, the stubble dark against my sunlit skin. But there was no sign that Phoenix had punched me. The blood was gone. My T-shirt was clean. I closed my eyes, briefly, and sighed with relief. I removed my clothes of the night before – my jeans still damp with sea water, my T-shirt still smelling of cigarette smoke from the Concorde – and went through to the sitting room. Phoenix was still there. Lying on the carpet under the window. Pale. Beautiful. Dead. I stood and looked down at her, and it was as if something inside me, that had been ticking steadily, stopped.

I think I had been standing there for some time when I next had what I might describe as a coherent thought. I wasn't sure what had brought me back to consciousness, and I felt a kind of numb curiosity about this, until I realised that it was actually the doorbell ringing. As a kind of reflex, I went out into the hallway to answer it, until I realised that, as I had a dead body lying in my sitting room, opening the front door might not be a good idea.

I stood there, aware that I could see a blurred silhouette through the frosted glass of the door, and also aware that they had probably seen me in just the same way as I'd seen them. I hesitated, wondering what to do next.

'Stephen,' I heard a voice call. 'Stephen?'

I looked back into the sitting room, at Phoenix's body lying there. It was too late to pretend I wasn't in, but then again there was no law that said I had to answer.

'Stephen,' the voice said again.

I walked up to the door, but didn't open it.

'No,' I said quietly. 'Go away.'

'Open the door, Stephen, this is ridiculous.'

I shook my head. The doorbell rang again. I found I wasn't angry. Just tired.

'Please, Helena, can't you leave me alone?'

'It's a little late for that, Stephen,' she said. 'Now, open the door and let me in.'

'No. Go away.'

'But you need me now, Stephen. I'm the only one who can help you get rid of Phoenix. She's real, you know. Genuinely. It was sweet of you to wake up this morning and imagine that she might have vanished. But she's real. Like me.

Like Seymour . . . like the scars that you've got on your side.'

I pressed my forehead against the lintel of the door.

'What are you going to do, then, Stephen? Chop her up and flush her down the toilet?'

I shook my head.

'We thought you were going to be friends with Phoenix. What a shame that you didn't manage it. Just like we thought – hoped – you'd make friends with Valerie. Why didn't you? You could all have been such good friends, if only you'd let them in.'

'I tried,' I whispered. 'I tried. I tried to get to know them.'

There was a short silence, and then Helena said, gently, 'Let me in, Stephen. Please. I can help you.'

I shook my head and said, 'No, Helena. Don't ask me again. You've done enough to hurt me, now leave me alone.'

I turned away and walked into the kitchen to put the kettle on, for something to do rather than because I wanted a drink. After I'd made myself some tea, I went back and looked into the hallway. There was no sign of Helena. I sighed with relief and went into the bedroom. I sat on the bed and wondered what to do next. I had no idea. All I could think of was that I had a corpse in my sitting room. If I went to the police, would they confirm that she was real? Would they confer upon her an identity?

In the end, I decided to try and live my life as if nothing had happened. Phoenix was from Thirteen. She couldn't remain dead on my carpet forever. That's not how Thirteen worked. It was only when I was in a certain frame of mind that Thirteen existed at all. All I had to do was genuinely forget that she was there, and . . . she wouldn't be there. It was simple.

I went out to the hall and closed the door to the sitting

room, then left the flat. I would go to Waitrose and get some shopping, as though nothing had happened. I could make my life normal by *being* normal. As I walked down Lansdowne Street, the summer sun and the breeze seemed to be agreeing with me. Western Road was as brash and busy with traffic as ever, and a couple passed me, laughing together at something.

I crossed the bottom of Lansdowne Place, and up by the beauty salon, hardware shop and Barney's café bar ... And there she was. At a table on her own in the window, a cup of coffee in front of her. Valerie. As I glanced in, she looked out at me and smiled, and waved, beckoning me in to join her. I stopped dead. She looked about fourteen.

I fled back to the flat.

How can I describe the next few weeks? I don't suppose I can, really. I looked into the sitting room every now and then hoping, I suppose, that Phoenix would be gone. But she wasn't. I kept the curtains closed and she simply remained there in the shade. On the second day I noticed that her face had taken on a waxy sheen, a pallid look that made her hair seem darker, and which, oddly, made her even more beautiful, albeit in a bloodless sort of way. I found that I couldn't bring myself to look directly at her. I would just open the door slightly and look at the carpet, and see the shape of her body at the periphery of my vision. After that, I suppose it was absurd to think that I could ever get back to feeling 'normal', that I could simply think Thirteen into non-existence. Because I felt weird. I couldn't help it.

That first week was hot, one of those sultry summer weeks that make you want to fling the windows open. But I didn't. On the fourth day I began to notice the smell. Sweet at first, but then progressively more nauseating, creeping beyond the room and into the rest of the flat. I sat in my room and thought, *The neighbours will start to smell this soon . . .*

I was paralysed. I heard my phone several times, but didn't listen to the messages. After the first couple of nights, when I kept waking up convinced that I'd heard someone saying something to me – moaning, or something – I began to sleep more deeply. Too deeply, in fact. More heavily than I'd ever slept before, so that waking up in the morning was a strange, painful and protracted business. Towards the end of that first week I realised I was supposed to go and meet Russell and his girlfriend in the Great Eastern. Part of me wanted to go, but in the end I couldn't do it. What could I say to them, especially as Russell would undoubtedly ask me about Phoenix?

What really shocked me, eventually, was looking in the mirror when I went for a piss and noticing that I had a short beard. It seemed impossible that so much time had passed. I guess I must have smelled pretty rank, by then, and not just Phoenix. I'd eaten the rest of the food in the flat several days before, and only had black coffee left now. I kept having odd bouts of queasiness and light-headedness, but was still no closer to any kind of decision about what to do.

In the end, I faced the sitting room. Phoenix was lying where I'd left her, and the smell in the room – not particularly strong, but sickening nevertheless – made me retch. I noticed several flies buzzing, and ran back to the bathroom to puke into the basin. I only brought up a small, but searing, smattering of bile, and my stomach burned with pain as I retched again and again. When I'd finished, I stood leaning forward with my weight on my arms, panting shallow breaths, a prickle of sweat on my forehead. But I knew I had to go back in there and face her.

I went back and looked down at her. Her face still seemed serene. From close up, I could see that she'd bled copiously from the back of her head and had been sitting in a pool of blood. This, and the fact that she'd fouled herself, seemed to explain a lot of the smell. I went into the bedroom and got myself a pair of scissors, then a flannel from the bathroom and a bowl of warm water from the kitchen. Then I came back to Phoenix and, taking a deep breath, rolled her onto her side. Turning away every thirty seconds or so to take a breath, I cut the clothing from her. No big deal – she was only wearing jeans and a T-shirt. The flesh underneath was pasty pale under her tan, and her stomach was bloatedly distended with gas as though she was heavily pregnant, but once I'd washed the blood and shit from her, she seemed oddly unchanged, somehow – especially her face, with her long, dark lashes and her stern, almost arrogant lips – as though she might really only be unconscious rather than dead. I pulled her over to the other side of the radiator. She was floppy when I'd expected her to be stiff with rigor mortis, which made things easier, and I left her against the wall, then set to work cleaning up the various fluids that had dribbled down the wall and soaked into the carpet, setting into a sort of weird gel. This took longer than I'd expected, and it wasn't possible to completely get rid of the stains, but I managed a reasonable job.

Having Phoenix sitting there so close to me made me feel creepy, so I got one of the spare blankets and wrapped her in it, which made me feel a little better. Then, I took a risk. It was three o'clock on a Wednesday afternoon, so I guessed there was a moderate chance that no one in the rest of the building was around, as I knew all the other tenants worked during the day. I dragged Phoenix's covered body behind the sofa, where it would be out of sight, then opened the curtains and the windows of the bay. Then I opened the front and back doors and the window in my bedroom. There wasn't much of a breeze, but enough to make the curtains stir slightly, so I knew there was at least some movement of air. Having the windows open like this made me feel nervous, to say the least, but I forced myself to leave them for half an hour before closing them. Then I went and had a shower.

As I was washing, I looked down and startled myself with the realisation that I could make use of the bath. It was so obvious, I couldn't imagine why I hadn't thought of it before . . . I wrapped a towel round my waist and went back into the sitting room. I closed the curtains once more, then dragged Phoenix through to the bathroom, which was awkward, especially trying to heave her up and into the bath. But once she was in, and I had arranged her so that her head was down, I ran a cold bath right up to the overflow. Now, the only part of her above water was her knees. I knew that all I had to do was run the bath water away and refill it on a regular basis, maybe once or twice a day, and there would be no smell. I didn't have to worry about disposing of the body, because all I had to do was disengage myself from Thirteen, and the body would deal with itself. Or so I hoped . . .

Under water, Phoenix's face looked more ethereal than ever. With the distortion of the water, it was less possible to see the distension of her stomach, and, as I looked down at her, at her naked beauty, I felt a strange pang of wistful despair. It occurred to me, then, that she had completely taken over my existence. This was now all that I could think of – the fact that I had her body in my bath. It made no difference that I hadn't let Helena into the flat when she'd asked me to let her in. Thirteen was a constant – unpleasant – presence nevertheless. Still, I found that when I went through to the bedroom, I was sufficiently tired to fall asleep almost immediately, though perhaps it was more like a heavy doze than what you might call restful sleep, lasting for maybe a couple of hours, and from which I woke feeling bizarre and empty.

And the emptiness remained. A literal emptiness of course – I could see myself getting thinner – but also a deeper emptiness that had nothing to do with food. I drank several litres of water each day, and going to piss became a painful neurotic ritual. I would realise that I needed to pee; a thought that would be accompanied by a dull sensation of dread at the thought that I would have to go and stand in the same room as Phoenix's corpse. I knew that all I had to do was drink less and I would have to go to the toilet less often, but there was a strange compulsion in me to drink – to force myself to check over and over again whether she was still there. I could just as easily have peed in the kitchen sink instead of the toilet, and the fact that I chose not to made it clear that on some level I wanted an excuse to go and check the bathroom so regularly and so compulsively. But neurotic behaviour of this kind is not susceptible to logic, and Thirteen seemed to be one long neurosis that I was succumbing to gradually and without resistance. It occurred to me several times that I was going mad, and the thought was rather comforting. Madness would be so convenient an explanation for what was happening to me . . .

I don't know when it was – early evening, I'm not sure which day – but I got up yet again to go to the toilet and I found that my legs could hardly take my weight. They buckled slightly and I had to grab the arm of the sofa to right myself before I could move with a kind of geriatric hesitance. As I opened the bathroom door, I could see Phoenix in my peripheral vision, but I could also see the shadow of someone standing behind the door. I didn't have the energy to do anything but give a yelp of fright and try to step back out into the hallway.

As the person pulled the door open, I found myself unable to move. I could feel my heart beat unpleasantly and I wanted to close my eyes, but couldn't. It was Seymour, Helena's disapproving brother, standing there in his dark suit, looking composed and – disapproving.

'Stephen,' he said.

'No,' I said. 'Don't say anything. I've had it with all of you. Helena's tried to entice me using Phoenix and it didn't work. What chance have you got?'

'Stephen' he said, 'you're going to die if you don't eat something.'

'You care?'

'Does that seem so impossible?'

'Right now, it seems utterly ridiculous.'

'Look,' he said and leaned down to pick up a carrier bag. 'I've brought you a curry from the Curry House on Prestonville Road – a dansak, your favourite, with a puri instead of rice.'

I looked at him.

'This is a trick?'

'No,' he assured me, 'I just want you to eat something.'

'Okay,' I said, 'I tell you what. I'll eat the curry if you tell me what's going on. Why is Phoenix still in the bath?'

Seymour shrugged slightly and said, 'She's in the bath because you put here there.'

'You know that's not what I mean. How can I make her disappear? How can I make sure that I never see any of you again?'

He smiled, and I noticed that he looked tired.

'I never wanted to see you in the first place,' he said, 'but now that you're here, I want to give you at least a reasonable chance of survival.'

A cold shiver travelled up my spine as he said this, but there was that cryptic edge to what he was saying that also gave rise to a creeping fury.

'Just leave me alone,' I said, 'you're as bad as the others aren't you? You have no intention of telling me anything useful.'

'Stephen,' he said, 'I'll admit that some of the others do take a certain pleasure in withholding information from you, but that is not true of me. I can't say anything because I am bound by my ethical code to remain silent on certain things. Believe me, if I could save you from Thirteen by giving you information, I would do so. But I can't.'

'So, go away,' I told him. 'You're of no use whatsoever.'

He smiled slightly and said, 'Okay, Stephen, I'll go.'

He walked past me and opened the front door, letting himself out into the dusk. I didn't watch him go, but looked down at the carrier bag for about five seconds, and then picked it up, ripped the food carton open and, using my fingers, started to cram handfuls of curry into my mouth. This was so messy that after two or three mouthfuls I managed to control myself enough to go through to the kitchen to get a spoon. The food was as rich as I could manage and when I went to bed I lay awake for some time feeling by turns nauseous and overfull.

The following day I felt slightly saner. Phoenix was still in the bath and I felt a whisper of disdain for Seymour as I ran the bathwater away and topped it up again. His visit hadn't changed anything. In the late afternoon, however, I found that my meal of the previous evening had reactivated my appetite and whereas previously I'd been too languorous to think particularly about food, today I felt my hunger as a gnawing and all-encompassing imperative.

At around 7.00pm, I dressed carefully, leaving the beard, and put my wallet in my pocket. I didn't feel confident enough to set off towards Taj or Waitrose, so made do with Grubbs, which was just a couple of hundred metres from my front door, and which did pretty good burgers. Walking up the steps to the pavement was a surreal experience. I felt as though I was walking up into a hostile world. I wondered if Helena would be waiting for me, and what I would do if she was.

But she wasn't. I made it to Grubbs, and ordered myself a large burger, chips and Coke. It would do for the time being. The man seemed to be watching me as though he thought I looked mad, but I tried to persuade myself that this was a natural paranoia thought, because I was so wary. While I waited for my food, I looked at some of the flyers on the side wall, and at the posters advertising club nights. They were comforting, somehow, referring to happenings in the ordinary world. I looked out at the traffic, and the occasional taxi that passed, and wondered at how quickly things can come to seem unreal. It was almost impossible for me to imagine that I had ever been a taxi driver.

'Your order, sir,' a voice said behind me, and I turned, surprised that the voice was female.

It was Valerie. Holding up the brown paper bag with my food in it, in one hand, and a can in the other.

'Double veggie burger, large fries, Coke,' she said, and smiled. She looked about twelve.

I felt that familiar lurch, that familiar hostility.

'You,' I said. 'What are you doing here? What the fuck is going on?'

'If you won't come and talk to me,' she said, 'then the least I can do is give you something to eat, to keep you going until you change your mind. It's free, by the way,' she added. 'On the house.'

She held the food out towards me and smiled encouragingly. I took a step towards her, wondering if this was a trap of some kind.

'You're getting younger and younger,' I said, and reached out to take the food, which she relinquished gracefully.

'When I'm young enough,' she said, 'you'll understand.'

When I got back to the flat I noticed that the foul, sweet odour had diminished. True, there was something that didn't smell quite right, but it wasn't unpleasant or suspicious. I sat in the sitting room, found something bland on TV, and ate my meal. It wasn't really enough to satisfy me, but I didn't feel able to leave the flat to get more.

'When I'm young enough, you'll understand,' Valerie had said. I looked down at my friendship bracelet. Was this significant, a symbol of her kind intentions, or was it just another piece of 'bait'?

I shook my head and switched off the television, then went through to the bedroom. Considering how weird a time I was having, it was strange how easy it was for me to sleep. Even the fact that I'd been dozing earlier, and the knowledge that there was a dead body in the bath, didn't stop me from drifting off with ease.

I was surprised, therefore, to wake up that night, suddenly alert. If it hadn't been dark, I would have thought I'd had a full night's sleep. I wasn't sure why I'd woken, but thought perhaps someone had called my name, or perhaps whispered it in my ear. I got out of bed and went to the window. Outside, beyond the patio, the taller buildings in Lansdowne Place reared so that only a portion of sky was visible, a rough orange glow from low cloud that had rendered the air cloying and humid. I found myself standing there, listening.

And then I heard it, out on the patio. The quiet, barely audible, sobbing of a child. I pulled the window open to try and see who was there, and the sobbing stuttered for a moment as though disturbed by the noise of the window. The patio belonged to the ground floor flat upstairs – I only had a tiny area outside the back door, barely the size of a table top – so I couldn't go out to where the noise was coming from. Here, I was more or less as close as I could get. I was aware, however, that this sobbing – a sobbing I'd heard on and off throughout my time as a taxi driver – set off some kind of specific response within me. It echoed, somehow. Reverberated, and brought tears to my eyes.

I stood there for some time, the sobbing continuing in quiet, rending intensity, the night air somehow lacking enough oxygen, and I remembered what Valerie had said: "When I am young enough, you'll understand".

I leaned from the window.

'Valerie,' I whispered. 'Valerie?'

Silence fell, suddenly.

'It's Stephen,' I said, then stopped, unsure what to say next – unsure whether I wanted to establish contact with her. Was this another trick?

I stood there, waiting. I could feel the night progressing, time moving forward, but the sound didn't come again, and eventually I closed the window and got back into bed. So, I thought, I'd been hearing Valerie all this time: Valerie as a child. But in what way did this have anything to do with me? And why was she so disconsolate?

9 year old boy to SB: My new mum's called Sarah. My bad mum is called Angie. Rutland Gardens, Hove, July 1st.

11. How can you ever trust anyone?

I'm dropping someone off up on Kings Road for the Honey Club at about 12.30am. The wind is nearly gale force, and there is a certain amount of water in the air. It may be a light drizzle, or spray from the sea, which is only a hundred metres or so away, raging against the shore. There is a woman standing on the pavement, wearing club clothes, with no coat or jacket, clearly suffering in the bad weather. Her long, dark hair is being whipped round her face by the wind. She opens my door and says, 'Please, *please*, are you free?' Driving a private hire cab rather than a hackney, I'm not allowed to pick up fares like this, from the street, but it is Saturday night and she'll find it difficult to find another cab, and she's so inappropriately dressed, that I take pity on her and say, 'Get in.'

She smiles with gratitude and jumps in beside me. As I drive off towards the address she's given me in Hangleton, I say, 'Were you waiting long?' 'Not really,' she says, 'I've just come up from the Honey Club.' 'A good night?' I ask. She doesn't reply immediately, and when I look across at her, I notice that she's started crying. Hard. Having distressed people in your cab happens regularly, and it is always difficult. At least I know not to say something stupid like, 'Are you all right?' As we come up by the clock tower, she manages to say to me, through her tears, 'Look, I know I'm going to regret this, but could we stop off at Albany Villas on the way?' 'Of course,' I tell her, and turn onto Western Road. As I drive, I can hear her murmur to herself, 'I'm going to regret this, boy am I going to regret this.' As we approach Albany Villas, she says, 'Okay. Keep the engine running while I get out. Be ready to make a quick getaway.' She directs me to stop outside one of the villas there, and runs up the steps to the door. The rain has started in earnest, and her hair is being whipped into rat's tails, making her look deranged. It is one of those houses that has been split up into luxury flats. The exterior of the building is immaculate. She leans down to the entry system and presses one of the buzzers. She waits a few moments, then starts screaming into the intercom. Although she is so close, it is impossible to hear anything she is shouting. The wind is furiously buffeting the vehicle. As suddenly as she started, she stops, and runs down to the cab and jumps in. 'Go!' she shouts. 'Go!' I get wheel-spin as we set off. At the top of the road, I look in my rear view mirror. No one has come out onto the doorstep. I turn onto Church Road, and the woman beside me lets out a low moan. 'Oh, God,' she whispers to herself, 'I shouldn't have done that. I really shouldn't have done that.'

*

I lay in bed after calling out to Valerie on the far side of the patio, her sobbing still reverberating in my head, in a series of disconsolate echoes. I realised that this sobbing had been inside me forever – that, in some way I couldn't understand, there had always been sobbing. It wasn't just since I'd become a taxi driver that I'd heard children crying. Although I'd never recognised them, these things had been there for as long as I could remember.

I got up and went through to the kitchen to make myself a snack or get a cup of something soothing and restful to help me get back to sleep. But I only had caffeinated coffee. Just thinking about this made me feel a creeping exhaustion coming on. It was harsh and insistent, and I recognised it immediately as the terrible necessity I'd had, when I was driving, to stop what I was doing and allow myself to dream. This oncoming dream-puncture was scary because, in the past when I'd succumbed to sleep in this way, I'd sometimes woken up elsewhere. And this time, I was sure, I wasn't going to wake up somewhere as prosaic as Tesco's car park . . . But I couldn't resist it. I staggered back to bed, and the dreams started – *bang, bang, bang* – as I closed my eyes.

Then I was in darkness, but gradually, like a mist clearing, I began to see a room, in which I realised I was standing. I recognised the room immediately – the trashy gold-framed mirror, the vinyl floral wallpaper, the candles. In front of me, I could see . . . myself. Unconscious, head flopped forward, and tied to a chair. Although I couldn't see the face of the person tied up – my own face – I recognised the vignette immediately. I'd been here before, after all. I'd had this experience. And none of it seemed real, more a kind of dreamy, film-like sequence but with blurred emotions attached. I looked down and noticed that I was wearing a dark blue suit. And that I was holding a knife.

The door opened and I looked up as someone came into the room. It was Helena. She was wearing a well-cut navy blue business suit. She smiled when she saw me, but not in a pleasant way. She said something that I couldn't hear, as there was some kind of buzzing in my head, a sort of fuzzy tinnitus, as though I'd been to an overloud gig. She repeated it again, and then gestured angrily towards the man in the chair, and raised her voice and said, loudly, so that I could hear her this time, 'Aren't you going to let him go?'

I still found it difficult to gather my thoughts, I was certainly not clear enough to get a handle on the complicated set of emotions that were welling up on seeing Helena like this. But her question made sense, and I leaned forward and swiftly cut the bonds of the unconscious man. As I did so, I could clearly see that it was me, and I felt a wash of sadness, seeing 'him' like that. There was a swelling round his right eye, and the bash to the back of his head had bled down onto the pale blue collar of his shirt.

Seeing him like this made me blaze with anger against Helena, a kind of blistering anger, and I looked down at my knife, and then up at her and she laughed.

'You're not angry at me,' she laughed. 'Think about it, just *think*. You're angry with *him*. Not me.'

I realised, then, that she was right. But I didn't know why. And in the confusion that this caused, I seemed to cease to be able to conduct rational thought. The dream-like feeling descended even further, and I felt as if I was falling into a deep, dark constricting hole of utter anguish. I saw the man in the chair, coming round slightly, and heard Helena say, sharply, 'Do it. Just do it!' And she laughed. And I could hardly think what she might mean, except that I had to do something to lance this great welling of pain. The man that was in the chair shook his head slightly, which seemed an impossibly provoking act of negation, of denial of my anger, and almost without thought I leaned forward again, and plunged the knife into him.

It was an extraordinary moment. Not only did I feel myself plunge the knife in, I also felt it entering my flesh. Felt the searing pain, for a second time, felt myself go rigid, and saw – from the vantage point of standing above it – myself fall to the floor. I didn't know what to do, but stood looking down at him, feeling the wound but unable to move to help in any way. I looked up. Helena had turned and was leaving the room. I looked back down at him, and the pain in me receded. We were becoming separate again. I saw the agony twisting his body as he lay, cheek against the carpet, and I knew what was going to happen. I knew he'd be in hospital soon, being stitched up.

I had a split second to make my decision. Should I try to help him, or should I . . .

I ran after Helena, out into the hall. There was the round mirror, though it wasn't convex this time, and didn't distort its reflection. There was the grandfather clock, too, though a more sturdy one than before, and with a louder ticking. There was the front door closing. I ran and grabbed it, flinging it open and stepping outside. Helena was starting down the path. I caught up and grabbed her arm. She turned to me and said, 'How far do you want to go with this, Stephen? Just how far do you want to go?'

I was awash with emotion. I didn't want to have anything to do with Helena, but avoiding her seemed to be an even more dangerous option.

'If I come with you,' I said, 'will you tell me what's going on?'

'If you come with me,' she replied, 'you will learn ... certain things ... about yourself.'

'That's not good enough,' I said. 'I want you to tell me whether you're going to stop pursuing me. I've got a corpse back in my flat, Helena. I want to know what you're going to do about it.'

'What *I'm* going to do about it?' she sneered, looking suddenly so disdainful of me that I caught my breath. 'You want to know what *I'm* going to do about it? Listen to yourself, Stephen. I took you along to that party where you met Phoenix. Did you make any effort to get to know the interesting people that I'd arranged to be there for you? Did you? No. Every time I offered you pleasure, you turned it into pain. Why did you do that?'

I stood there and her anger blasted over me.

'I could have taken you so much further,' she said. 'But you blew it. Of course I can give you new experiences – new and valuable experiences – but only if you know how to engage with them.'

She turned to leave, shaking her head.

'I'm so disappointed in you, Stephen. You're locked into that cycle, aren't you? You can't escape it. I give you chance after chance, and you end up plunging that knife in, over and over again.'

I looked at her. She seemed to hate me at this moment.

'But how do I stop?' I whispered. 'How do I stop hurting myself?'

She laughed, nastily this time. 'I'm afraid you're asking the wrong person.'

'Please,' I asked.

'You don't mean it,' she told me.

'I do,' I assured her.

'Do you?'

She looked hard at me, then turned away and strode off purposefully, not looking back. I watched her walk across the road, on under the eaves of the trees that bordered Wish Park, and into the darkness of the night. I followed more slowly, out onto the pavement. As I did so, I noticed that the Galaxy was parked on the far side of the road, empty. I wondered briefly why my old taxi should be there, now that I no longer drove it. But I didn't have to wait long for the explanation. I heard the front door opening behind me, and saw *him* stagger out of the house, clutching his side, closed in on himself with pain, blood soaking down the leg of his jeans.

I watched as he lurched across the road to get into the taxi. I didn't have a chance to witness any more, because at this moment a hackney pulled up beside me and stopped. I looked down. The rear door of the cab was right beside me. I hesitated for a moment, then opened the door and climbed in. It was Seymour at the wheel, but he was looking ahead and hadn't acknowledged me, so I leaned back and looked across to where I could see the silhouette of *him*, in the Galaxy as he pulled out into the road, slewing to the other side before righting the wheel and getting back on course. Without any instruction from me, Seymour pulled out behind it, following it down to the bottom of Wish Road and then out onto Kingsway.

The Galaxy pulled away from us. By the bottom of Hove Street I saw it shoot the red light at maybe sixty miles an hour. Seymour stopped at the light. Yes, there was the police car, siren suddenly flaring sound out into the night as it flashed its way onto Kingsway in pursuit. I saw the Galaxy braking hard and pulling over, bumping up onto the kerb.

The lights turned green and Seymour accelerated and passed the police car, which had now stopped and from which a policeman was stepping. I could see *him* slumped against the wheel of the Galaxy, blue lights flashing around him. It seemed so garish. So . . . fake. Somehow. I put my hand to my side, and felt the silicone dressing that was there, attesting to *some* kind of injury at least.

The taxi sped on past this scene. From the window of a car it looked – quite frankly – like another Saturday night 'moment', of which there would be several over the course of a single evening for a taxi driver in this city, or any city. Only as I thought this did it occur to me to wonder where I was going.

But it was so mesmerising, somehow, to be travelling these late-night streets: the sea, so quiet and open on one side, the teeming 'otherness' of clubland on the other. I still didn't feel that I was properly awake, and had a sensation of being detached from what I was experiencing. It occurred to me, as we passed, that it was Saturday night and that, in the city centre, it was just as busy as it would be in the middle of an ordinary working day, but with totally different people.

We went on past Brighton Pier and up Marine Parade. I looked at my watch, but realised, only then, that I wasn't wearing one. I saw Eastern Terrace up ahead, and for a moment, I thought we were on our way there, but before we got to it, Seymour pulled into the short street leading to a development of modern houses. He stopped the cab just there, and, as the vehicle had clearly and definitively stopped, I wondered whether I should get out. Or perhaps I should say something, or offer to pay the fare of this taxi that I hadn't

ordered. As I considered what to do next, I noticed the name
of the place where we'd stopped.

Seymour Square.

As I clocked this, Seymour turned round, a kind of wry
smile on his face – almost a smirk. He put his finger up to his
lips, to indicate that I should say nothing. I remembered the
occasion of our first meeting, when we dined at Septimus with
Helena, and he'd earnestly advised me never to visit Thirteen
again. And then his words to me in my flat only the day
before: 'I never wanted to see you in the first place'. But here
he was again, driving me across the city.

'Seymour?' I said.

'*Don't* say anything,' he told me. 'We'll talk later. First, I
have to take you somewhere.'

He backed out onto Marine Parade, then set off towards the
city centre. At Brighton Pier, he set off up the Old Steine, past
the Pavilion, Victoria Gardens and St Peter's Church, where
he turned by The Level towards Richmond Place. I remembered how much I'd disliked Seymour; that I'd thought him
arrogant and self-consciously superior. But here he was, a taxi
driver now. Driving me through the city.

Did I have an inkling of what he was doing? I suppose I did,
because it was with a feeling of inevitability that I watched
him slow down and turn into . . . Phoenix Place. I could see
the street sign, up there on the wall. Phoenix Place. He didn't
stop, but turned and made his way back to Richmond Place
and up Southover Street, then along Queen's Park Road. But
before he got to Elm Grove he turned off along . . . Bentham
Road. Seymour Bentham. Seymour Square. Bentham Road.
Why hadn't I seen it before? My god, I was a *taxi driver*. I knew
all the streets in the city . . .

As Seymour drove down Bentham Road, it struck me, like

215

a blow to the chest. Helena! Valerie! They were two closes off Fairway Crescent in Portslade. And Helena Caburn! Caburn Road was up near Seven Dials. Jesus, they were all street names!

Seymour turned right up onto Elm Grove, then immediately right again onto Carlisle Street, and said, 'You needed to name the nameless, Stephen. You had no words for us. If you had no words for us, how could we exist for you?'

I looked out at the dark of the night.

'Where are you taking me?' I asked.

He didn't answer.

I felt too shaken to ask any further questions. Instead, I sat and tried to relax, looking out at the passing streets. Strangely, beneath my confusion and curiosity, there was a sense of calm, a settling, somehow, as though a weight had been lifted from my shoulders. The city passed by, and it was almost as if I was watching it on television. It was 'real' but I was separated from it, and not just by the glass of the window from which I was observing it.

It was only as we pulled into the top of Lansdowne Street that I realised Seymour was taking me home. When he pulled up outside the flat, I said, 'You are coming in aren't you?' and he laughed and said, 'Yes, of course. Unlike the others, I will never abandon you.'

It occurred to me that he'd given me food when I was starving, which wasn't the kind of thing someone would do if they wished me harm. But everything that I had witnessed in Thirteen was so difficult to interpret, and had so relentlessly turned sour that I was still faced with this major question: did I trust him?

He touched me, gently, on the shoulder and said, 'Did you trust Helena?'

I turned to him, and he smiled with a gentle encouragement. 'Yes,' I said.

'Did she prove to be trustworthy?'

'I don't know,' I told him. 'Ultimately, all she seemed to do was cause me pain.'

'Then can you trust anyone?'

'I don't know.'

'So let me in,' he said. 'You're asking yourself a question that has no meaning. You're asking yourself whether you can trust me. But you haven't even answered the question of whether you're capable of trusting anyone.'

'Okay, okay,' I said, opening the door. 'I'm letting you in. Okay . . .'

Inside it seemed different. Lighter, somehow, as though the place had been aired. I went straight through to the bathroom. It was empty. Phoenix was not in the bath. I came out.

'Did you do this?' I asked. 'Did you get rid of Phoenix?'

He shrugged slightly and said, 'Look, let's go into the front room, where we can talk.'

I opened the sitting room door, and as I did so, I noticed the light smell of lavender and citrus. Even before I turned the light on, I knew that she was going to be there.

'Hello, Stephen,' Valerie said as light flooded the room. She was about nine, dressed in a pale dress with a blue floral pattern, her dark hair pulled back in a pony tail. What had she said to me? "When I'm young enough, then you'll understand."

I sat down opposite her. Seymour came in behind me and closed the door.

I took a deep breath.

Was I ready for this?

No.

But when would I ever be ready?

'What have you got to say to me?' I asked.

She looked as happy as she'd been when I gave her the friendship bracelet on the seafront – back when I'd still thought of Helena as my friend. She held my gaze and said, 'You're still asking the wrong kind of question, Stephen.'

I glanced a query at Seymour, who was sitting there, looking as though he was invigilating, somehow. But he looked impassive. He shrugged. Where else did I have to turn?

Valerie could clearly sense my turmoil and she nodded slightly to draw my attention. 'I suppose you feel cornered?' she said.

Something in the way she asked this made me take a couple of breaths and think carefully before I answered. Cornered? Cornered by what? By Helena? By Thirteen? I'd just been to a horrific scene of violence in Thirteen. An act of violence perpetrated on myself, by myself. Did this make me feel cornered?

I took several more deep breaths. It felt as if there was no oxygen in the air. I closed my eyes. If I pulled away from this encounter, would I simply end up spending the rest of my life plunging the knife in over and over again? But was I prepared to hear what these people I was sitting with had to say? I opened my eyes and said the words that were, I suppose, the most difficult I had ever spoken.

'Okay,' I told Valerie. 'I'm ready.'

Silence.

I waited for a while, but the silence remained. Valerie sat, immobile, looking closely at me and smiling her bright, friendly smile. Waiting.

'I'm ready,' I said.

She raised her eyebrows slightly.

'Okay,' I admitted, 'maybe I'm not ready. But I recognise

that I'll never be ready. So you might as well get on with it, ready or not.'

'Good,' she said quietly.

I closed my eyes again and tried to remain calm.

'Now,' she said, 'I'm going to ask you a few questions. I'm sorry that in doing so I'll cause you pain, but . . .'

She stopped. I opened my eyes and saw that she was watching me closely.

I nodded for her to go on.

'Okay,' she said. 'First question. Where do your scars come from? The scars on your side, that you're getting treatment for.'

'Someone stabbed me,' I said.

'No,' she said, 'I mean the scars that were already there before that?'

'I was burned,' I said. 'In a fire.'

'How did that happen?'

'It was a silly schoolboy prank that went wrong,' I said. 'We never meant it to get out of control.'

'We?'

'Graham and I. Graham Kingsley . . .'

It was Graham who'd told me to become a taxi driver. Graham. Holidaying in England from California.

'Who is Graham Kingsley?' Valerie asked.

'We were at school together,' I said.

'And, together, you started a fire?'

'Yes.'

'Who lit the fire?'

'Graham,' I said.

'Tell me what happened.'

'I can't remember.'

I looked at Valerie. She was still smiling but in a way that verged on pity, and I felt a sudden resentment that this child was pitying me.

'God,' I said, 'this is ancient history. Graham and I were just schoolboys. We got up to a few pranks. Okay, some of them were a little extreme, true – bricks through windows of people we hated and so on. But nothing like the things you hear about today. Even minor delinquent behaviour that you get nowadays would make anything we did seem like nothing. The fire getting out of hand was just an accident.'

'Tell me about the fire.'

I paused. 'Look, I was a child. What am I supposed to be able to remember?'

'Tell me what you remember.'

'Okay,' I said. 'Okay.'

I tried to relax, and looked up at the ceiling, noticing a crack there that I hadn't seen before. The muscles in my back had knotted and I realised I was clenching my fists. I unclenched them and placed my hands on my knees.

'Graham had this annoying relative,' I told her. 'An aunt, I think. Yes, an aunt. Aunt Eileen. He used to hate being tyrannised by her, and wanted to get his revenge, so one afternoon we climbed over her wall and set light to her garden shed. That's all it was. It seems so ridiculous to make an issue of it now. All he wanted to do was upset his aunt.'

'But what happened?'

'One side of the garden shed was up against the main body of the house. We didn't really know that at the time. Well, we had no idea that the shed was going to make such a major fire in itself. I mean, it went up like ... like ... I don't know, it was like a furnace. Of course anything next to it was going to ignite.'

'What did you do then? When it went up like that. Did you run away?'

I shook my head.

'That was the major flaw in our plan. We climbed over the wall at the foot of the garden without any trouble, to light the fire, but it was too high for us to get back over it. Once the main house began to burn, we wanted to run away, but we were stuck in the back yard. Trapped.'

I stopped, suddenly caught up in the memory – for the first time in years. For the first time, I suppose, since the fire itself and the gruelling inquiry afterwards.

'Yes,' I said, 'we were trapped. The flames were so fierce we were beginning to get burnt ourselves.'

'So how did you get away. How did you survive?'

'We had to run through the house.'

'Describe the house to me.'

'I can't remember,' I said. 'What is this? I was only nine.'

'Nine's old enough to remember things with complete clarity, Stephen,' she said. 'Whatever you can remember, tell me.'

'Okay, okay.' I tried to focus on what had happened.

'The house was full of smoke,' I said. 'We could hardly see anything. Graham had a handkerchief that he held over his nose, but I didn't have anything, and choked quite badly. It was so acrid in there it was hard to keep my eyes open. I had tears running down my face and found it hard to see to follow him. In fact, now I think about it, I got lost and ran into the sitting room, instead of the hall and the exit from the house, which made me start to panic, big time. I ended up crashing blindly about for what seemed like ages, before getting back out into the hall. That's how I got burned when Graham didn't. He'd got out some time before I did. Even when I did get out into the hall, I tripped and fell against something.'

'What?'

'A clock. A grandfather clock.'

I looked at Valerie, and she smiled encouragingly back at me.

That was what Thirteen was all about, why it was an address . . .

'The house that I've kept on visiting – the house where I used to pick you up in my taxi – it's the house we burned down, isn't it? I didn't recognise it because it kept changing every time I visited it.'

Valerie paused before continuing.

'So what happened when you fell against the grandfather clock?'

'It came down on top of me. It was already in flames, and I had to scramble out from underneath it.'

'Did you get out all right?'

I sighed. 'No, *obviously* I didn't get out all right, otherwise I wouldn't be undergoing treatment for the scars.'

'Was there anyone else involved?'

No. No, I thought. *Please, don't make me go through this. It's not fair. It was just a schoolboy prank.*

'Was there anyone else involved?'

I took a deep breath.

'Yes. Yes, there was. Graham's cousin. She was upstairs.'

'And what happened to her?'

'She . . . was killed in the fire.'

'What was her name?'

'I don't remember. I never saw her – she went to an all girls school out towards Steyning. Graham and I never talked about her. We knew each other for eight years after the accident, before he went abroad, and we never mentioned it. Not once.'

'But how old was she?'

'Nine,' I said, and opened my eyes. 'I heard her crying as I ran from the house.'

Why was Valerie so happy? Why was she so benign?

I opened my mouth but couldn't speak for a long moment. It was only when she looked briefly at Seymour that I managed to whisper, 'So, you're the little girl that died?'

She smiled and hesitated slightly before she spoke.

'Death, to you, is a little girl,' she said.

Seymour glanced at Valerie, then stood.

'Okay,' he said, 'I think it's time for us to leave. I'm sure Stephen would like a chance to be alone with his thoughts.'

'No, no,' I said. 'Please stay for a while.'

Valerie smiled and said, 'Really, we must go. But we're not abandoning you his time. I promise we'll meet again, soon.'

On the way to drug rehab clinic to get more methadone.
1st addict: They'll never give you more, Steph. You're only two days into your week's supply.
2nd addict (desperately hopeful): Do you think they'll believe me if I say I lost my first scrip? Preston Circus, Brighton, July 5th.

12. Visits.

I woke up in the morning, feeling light and, well, I can't quite find the word for it. Cleansed, perhaps. As if I'd been suffering from a fever from which I was now cured – only this was a fever from which I'd been suffering for the whole of my adult life. There were other feelings in there too though, such as grief, which, although it was present, was somehow unable to stop this surge of wellbeing. Clearly, I was feeling grief for the girl – Graham's cousin – who'd died in the fire that Graham and I had set. And there was a whole series of other, more complicated emotions, such as remorse and regret and shame around the part that I'd played – however unintentionally – in her death. Then, too, there was grief for my loss of innocence at such an early age, for the pain I'd suffered, both physical and emotional. For the scars that I'd carried around, quite literally, ever since.

But my scars were healing. I could feel them shrinking beneath my silicone dressings.

I realised that I wasn't sure what day it was, and so I went down to Budgens to get bread and saw that the Sunday papers were out. I went to the grocer on the next block and bought myself some mushrooms, then came home and made myself a late brunch of cereal followed by mushrooms on toast, with freshly brewed coffee. Then I went for a swim. A long slow swim in the cool waters of the English Channel.

At 4.00pm I phoned Russell, but he wasn't in, and so I left a message: 'Sorry I stood you up the other day,' I said, 'I was . . . called away, suddenly. By a family emergency. I didn't have a chance to let you know. But I'm back now and I'd really like to meet up for a drink sometime. Give me a call.'

Then I phoned Lou.

'Hi,' she said, 'yes, both Colin and I are free. We've been gardening all day, so we're gagging to down tools and go for a beer. Why don't we meet up now?'

'It's such a beautiful day,' I said, 'let's go to The Boardwalk.'

'Okay,' she said.

'Right,' I told her. 'I'll leave now and see you in about twenty minutes.'

It was warm, and the entire population of the city was out, it seemed, enjoying the sun. I remembered walking along here the previous summer and bumping into Graham. I'd been relentlessly gloomy then, actually a little bit mentally ill, I now realised, and in need of help. But unable to admit this to myself.

Graham. I'd promised to keep in touch with him and tell him how I fared. But it had all been so confusing, so difficult to put into words. Even now, what could I tell him? How could I send him an email that even vaguely described the journey I'd taken? But then, perhaps he'd known I would encounter Thirteen? Of course, he must have.

I looked out at the quiet sea, sparkling in the sun, at the hoards of sunbathers, at the kids splashing and screaming in the paddling pool down towards the West Pier, and I thought, *Thank you, Graham.*

Lou and Colin were already there, waiting to be seated, when I arrived at The Boardwalk, and we queued for a while to get a table. When we did manage to get one, it was at the edge of the seating area, and we sat, looking out over the beach and both the Brighton and West piers. Lou was wearing sunglasses and looked bright and happy.

'And why are you so cheerful?' she asked.

I laughed, but a little warily, not sure how much I could tell her. 'I could ask you the same question.'

'I'm often happy like this,' she said, 'as you know. But what about you?'

I laughed again, not sure quite how to explain. 'Do you really want to know?'

She looked at me carefully, and realised immediately that I was referring to Thirteen, and she glanced at Colin and said, slowly, 'Yes, I suppose so. I suppose it's something you need to tell us, isn't it?'

I nodded.

I told them pretty well everything, then. When I explained about the fire – which Lou already knew something about, having known me at the time – I cried a little, with real sorrow, and the tears felt clean and genuine. It does Lou and Colin a lot of credit that they neither laughed nor told me that I was mad. They even took the 'everyone was called by a street name' bit without flinching. In fact, Colin leaned in slightly as I talked of this, and narrowed his eyes as if listening particularly carefully.

When I finished, Lou said, 'So, how objectively real do you think this has been?'

I looked at her and considered. 'Perhaps it depends on what you think of as "real",' I told her.

'Has anyone but yourself seen anyone from Thirteen?' she asked.

'Yes, a passenger in my taxi saw Valerie—'

'I mean, someone you know, a friend.'

'You saw the snowdrop that Valerie gave me. That's pretty convincing circumstantial evidence in itself.'

'And do you think something's been resolved?' Colin asked. 'Do you think that you've exorcised Thirteen. Do you feel you've now been given the "key" and can have access to it whenever you want?'

'I don't know,' I told him.

The waiter came up to us then and asked us if we wanted any more coffee and Lou asked for menus for lunch. I recognised him, immediately, and as he walked away, I said, 'That's the waiter who served us when I came here with Helena. I'll ask him about her when he comes back.'

'No, don't,' said Lou.

'I won't make a scene,' I said, 'I promise.'

Lou looked at Colin, warily I thought, but didn't say anything.

When the waiter came back with the menus, I remembered his name.

'It's Michael, isn't it?' I said to him.

'Yes,' he said.

'I came here with a friend of mine a while ago. Helena Caburn. I wonder if you remember?'

He looked at me kindly and said, 'I'm afraid we have quite a lot of customers here, sir.'

Lou looked warningly at me, but I carried on.

'Yes, but Helena knew you by name. Beautiful woman. Maybe forty-five, long dark hair? She bought the most expensive wine on the menu.'

'Oh, yes, of course. But she never told me her name. And I wouldn't say I know her. She's just one of our more . . . memorable customers. She comes along here from time to time and always buys the most expensive wine we've got. And tips very well.'

'Okay, thanks,' I said.

'Is there anything else?' Michael asked.

'No, no thanks.'

'Actually,' said Lou, 'I'm starving. Don't go. We'll order straight away.'

She and Colin ordered fish with salad and new potatoes. I found I was ravenous and ordered a plate of pasta with a side order of chips and some ciabatta.

When he walked away with our order, I smiled at Colin and Lou.

'You don't seem at all surprised by any of this,' Lou said to Colin.

Colin shaded his eyes and looked out at the horizon. 'I've always told you that this world is more mysterious than it appears on the surface,' he told her.

Lou drained the last of her coffee, then said, 'You were interested in this, right from the start. Right from the incident with the snowdrop, weren't you? That's why you looked it up on the Net.'

'Mmm,' he said.

I laughed.

'Have you ever had anything to do with Thirteen?' I asked him.

'No, no,' he said. 'Well, not exactly. It's just that one or two things happened to me when I was a student that I couldn't properly understand at the time. Nothing that I could really describe now. Let's say, I experienced a couple of things that left me with such an air of mystery that this tale of yours doesn't completely surprise me.'

Our wine arrived, the house red this time, considerably cheaper than the wine I'd drunk with Helena and a slightly older Valerie. We toasted each other and I found myself smiling widely. A happy silence lasted until our food arrived and then we concentrated on eating for a while.

Later, Lou said, 'So, are you going to get in touch with Graham to tell him about all this?'

'I've got his email address,' I said, 'so I suppose I'll drop into an Internet café at some point and contact him.'

I took another sip of my wine, and almost choked as I made the connection.

'Oh my God!' I gasped.

'What?' asked Lou, startled. 'What!'

'Graham,' I said, 'Graham Kingsley. *Graham Kingsley!* They're roads! Graham Avenue, Graham Close, Graham Crescent. And Kingsley Road – up by Preston Park Station.'

I shook my head. How far back did Thirteen *go?*

'It's impossible that Graham is from Thirteen,' said Lou. 'I

mean, we were all at school together. He was just as much a
friend of mine as he was of yours.'

'Curiouser and curiouser,' murmured Colin. 'At least you
don't have to worry about us. There's neither a Colin nor a
Louise road in Brighton. As far as I know.'

'No,' I said, 'there isn't.'

I thought for a moment. 'As well as being the one who told
me to become a taxi driver, Graham was the one who lit the
fire,' I said. 'The fire in which I got my scars. Why didn't I
make the connection before?'

'Because we bury things like that,' said Colin, 'we bury
them deep.'

I shook my head, and then had *another* thought.

'Russell,' I said.

'Russell?' Lou asked.

'He's this guy I met the other week. I knew him slightly
anyway, but we got on well and we arranged to go out for a
drink. There's Russell Crescent, Russell Mews, Russell Place,
Russell Road, Russell Square . . .'

'But Russell's such an ordinary name,' she said. 'It might be
a coincidence. I mean, how many people that you meet would
have names that corresponded to a street in Brighton.'

'Yes, well . . .' I conceded.

'I mean, names like Helena Caburn, Seymour Bentham, or
Phoenix are kind of unlikely. But *Russell*?'

'There's a George Street just round the corner,' said Colin.
'Edward Street, Veronica Way . . . and that's just on the way
back to our place.'

'Edward, Eileen, Elizabeth, Ellen, Ethel . . . and that's only
the E's,' I said. 'There's even a Kevin Gardens, would you
believe, in Woodingdean. But how can I *know* about
Russell?' I drained my glass. 'I suppose I can't. But that's

irrelevant, because right now I need to get to an Internet café.'

'I'll pay for this,' said Colin. 'I can't remember the last time I had a more interesting lunch.'

He paid and I threw in a few pounds for a tip.

'You could come home with us and log on there,' Lou said. 'Isn't there somewhere nearer?'

'There's an Internet café on Middle Street,' said Colin. 'Do you remember Graham's address.'

'Yes,' I said as we left. 'It was a Onetel account. The user name was simple, GK for Graham Kingsley, and the word "baggage" because of the job he does. GKbaggage.'

We walked up Ship Street, by the side of the Old Ship Hotel, and The Enigma. The street was narrow, and dusty and a little claustrophobic. We didn't speak. I was too keyed up for that. When we got there, the café wasn't particularly busy and I was swiftly assigned a terminal. Lou and Colin stood behind me as I logged on. I wrote:

Dear Graham,

You knew about Thirteen all along didn't you? That's why you told me to become a taxi driver. Well, it worked. Can you reply to this message as soon as you get it, because I'd love to talk to you about it? Could you give me your phone number in California, too? Maybe I could scrape together some cash to come over and see you? What do you think? Don't reply to me here, but via Lou – Lou Butler – do you remember her? She sends her regards by the way, as do I.

I added Lou's email address and sent it off. Within seconds, the message "The following address had permanent delivery errors" popped up on screen, followed by Graham's email address.

I smiled to myself. 'I knew it,' I said.

'Are you sure it's correct?' Lou asked.

'Absolutely,' I told her, getting up to go and pay. 'I wouldn't forget something like that. And it's no surprise to me now that he gave a false address.'

We came out onto the pavement, and I turned to them. 'Look, thanks for listening. I'll get off now.'

Colin looked as though he might be about to say something, but he stopped himself.

'Okay,' Lou said, hugging me. 'Be careful, though, and come and see us soon.'

'Yes,' said Colin. 'Like in the next few days. Or tomorrow if you're free. I want to talk to you about this some more.'

I agreed and, as they went off towards Duke Street, I wandered back to the seafront, which was even more busy now than it had been earlier.

Right, Phoenix, I thought. *Where are you?*

I was on my own. There was no reason why she couldn't put in an appearance now. I went and leaned against the railings above the carousel and the palmist's booth and closed my eyes to visualise her. The image that instantly came to mind this time was of her lying naked on my bed. I could hardly bring a more powerful image to mind and I half expected to feel her touch on my arm before I opened my eyes. When I did so, I looked down over the seafront, at the restaurants and bars, and at a shop selling plastic shoes and inflatable hammers. But there was no sign of Phoenix. I held her image in my mind as I started to wander off up to Hove Lawns and Lansdowne Street, looking closely around me as I went. But there was no one.

I crossed the road at the bottom of Lansdowne Place, and half way up that block, just as I was passing Lansdowne Square, a car pulled in beside me. I turned.

It was a taxi.

A hackney.

Phoenix was in the back.

She opened the window and looked out at me. 'You can't just summon me every time you want to have a conversation, Stephen,' she said. 'That's not the way it works. Besides, there's some unfinished business you need to get sorted out first.'

'What do you mean?'

'You still need to talk to Valerie.'

'How? Where?'

'Sanctuary.'

'Where's that?' I asked. 'You mean The Sanctuary café? No, no, don't say anything. I know what you'll say.'

I looked in to see if it was Seymour at the wheel. It wasn't. I couldn't help feeling yet another welling of hostility at all this. What did she mean, unfinished business?

I nodded towards the driver and said, 'What's his name? George, or John, or Norman, or maybe his name is Old Steine, perhaps, or Prince Albert or "The London"?'

'I know you must be sick of this, but please give it one more shot, Stephen.'

'When,' I said, 'when is this going to end?'

'End?' she said.

The car started to move off, and Phoenix leaned out and called, 'Sanctuary, Stephen. Remember. Sanctuary.'

I walked up to the flat, and thought, *What do I have to do? How do I do this?*

When I got in, there was a message waiting for me from Russell, asking if I was free the following Thursday, 8.30, at the Great Eastern once more. I phoned him back and he answered, so I told him that I really would be there this time.

'Looking forward to it,' he said.

'By the way,' I asked, 'before I go, can I ask you one thing?'

'Mmm?'

'What's your surname?'

He paused.

'Why do you ask?'

'I think someone might have mentioned you – mutual friends.'

'It's Freely, Russell Freely.'

I sighed, amazed at how relieved I was.

'Oh, well,' I told him, 'it must have been someone else, then. See you Thursday.'

I went through and turned the television on. But that seemed too trivial, somehow, and so I turned it off again. Instead, I picked up a light jacket and went down to the seafront. The sun was lowering, and I could see the smoke rising from a barbecue on the beach where a bunch of people were sitting around on blankets, drinking wine. It was good to be out in the open air.

It was all very well for Phoenix to tell me to do X or Y, but if she didn't give me further information about *how* to do what she was advising me to do, the advice was worse than useless.

No, I thought. I would not consider this further for a while. I would go for a walk, clear my head, and then consider things later. Much later.

I wandered along past the King Alfred Centre and Hove Lagoon, and on up by Shoreham Harbour, and the power station, to the breakwater at the harbour mouth. It was a little over three miles, and I found myself in a light reverie as I walked. Maybe, I thought, Thirteen would always be a kind of unfinished mystery. Maybe its very unfinishedness what was it was. Maybe it was one of those things that identified me,

235

made me who I was, Stephen Bardot – the fact that I would always 'need to talk to Valerie'.

I stood at the harbour wall, looking down into the dark water – water that remained utterly mysterious. It would never yield its secrets. But then again, it would never ask me awkward questions. As I turned to walk back to the flat, I could see the lights of Brighton sparkling again in the late dusk. The breeze was still warm, and I walked with my jacket over my arm. As I came back past Hove Lagoon, I realised that the end of the lagoon was at the foot of Wish Road. Did this fact seem significant? I felt open and expansive, but not exactly zoning. I wondered whether to wander up there or not, just to have a look.

It was while I was trying to decide that I saw the smoke, and the flicker of light from the flames. I closed my eyes, and felt that odd thump of emotion, that 'not again' feeling. Tears sprang to my eyes and I thought, *do I have to confront this AGAIN?*

As I watched, I heard the approaching fire engines. What good would it do to go and look at the fire? What could I do?

And then, I had the thought. *Valerie! Maybe she's still inside! Maybe if I intervene . . . maybe I can RESCUE her this time!* I sprinted round the lower half of Hove Lagoon and then over Kingsway and up Wish Road. Again, the house was different. I recognised it immediately. Graham's aunt's house. It was modern fake-Tudor with a gabled porch. I could see two fire engines, already pumping water into the house, and I could also see the flames roaring up to the sky from the back of the building. But the front of the house was still more or less intact – that room above the front door was free from flame, even if the downstairs was an inferno. Did no one have a ladder? Did no one know that there was someone still inside!

As I arrived, breathless but ready to scream what I knew to the firemen, the frame of the roof of the house cracked and, in weird, graceful slow motion, it collapsed in on itself, sending up a great spume of flame and smoke, and I thought, *There's someone in there!*

To die in a fire.

Even from here, thirty or forty metres away, I could feel the searing heat of the flames. A fireman turned to me and waved me away. I walked back across the road, sat on the far pavement and put my head in my hands. I had never really faced up to this, had I? Not what it really meant. Graham had started the fire, but I'd been his accomplice. Would he have done it on his own? I don't think so.

I heard, rather than saw, the tyres of the taxi that pulled up just then, and I looked up to see Seymour at the wheel once more. I sighed and wiped my eyes, and opened the taxi to get into the front passenger seat. Seymour looked at me, and said 'Where can I take you?' and I said, 'Sanctuary?'

Woman to companion: When he said yes, he only sometimes meant yes. When he said no, he only sometimes meant no. I only knew where I was when he said maybe. Lansdowne Place, July 12th.

13. Life is . . . an open-topped sports car.

I was hardly watching where Seymour was taking me, but was surprised that the journey was so short – just a block or two. We pulled up outside an Edwardian semi. The house was one of those ones that should have been characterful, but which had been ruined by having white plastic UPVC double-glazing fitted throughout. As I got out of the cab, Valerie opened the door and beckoned us in. I got out and started up the short path to the door. It seemed just a little too bizarre that I had just witnessed the fire in which she'd died, and I had no idea what I might say to her. But as I approached, she said, 'Don't worry, Stephen. Don't say anything. Just come inside.'

I followed her in, Seymour behind me. The interior was

stark. Bare. The floor was stripped in the sitting room, and on the brilliant white walls were limited edition prints showing vases of flowers on tables in front of Venetian blinds. Valerie was pouring me something at the drinks table – a beer. Lager. It seemed strange, a nine year old acting as an adult.

I sat down and Valerie left the room. I turned to Seymour, who'd sat down in a large, comfortable chair by the door. 'I'm beginning to accept,' I told him, 'that remembering the bald facts about the fire is not enough.'

Seymour looked at me questioningly.

'I mean,' I said, 'seeing the fire, now, like that, made it real to me in a way that it has never been real before. Facts are very different from feelings, aren't they?'

'And has seeing what you have seen helped?' asked Seymour.

I thought about this for a few moments. 'I don't know. I suppose it's made it impossible to ignore, or "forget" what has happened.'

Seymour sat there, inscrutable. I looked at him and – in spite of myself – felt a sudden warmth towards him that was shocking, seeing as it seemed to come from nowhere, and so contradicted what I'd felt about him before. I looked around. 'Is this "sanctuary" then?'

'Sanctuary is not a place—' said Seymour.

I chuckled. 'No, no, of course,' I said, and shook my head – with what? Mirth? Resignation? Realisation? 'It's not a place, it's a—'

'—state of mind!' we both said together, and laughed.

Seymour looked so different, laughing like this, as though he really liked me.

'I think I owe you an apology,' I said.

'Oh? Why?'

It was actually quite difficult to say this, with Seymour sitting there in front of me. But I needed to make the effort. 'Because,' I said, then hesitated, not sure of the best way to continue. 'Because, when I first met you, I thought you were both pompous and arrogant. Not only that, I assumed that you disliked me. I mean, you have to admit you were dismissive of me, weren't you, that night at Septimus? You said you hoped we would never meet again, do you remember?'

'Of course I remember,' he said, 'and in that respect, I suppose I have an apology to make to you.'

I was surprised by this. 'You,' I said, 'apologise to me?'

'Yes, well . . .' he said. 'I do have a tendency to come over a little distant and . . . unfriendly.'

'That's certainly true,' I said.

'In a way,' he said, 'I regret that. But that's how I *am* when I meet people. I find I can't put on some kind of front, like Helena can, just to make a good impression. I can't be anything other than myself.'

Just then the door opened and Valerie came back into the room. She came over, sat down and looked at me. She reached out and took my hand, holding it loosely. I understood this to be a gesture of some unconditional kind, and smiled at her. She smiled back and said, 'Seymour's got a couple of questions to ask you. Do you mind?'

Did I trust him? I looked over to where he sat, watching me. 'Of course I don't mind,' I said.

Seymour smiled.

'Go ahead,' I told him.

Here we go, I thought.

'Okay,' Seymour said. 'Think back to the time of the fire. Do you remember Graham's aunt. Aunt Eileen?'

'Yes.'

241

'Graham hated her?'

'Yes.'

'How about you?'

I thought about that for a moment. 'I didn't hate her,' I said. 'I *loathed* her. Or not even that – I genuinely believed her to be evil.'

'Why?'

'I . . . I . . .' I paused and thought. I picked up my drink and took a gulp. Thought some more. 'I don't know,' I said. 'Because Graham thought so, I suppose. I mean, I trusted him. I accepted his opinion of her. And I'd met her a few times, too. Well, not met her, but she used to come and pick him up from school sometimes, when Graham's parents couldn't get there, and she'd take him home on the bus.'

'On the bus?'

'Yes, Graham used to be so ashamed of it. Not that other kids didn't go home on the bus – some of them did – but his dad had a Jaguar convertible, and Graham used to get a real buzz out of going home in that, in an open-topped sports car. His aunt had a car too, but Graham's parents didn't trust her, because she drank. I mean, she was an alcoholic. They didn't trust her not to be drunk during the day.'

'And Graham hated her because of that?'

'Yes,' I admitted. 'And I hated her too.'

Shame washed over me, and I felt a kind of humiliation well up from inside me – as if it had always been there but was only making itself known for the first time. I could see her so clearly in my mind's eye – a friendly, attractive woman, trying to deal with a hostile nephew and his friend. 'Poor woman,' I murmured. 'She was always nice to me. And I really did *hate* her.'

I looked at my beer and as I picked it up to drink from it, I suddenly felt the burden of the complexity of life bear down on me, like premature old age, and I thought for a moment that I might buckle beneath it.

'Okay,' Seymour said, 'tell me the story. Tell me this time, not Valerie.'

'The story of the fire?'

'Yes.'

'I'm not sure I can remember anything more than I told Valerie.'

'I'm not asking you to remember any more facts. I'm asking you to remember how you felt.'

Valerie stood up and went to open the curtains at the back of the room – the curtains of the French windows that opened onto the back garden. She opened them in a way that made them seem like the curtains of a theatre, and as she did so, I saw the flashing blue lights of the fire brigade, on the far side of the garden wall. I could see the top of the arc of a jet of water as it came over and onto the fire – a fire that was now more or less under control. I could only see the upper section of one side of the house from where I sat, which was roofless now and belching black, sodden, waterlogged smoke. It was difficult to see more as the garden wall was so high, and on this side there were a couple of apple trees that obscured the view even more.

Now I realised, with a jolt, where I was. Graham's house. Not as it really had been, but a kind of unreal version of it – an unlived in version of it. Which was why I hadn't recognised it.

'I'd forgotten,' I murmured, 'that Graham lived back-to-back with his aunt like that.'

I tried to ignore the view outside, but even if I looked away, I could still see the flashing blue reflected on the walls around me.

243

'Go on,' said Seymour. 'Tell me about how Graham came to light the fire.'

I shrugged.

'Okay. We started off by climbing over the wall,' I gestured out of the window, 'as you can see, it was pretty high. But we climbed into one of the apple trees to get up onto it, and then dropped over into the garden on the other side. Well, it was hardly a garden. Just a sort of patio and tiny lawn.'

'How did you feel?'

'It was kind of fun, I suppose, and it felt a bit daring – though not *that* daring. I mean, what would have happened to us if we'd been caught before we'd actually lit the fire? Been invited in for tea and cakes, probably.'

'Did you worry about being caught?'

'Not really. It was just a prank, you know. Burning someone's shed down.'

I smiled, mirthlessly. 'Oh, the innocence of childhood!' I sighed. 'Everyone would have guessed straight away that it was us, even if it hadn't got out of hand like that. I mean, it was an enclosed garden. The only way into it was over the back. It would have been obvious.' I shook my head. 'Still, we didn't think of that. We just went into the shed and got a few bits of cane and stuff, and some old newspaper that was on the floor, and Graham lit the fire.'

'How did that feel?'

'It didn't feel like anything particularly,' I said, 'except exciting. Graham was livid, of course. I mean, shaking with rage at his aunt. I'd been invited round to visit him that afternoon, and so I went on the bus with them when she came to pick Graham up from school. She was drunk when she arrived to pick us up. It was the first time she'd done this, or at least *obviously* done this – everyone else from school could see quite clearly that she was drunk – and he went white with fury. She said something to him about how if Graham's parents didn't trust her, how should they *expect* her to behave? I was embarrassed by it, because even though I hated her, I still felt sorry for her, having to deal with Graham's hostility like that. When we got to Graham's house, she came in, settled us down in front of the TV, and then went off to collect Lisa—'

So . . .

I blinked a couple of times quickly, then looked across at Seymour.

'The girl was called Lisa,' I said, trying to work out what this might mean. 'Not Valerie at all. I hardly knew her. Graham's aunt and uncle kept her away from us because they thought we would be a bad influence on her. Which Graham resented, of course, even though it was absolutely true. But that was just another reason why he hated them.'

Seymour nodded, and waited for me to continue. I tried to concentrate.

'So,' I said, trying to get back to the narrative of my memory, 'we climbed over the wall into Aunt Eileen's garden and Graham lit the fire . . .'

For something I hadn't consciously thought of for so many years, it was amazing how fresh and vivid the memory was. I could remember the dusty green bark of the apple tree, and the particular orange-red of the bricks, and the slightly canvassy black trousers I was wearing that day. And, of course, I could remember the fire.

'It just wouldn't start,' I said. 'I mean, it kind of spluttered, and crackled a little, and a few tiny flames started up, with a thin trickle of smoke, but I thought it was going to go out

245

altogether. Graham tried fanning it and so on, and the more it didn't get going, the more angry he got – in that quiet, almost violent way, which characterised all his feelings towards his aunt. Looking back on it, I realise he felt a kind of impotent rage against her. He'd finally got so wound up that he was committing arson – and it wasn't even working.'

'What happened then?'

'Then? I saw the thinners,' I said. 'I mean, the front of the shed was full of plant pots and so on, but the back had a stack of old paint tins, and brushes and that kind of thing, and I saw the container of thinners, and I also saw the label warning that it was flammable. You know, that red diamond with flames coming from the top of it.'

Seymour nodded. Valerie seemed to be entranced by my story. Her hands were folded in her lap, and she looked incredibly formal.

'So,' I continued, 'I went over and took the top off, and took a sniff and realised immediately that it was a bit like petrol. Once, only a couple of weeks before this, my dad had a barbecue for friends, and he just couldn't get the charcoal to light, so he went off and got a container of stuff like this, and poured some of it out into an old paint tin and threw it onto the barbecue, and that got it going all right.'

I remembered this occasion, too, now that my memories of that time had been so clearly evoked. I also realised that I'd forgotten how much I used to like to go and have tea round at Graham's house – this was the year before my mother left, and at that time I was always pleased to be invited elsewhere.

'What did you do when you saw the thinners?' Seymour prompted me.

'I did what my dad had done,' I said. 'I got an empty paint tin – though there weren't any small ones, so I had to use a big one – and I poured thinners into it, and told Graham to stand back, and then I . . .'

I found it suddenly hard to grasp the thought, given how I'd always categorised this moment to myself.

'*I* did it,' I said, '*I* made the fire what it was. It was me, not Graham . . .'

And I had genuinely forgotten it. I stared at the wall, at the blue lights flashing rhythmically against it, then briefly out into the garden.

'And then?' Seymour asked.

I shook my head, as though this might settle my thoughts. 'And then,' I said, 'I had this kind of duality moment, because I knew what I was doing was wrong, but I couldn't stop myself. It's difficult to describe something like this – something that I did when I was child – in the vocabulary of an adult. It was as if I had this voice in my head, encouraging me, in spite of another part of me that was horrified at what I was doing.'

As I said this, I stopped.

Helena had said we'd met before, when I'd struck that match to light her cigarette in Septimus, and I'd looked at her over the flash of flame as the match ignited. And now I remembered that soft, sweet voice, that utterly seductive, alluring voice, murmuring . . . *Do it. Just do it.*

What could I say?

I sat with the memory, turning it over in my mind, trying to understand the emotions that it provoked. I drank some more beer, sighed, and looked at Seymour.

'In a way,' I said, 'I suppose I knew what was going to happen, but it was still a shock, I mean the way the whole place went up – *whoom!* – like that. It was incredible, and Graham screamed with laughter and pleasure, and for a moment everything was . . . perfect, I suppose. I had done

SEBASTIAN BEAUMONT

something that proved my friendship for him. I had recognised his anger and how much he hated his aunt – and I had
done something appropriately *incendiary*.'

If only it had stopped then. If only it had all stopped in that
moment.

'Then, there was that awful horror,' I said, 'of knowing that
everything was out of control. That something relatively small
that we'd done, was turning into something huge and terrible.'
I sighed. Still not fully able – or ready – to face what had
happened as an entire event, a sum of all these smaller parts.
'And then it's pretty well as I told Valerie before – about not
being able to get back over the wall, and having to get in
through the house. And getting lost . . . and getting burned.'

'And Lisa died?'

'Yes,' I said. 'Yes, she did.'

He nodded slowly.

'Just Lisa?'

I put my head in my hands.

'Lisa died,' I said, '*and* her mother. Graham's Aunt Eileen.
She died too.'

I closed my eyes because I couldn't bear that terrible blue
flashing light on the wall in front of me, it was so *relentless*.

'They were both overcome by the smoke,' I said. 'They
didn't suffer the agony of being burned.' At least that was true
– or at least, that was what I had been told at the inquiry, and
what I had chosen to believe.

'But you did,' said Seymour. 'You suffered the agony of being
burned.'

'Yes.'

'And what about *your* pain?'

I looked at Seymour. 'What about my pain?'

'You were a child,' he remarked, 'as you've already told us.'

248

'Yes,' I said. 'I was a child.'

'Your pain was real, Stephen. You blamed yourself for what happened. And you always assumed that you deserved the pain that you suffered.'

I leaned back and looked up at the ceiling, and as I did so, I . . . I'm not sure what happened, but I guess I must have passed out.

As I gradually came to my senses, I saw everything through a fog of incomprehension. I realised that I was sitting in a chair with my hands tied behind my back. I had a thumping headache and my eye was half closed, it was so swollen. There was also a kind of roaring in my ears, and a sort of reverberation that made it difficult to gather my thoughts in any coherent way.

I saw the gold-framed mirror straight away, and the candles, and knew that this was significant, but couldn't quite put my finger on why. When the door opened and Helena came in, wearing that now-familiar blue suit, I started crying. She looked at me as if she didn't recognise me, then started saying something to someone in front of me. I was still fuzzy and unclear, but when I felt my bonds being cut, I felt a great gobbet of something, that was clenched and stuck in my abdomen, break forth, cracking open and upwards with an explosion of pain. I heard the words 'Do it. Just do it!' and I yelled, 'No!' and tried to leap to my feet, falling forwards instead to sprawl face down on the carpet, because my legs were so numb and useless. I could feel the carpet against my grazed cheek, and this focussed me somehow, so that I could scramble to my knees, and manage to half-stagger past where Helena stood, without looking at her, and out into the hallway. I glanced back into the sitting room, and there *he*

249

was, standing with a knife in his hands. He looked at me, eyes slightly glazed, unfocussed, and then I saw him recognise me.

The knife fell from his hand.

Helena, who was still in the room that I had just left, turned and walked to the door without seeing me, and closed it, shutting me out so that I was alone in the hall. I looked around me, at the clock, at the mirror, at the red carpet. I found that I was totally calm. I walked down the corridor into the kitchen, then across to the back door and out into the balmy warmth of the summer evening. I passed the shed, standing there intact and seemingly insignificant, then across the patio and small lawn. At the back wall, with my adult height, I could easily jump up and grab a branch from the apple tree. Using the branch, I hauled myself up onto the wall, and then jumped down the other side. When I went up to the French windows, Valerie – aged about twenty – opened them for me.

'Welcome,' she smiles, 'to Sanctuary.'

'You're not Lisa, are you?' I say.

'No,' she agrees. 'I never was.'

The interior is completely different to how it was when I was here, what, only a few minutes ago? It is darker, the walls a kind of orangey ochre, the furniture in the sitting room is dark too, as well as the paintings – open colour-fields of black and dark blue.

Valerie has gone off somewhere, but Seymour is there, and Helena, the sight of whom makes my heart thump un-pleasantly, but she smiles and embraces me as I come in and says, 'Let me get you a drink, Stephen.'

I sit down, and realise that the room is bigger, too. Far too large in fact to be a room in the house I've just been standing outside. The windows are fake leaded, for a start, and not double glazed as they were a few minutes earlier.

Seymour smiles kindly. 'How are you?' he asks.

'Dazed,' I say.

He nods. Helena comes over and hands me a drink. I sip it and laugh. A Harvey Wallbanger.

'But,' I say to Helena, 'you were so unpleasant to me.'

She looks at me and says, 'I accompanied you to the start of a journey, Stephen. Where you went after that was up to you, not me.'

'I thought I was going to go mad at one point,' I say. 'I didn't think I'd survive . . .'

Seymour nods. 'But I knew you'd be all right,' he tells me. 'I knew it because the first time you saw Helena, you saw her as a nurse. Otherwise, I would simply have stopped you from seeing her again.'

'Bless you for seeing me as a nurse,' Helena says to me. 'I've been known as lots of things in my time. A lot of them derogatory.'

'But,' I said, 'you've always been around. That's what you were trying to tell me when we first met, at Septimus, when you asked if I recognised you.'

Helena shrugged and smiled and sipped her drink.

'And do I ever have to come back to Thirteen again?' I ask her.

'Not for this. Not for what you've looked at today. But as for other things? Well . . . And then, of course, there's the future.'

'You mean,' I laugh, 'I might have to if I fuck things up again?'

'Oh, well now,' she laughs. 'I'm sure your past isn't squeaky clean, even now. But, whatever happens, you can be sure that we'll meet again, Stephen. The circumstances will be up to you.'

The door opens and Phoenix comes in. It is strange – she is still beautiful, but beautiful as a picture you might hang on your wall. I feel no sexual attraction for her whatsoever. She comes over and kisses me, and sits beside me, and says, 'Stephen. Hi.'

In some ways, I think, she is too beautiful for me. Intimidatingly beautiful.

'Is there such a thing as "too beautiful"?' she asks.

I shrug. I look down at the friendship band round my wrist, and tears well up.

'So, what do you want to do now?' Phoenix asks.

What do I want to do? With all this pain, and relief, and newly awakening, something inside me is tender and vulnerable, and yet stronger than I could ever have thought possible . . .

I shrug, and say, 'Isn't there a party we can go to?'

Helena laughs. 'There's always a party,' she says.

'Where?'

'You tell me.'

I look at them; they seem primed, somehow, expectant.

'Come on,' I say to Valerie. 'Come on,' I say to Phoenix. 'Come on,' I say to Seymour. 'Come on,' I say to Helena. 'Let's go.'

I get up and open the door into the hallway, which isn't the hallway of the house I so recently came into. It is now, quite suddenly, vast and tall, with a black and white marble floor, and a long, sweeping staircase lit by a glittering chandelier.

'Sod it,' I say to Helena. 'So what if it's formal?'

Together the four of us walk up the plain, perfectly polished carpetless stairs and onto the landing. Here there is a maroon carpet and dimmer lighting. I look round at the four doors leading from it, three of which are silent. From the fourth comes the sound of pumping music. I smile to the others and cross to the fourth door and open it to let them in: Helena, who kisses me; Seymour, who kisses me; Valerie, who smiles and nods a little nod of complicity; Phoenix, who playfully puts her arm round my waist and pulls me in with her.

'Take off your shoes,' I call to them, leaning down to take mine off as I close the door behind me. '*And* your socks.'

It is as it was the first time I came here. There is the bar. There is the DJ. There is the child Valerie, happily playing the cello, in her formal white blouse. But this time there are many more people here. The room is packed. Heaving. Everyone seems to be happy, under the lights, with the cross-projections and the music. I look at it and feel that all before me has a kind of cohesive, happy unity.

But I can't quite believe it.
I just can't.

It is so seductive.

So seductive.

Phoenix, who I haven't seen for a few moments, comes over and thrusts a glass into my hand. I sip it. Another of those odd almond, apricot and absinthe cocktails I had last time I was here. She laughs and kisses me.

'Let's dance,' she murmurs, grabbing me loosely by the waist.

I laugh with her, but can't quite get it. Can't quite connect. I drink my cocktail down in one and drop the glass, which falls noiselessly onto the thick pile of the carpet. What about the part I played in the death of Lisa and her mother? Can I forget that? Can I just come here and be happy? And what about the pain that I have brought to the surface again after so many years?

I'm looking for something. I'm not sure what. There's Helena, laughing with Seymour. There's Valerie playing her cello. There's the older Valerie standing by the tall windows. Here's Phoenix, holding me tight.

I crane round to see what I can see.

I see Charlotte. She's wearing a formal evening dress tonight, rather than rubber – purply dark blue crushed velvet that scintillates subliminally in the light. I notice, now that she is so conventionally dressed, just how pierced she is. I hadn't noticed before – or perhaps she hadn't been wearing this facial jewellery at the time. The bridge of her nose is pierced, as is her eyebrow. She has a labret through her lip, and many rings in her ears. She recognises me and comes over, laughing. As she approaches, I see that her laughter is not happy. It is not friendly.

She leans in, apparently to kiss me and, instead of doing so, says, 'For *fuck's sake*, Stephen!'

I look at her.

'What?' I say. 'What!'

'You didn't come to see me, did you? You said you would, last time you were here. I even gave you my card. But what did you do? You forgot all about me and went off with Phoenix.'

She says Phoenix's name with a venom that is truly shocking, and I'm about to respond when she looks over my shoulder, distracted by someone approaching from behind me. I turn and see Kenton. I realise I had completely forgotten about him.

He smiles and leans in to speak to me and says, 'Don't worry about Charlotte, she's always pissed off at *someone*. It's her vocation. Enjoy yourself, Stephen. Let yourself go. Just have a good time.'

He smiles, but there is something not quite right about his expression, which freaks me out a little. He notices this and says, 'Don't you remember, Stephen, that you promised you would come and see *me*? Last time you were here, we had a conversation, don't you remember? I told you that I could tell you a few things that would give you a perspective on Thirteen. And you said you wanted to hear them. And I believed you meant it.'

'Yes,' I tell him, 'I do remember now, but I'm afraid I forgot all about it. I'm sorry.'

He gives me an ironic glance.

'Story of my life, mate.'

He gives me a hug, a genuine heartfelt hug and says, 'Never mind. I'll be here whenever.'

'Okay,' I say to him, feeling suddenly as though I missed something important by not going to see these people, and I sense another mournful bleb rise to the surface in me.

'Look,' I tell him, 'I really *will* come and see you. I'm sorry I didn't before. It's not because I didn't mean to—'

Just then I am grabbed by the arm. I turn and see that it is Phoenix, and she leans in to me and says, 'For *fuck's sake*, Stephen, you're supposed to be having a good time. Come and have a dance. This is a party, not a wake.'

I smile, and allow myself to be pulled into her embrace, but I am fully aware that Phoenix's embrace is not a simple embrace. It is as complicated as an embrace can be. I glance over at Helena, who raises her glass to me, and laughs. I see Seymour, who is some distance away. He looks at me, then does a pantomime of looking at his watch and seeing how late it is, and he points to the door. 'I've got to go,' he mouths, and I wave back to him and feel, as he leaves – and this shocks me more than anything else – as though I'm being abandoned by my best friend.

I break away from Phoenix's embrace and say, 'Look, I think I'm going to go and have a word with Valerie.'

She looks at me as though trying to decide whether to be offended or not, then shrugs.

I look round the room, and it is a whirl of noise and colour, and I think, *Oh, for FUCK'S SAKE, Stephen!*

I walk towards Valerie, and the carpet is soft and I can feel the nap of it tickling the soles of my feet as I walk, and I think, *Can I experience this moment, just for itself? Can I lose myself in this evening without bringing baggage with me?*

Valerie notices that I am walking towards her, and she smiles, pleased, and I say, aloud, 'I can try.'